Mask

H. G. Wells Short Story Competition 2021

Also in this series

Mask

Edited by
Liz Joyce & Tony Scofield

St Ursin Press

First published in Great Britain in 2021
by St Ursin Press, 3 Broadfield Court,
1-3 Broadfield Road, Folkestone, Kent CT20 2JT,
United Kingdom

Sponsors

Cover picture by Jondolar Schnurr/ Pixabay

ISBN 978-0-9955730-8-6
St Ursin Press is an imprint of Trencavel Press
www.trencavel.co.uk/St Ursin.html

Contents

2021 Senior Prize

Foreword

This year's theme of 'mask' was a deliberate ploy to get under that very thing. Much of the world has spent the last year behind a protective face mask due to the Covid Pandemic. Would that it might melt away like HG Wells' aliens in *War of the Worlds*.

One hundred years ago, Wells published a kind of short story called *'The Grisly Men'* in which he imagined what Homo Sapiens might have felt when he encountered Neanderthal man. He saw this entirely through the mask of contemporary humanity. He made many of the common misassumptions of his time, that one civilisation had destroyed another. To be human though is to communicate and our destructive forces have largely been sublimated by creative ones.

Wells would probably have been delighted by our contemporary understanding that these were just parallel civilisations that mingled due to natural forces changing within the world they knew. Wells rightly predicted that time would see the dissolution of boundaries across the world. I think he would have seen the creative potential of the internet in linking us all.

The HG Wells Short Story Competition was the brainchild of Reginald Turnill who reported on all the Apollo Space missions for the BBC. He lived, like Wells, in Sandgate. This year's entries poured in from all over the world across the internet. The best stories did indeed look beneath the mask and show us a little more of ourselves. We are delighted to offer this year's anthology. Many congratulations to those who were shortlisted and to those of you who knew you wrote something excellent. We had again record numbers of entries this year and the conclusion must be that the creative forces of the world are stronger than ever.

CHARLES BAIN SMITH RIBA CA

Chair of Judges

Soup for Starters

Audrey

My husband stretches his mouth into an unnatural shape when he looks at me. It is not a smile. He sits rigid at the dining room table, half concealed beneath the oak. Glassy, bloodshot eyes protrude from his skull, unblinking. His lips curl at the edges, recoiling at my arrival. It's as if he's a puppet and someone is pulling the strings, encouraging his every movement.

My puppet. My strings.

The grandfather clock strikes the hour, my head pounding with every toll of the bell. I lean over, plant a kiss on his cheek, his stubble grazing my lips. I leave a red smudge in my wake. He glances at me. Nods. He takes his glass to his lips. Sniffs. Checks to see if I'm watching. He gulps it down too quickly, chokes.

He is afraid of me.

He should be. I've been reading through his messages. Every last sordid one. He's done things with her we've never even discussed in our twenty-two years of marriage. He's risking our lives in the middle of a fucking pandemic—to screw this stranger.

Only she's not a stranger.

I cried when I first read those texts. I lay curled up in the foetal position on our bed and I thought about killing myself. Just to spite him. Just so our son would never look at him the same way again.

I thought about the first time I met Matthew, back in college when we took the same sociology class. I couldn't resist when he asked me to tutor him, blinking at me with soft brown eyes, flicking his dark hair from his face. I remember that surge through my body when our hands grazed as he handed me a pencil. Walks on the beach in the hazy rain, sharing a bag of chips. A kiss. Dancing skin to skin, his calloused hands on my waist as I caressed his cheek and called him mine. Weekends in Prague and nights under the stars. August 15th, the day he gave me his name. The light in his eyes, and the darkness in my mother's when she told me I'd live to regret my decision.

"I'm just going 'round the shop to get milk, love," he would say.

There's already three bloody cartons in the fridge. All with the same stupid date. I think back now to all of those 'runs' he went on, unable to shed a single pound of fat. How stupid of me. It was as if I didn't know him at all. He was lazy when I met him and he was lazy now. That's what broke our marriage. He didn't put any effort into anything. As though the very idea of dinners and dates pained him. He didn't want to bother with polite conversation. Light flirtation. All I got from him were eye rolls and empty grunts. Even in bed.

I thought he was too lazy to cheat. That was my mistake. It's not like I didn't try. I bought the most beautiful negligees and leather lingerie sets. I invested in sheer stockings and spanks. Botox and liposuction. A personal trainer and a gruelling military diet. Do you know how fucking hard it is keeping to a consistent diet when you aren't permitted to leave the house? I work on myself every day—on my body and my mind and my hobbies—and he dares to sit there, looking at me like a bug that must be squashed. Sending pictures of his junk to other women. I'm trapped in this prison with the worst kind of offender.

How easy it must be, to be a man. He can walk away from us and fuck anything with a pulse. Lead this whole other life. He can forget about his family. Start a new one. Mothers don't have that luxury. *Women* don't have that luxury.

I hate him.

He has given me nothing while I've given him everything. OK— that's a lie. He gave me my son. My world. Xavier.

Xavier was born thirteen years ago. We bonded instantly, his tiny pink fist enclosed around my manicured thumb. He was always mine. I couldn't bear it when Matthew held him. He was clumsy, always forgetting to support his head. Changing him over the cooker. Leaving him unattended on the couch to answer the door. "I was gone one minute, Audrey," he'd huff. As if one minute wasn't long enough. As if we hadn't almost lost him once before.

Matthew left us for two nights when I told him I wanted to home-school Xavier. He said it wasn't normal to keep a child hidden away like that. He said Xavier would have no friends. But Xavier didn't need friends. He had me. The other children would make him sick. Expose him to germs. I'd never seen a child with an immune system quite like his. He was always sick. I spent most nights sitting in an armchair at his bedside, watching his chest rise and fall. Days checking his temperature and spoon-feeding him chicken soup. He never cried. He was always a good boy. When this pandemic started, I knew he didn't mind being at home. He was always there anyway.

"Would you like a glass of wine, dear? Pinot Noir? Chardonnay? Merlot? Cabernet Sauvignon?" I asked Matthew, blinking slowly, simpering.

"No thank you, I'm quite alright, darling."

His eyes didn't sparkle. They reflected only my plastered-on smile, pearly whites threatening to unleash themselves and become embedded in the flesh of his neck.

"How about a beer? Lager? Stout? Pilsner? P…"

"No. Thank you." He fidgeted with a table napkin, his expression souring.

"A short? We've got gin. Vodka? Perhaps some whisky?"

"I'm not thirsty, love," he said all at once, forcing a half-hearted chuckle. A vein pulsated in his forehead. I longed to reach out a slender finger and press down on it.

"As you wish." I gritted my teeth. I watched Xavier from the corner of my eye, sitting on the short side of the table, staring dreamily into space. Such a good little boy. He had set the table as I had taught him, carefully arranging the silverware and placing neat little folds in the corners of the napkins. He placed three glasses of milk on the coasters—of course Matthew couldn't handle the slightest hint of spice. Xavier even helped me prepare the dinner. We were having his favourite that night—chicken alfredo with tomato and basil soup for starters.

I would do anything to make him happy.

The family dog died last week. It was a terrible affair. Rupert was six, a healthy Doberman, in his prime. We'd been having a pest problem. Matthew left the shed door unlocked, and our Rupert ingested the poison. I will never forgive Matthew for that, even if Xavier does.

I will never forgive Matthew a lot of things.

"How was work, dear?" I ask as I stir the soup. I turn back to look at him, sitting with his head bent, staring at his stupid phone. Beads of perspiration etched across his forehead.

"Busy, love."

"Is Richard still micro-managing?"

"Richard?" His cheeks redden, and I know I've caught him in a lie. "Yes, Richard's a pain, I'll admit."

"I was always fond of his wife."

Matthew doesn't respond, and I wonder if he's slept with Richard's wife too.

I straighten my smock dress and smile at the boys, walking towards the table. I carefully balance the ceramic bowls of steaming soup. The bread is already buttered. I sit at the far end of the table, teasing out a blonde curl. I'd had to dye it myself, over the bathroom sink. I submerged my head in the lukewarm water until I couldn't breathe. Screamed.

I spent hours applying my makeup, focused intensely on each fine stroke of the brush and puff of powder. I pressed my dress to ensure there were no creases. Pressed it again. I wanted to look perfect. This was the image I wanted engraved in his mind forever. This is the last time he will ever see me.

Us.

Tonight I will announce that we're leaving, Xavier and I. I'll take the packed suitcases from beneath the dining table that I've carefully concealed beneath the oil cloth. He'll be green when he sees them. Then he'll be sorry.

All I have to do is wait.

Matthew

I don't like the way Audrey is looking at me, the way her left eye is twitching like that. In unison with the flickering bulb above the dinner table. 'Witchcraft', I think.

I never should have married the woman. I hate the bitch.

She leans in so close I can smell her sweat, masked by perfume. Citrusy, like a detergent. Like bleach. She kisses me, her hot breath on my cheek.

She knows something.

I tell myself I'm just being paranoid. That woman doesn't know shit. She didn't know about Gina or Heather or Sarah or Alice or any of them. I felt guilty after the first one. Couldn't touch Audrey without remembering Gina's taut skin beneath my lips, her thick thighs wrapped around my waist. I got depressed. 'Snap out of it'. Audrey said. So I slept with Heather.

It's Audrey's fault we're broken. She drove me away. That robotic little head tilt is making me antsy. The sickeningly sweet aroma of the soup wafts through my nostrils, forcing my stomach to swirl. I take the frothed milk to my mouth, sip. It's sour. I gag.

The bitch must have done it on purpose. Left the milk out all night. She does shit like that. Cuts holes in my favourite boxers. Throws away single socks so I'm left with no matching pairs. She tried to kill me once, I swear it. Cashew nuts in my fucking salad. She knows I'm deathly allergic. I wanted to die right there and then on our kitchen floor so she would spend the rest of her miserable life in prison. Or better yet, be institutionalised.

The woman is insane.

"Did you do something with your hair babe? It looks great," I say, winking at her as I place my napkin in my lap. It's better to play her at her own game. I know it aggravates her. And I play to win.

She whispers thanks, turning away from me so I can look at her ass, or lack thereof. She works out every day, but she looks worse for it. She is shapeless, a shadow of herself. I used to squeeze her hips as she washed dishes over the sink, but now when I touch her it's just bone. She used to have dirty blonde hair, and she'd let me brush my fingers through it each night before bed. Now she's dyed it peroxide blonde and gets it blow-dried once a week. It's crispy and dry and she pushes me away whenever I try to touch it.

She reaches inside our drinks cabinet, offers me wine. I say no. Do I want beer? No. She keeps listing all the drinks, as if I don't already know what fucking alcohol I keep in my own house. She recites like she's reading from a script.

She tries to get me drunk all the time, just so she can roll her eyes at me and tell me I'm a good-for-nothing alcoholic. Just like my father. My blood boils. God forgive me, but I want to hit her. Smash her head against the damned cabinet. Just to draw blood. Just to know she feels something. Just to know she's human. I don't know when or why she became a Stepford Wife. She's a dead-eyed robot. Even when we sleep together. It feels like I'm fucking a corpse. I can't even get it up anymore.

For her.

I remember loving her, what it feels like to be loved by her.

We used to be good. We spent three months in Thailand, four weeks in Vietnam, two years in Australia. We went on nature walks and had sex outdoors. We spent weekends drinking too much wine and smoking cigarettes with all of our friends.

But she decided she wanted a baby. Because her sister had a kid or some shit, I don't know. We tried. I don't know when it stopped being fun. We'd fuck and then she would roll over and cry herself to sleep. Ask me to fuck her again tomorrow. She was pregnant.

And then she wasn't.

I wasn't allowed to grieve. She cried for the two of us. She said it was my fault she miscarried. She said I didn't want our baby enough, and that's why God had taken him away. So I packed my bags. She got on her knees and begged me to stay. Used her body like a weapon. I ended up back in our marital bed, with the suitcase left gathering dust on the landing.

And then we had Xavier.

And then Xavier got sick.

Audrey thinks one of our friends kissed him on the mouth. I don't know if that much is true. All I know is he nearly died. And we don't have any friends anymore.

Xavier is cursed to live in this godforsaken house forever. She loves our son more than she loves me. He is her doll. Clean and perfect, unblemished and unblinking. Unable to fight back. I think that's another reason our marriage has fallen apart. I refuse to be her doll, and she thinks that means I refuse to be her husband.

She never lets him just be a kid. You know what he got for this thirteenth birthday? It wasn't new football boots or money to go to the cinemas with his mates.

He got a fucking ant farm.

What's worse is that he wanted one. The kid's never been around other kids. I got him to Facetime some of the cousins once. He shrank into a caricature version of himself, a mute, a freak. They asked if he was a bit 'soft in the head'. But of course, darling Audrey didn't find that one bit funny and now we don't send them Christmas cards anymore.

He's a strange kid. Sometimes I wonder if he's mine at all.

"Could you pass the pepper, Daddy?"

I shudder. That's what Samantha called me last night, when I had my hands around her throat. He's a teenager now. Too old for this Mummy Daddy bullshit. It's her that has him like this. I regret to think what the other boys will call him. To his face, definitely to his face.

I met Samantha at work. She's twenty-two, big hips, tiny waist. Horny little thing. She doesn't ask for money and she laughs at my jokes. She says she likes my 'dad bod' and calls me her silver fox. I'm her dirty little secret and she is mine. When she smiles I notice her crooked row of teeth. She's real. And I think I'm falling in love with her.

Samantha texted this afternoon.

'Daddy, I'm waiting on a covid test.'

'Fuck.'

Audrey would kill me if I brought that into this house...

It doesn't matter.

Not anymore.

The divorce papers came through today. They're in a sealed manilla envelope. I'm holding them between fingertips doused in perspiration, concealed beneath the table. We talked about it before. Separating. She refused. And I'm not thick. It's not because she loves me. It's because that woman is cunning and manipulative and she'll try to fleece me for all I'm worth. So I filed for contested divorce. I'm going to give her the papers after dinner. The Last Supper. Surprise bitch!

And that's just the half of it! I plan on suing her for custody of our son. She ruined my life, now she's ruining Xavier's too. I won't stand for it. She won't nag at him about the tiny nooks and crannies that need dusting, or swat him away from the cooker and sigh and insist on doing it herself. She won't tell him whom he can and can't speak to. She won't destroy any semblance of personality he has left. He will not be emasculated.

It's cruel, but I wish I had a camera so I could take a picture of her face when she realises I'm taking everything. I'd savour it forever. I take a mouthful of my soup, tell her it's delicious.

All I have to do is wait.

Xavier

I've always known my family was different. We are nothing like the people I read about in my books, or the images I see on television. We look like them, with our designer clothes and freshly cut hair and wide smiles. We sound like them too.

"This is marvellous, dear."

"How delightful, darling."

"I love you Mummy. I love you Daddy."

Our love is like stale bread. We are covered in mould. Sour. Decaying.

I see it in the way they look at me. My mother, fawning as though I am a precious jewel, something to be admired. Untouched. My father, sighing and rolling his eyes. Disdain. Disappointment. He thinks I'm effeminate.

I think he's an asshole.

I don't love him. I don't love either of them. She's like a cobra, always squeezing too tight. Eating all the other snakes. If she is a cobra, then I am a mongoose.

I don't appreciate being a pawn in this little arrangement of theirs. We've been locked away together for approximately ninety-one days, thirteen hours and forty-five minutes.

I have been locked away my whole life.

I tried to connect with others, but they mocked me. My mother would kiss my skinned knees and tell me I was special, much too clever to be around the likes of them. She'd gently place the plaster on before marching across the street to the accused's house. I expected her to knock on their door and shout but instead she would peer inside their windows, look over her shoulders. Key their car. Slash a tire. Steal their child's bike.

I'd watch it unfold from my bedroom window, stripping the plaster from my leg and tearing at the wound from my knee. Ribbons of flesh. I liked how it felt. Masochism. I read that somewhere.

There's a lot of things you can learn from reading. There's lots of things you can learn from the internet. Babies are not delivered by storks. People fuck. Naked, sweaty animals at their most primal. I've seen it. People hurt each other. Sometimes they fuck and hurt each other at the same time. People kill each other. They shoot and they stab and they gouge and they post videos on the internet for the whole world to see.

My father fucks his assistant and it kills my mother inside. My mother fucks that silver thing in the nightstand and that kills my father.

Neither of them are good enough.

My father searches for happiness at the bottom of a bottle. My mother is addicted to Xanax. She thinks I don't know. She tries to make me forget, but every ivory pill remains unswallowed beneath my curled tongue. I'm surprised the pills haven't killed her yet.

The mutt pissed on my fresh linens so I killed him. Pesticides rolled into thin slices of deli ham.

I keep my hands concealed beneath the table, tugging at the skin of my nailbed. There is a searing pain as the skin is torn away, droplets of blood pooling in its wake.

My father flexes his hands beneath the table and she smiles too wide, red lipstick staining her teeth. Do they really think they're fooling each other? They're not fooling me.

"Aren't you going to have some of your milk, dear?"

"No thanks."

It's in the soup. Enough to kill eight full-sized adults—and some in the buttered bread, just in case.

All I have to do is wait.

Masquerade

The building on the hill was a sturdy brick fortress, so severe that even the weeds growing from the cracks in the pavement jutted up with military fervour. One would almost think it was a prison, rather than a school. Perhaps it was a kind of prison, in a way, with parents hurrying toward the gated entrance in a determination that matched a warden's measured stride. 'SUMMIT SCHOOL', announced the sign nailed above the gate. In a few steps, I would pass under that formidable archway. Mama's voice floated back to me, carried in the brisk wind. *Cover your knees. Keep your eyes wide open.* I smoothed my skirt over my knobbly patellas. Could they really tell?

I walked with my head down, as though a view of the floor would lend me a veil of anonymity. *Anonymity,* Baba had taught me, *is proportionate to safety.* A pair of red leather high heels appeared out of the corner of my eye; a commotion was taking place, blocking the hallway.

The high-heeled woman wrinkled her nose, as though detecting a thin odor.

"You're on the wrong side."

I flinched, then realized she was speaking to the family of four in front of me.

"I'm sorry?" the father leaned forward calmly, the creases in his suit deeper than the lines of consternation forming on his forehead.

"You're on the wrong side," the woman said loudly, as though the repetition would offer clarity. When they failed to move, she pointed toward the door.

"We don't take your folk here."

There were two schools in Milford. Summit was the school on the hill. Bentley was the decrepit building behind it, separated by a rusted fence. Those denied entry to Summit went to Bentley. People who weren't white enough were sent there. It was an unspoken rule that everyone except the people at Bentley seemed to know about.

"But I thought we enrolled here just last week," the mother interjected. She turned and caught my eye, smiling placidly in reassurance. "And besides, there's still plenty of room, right?"

"You are being an affrontment to the learning environment," the woman interrupted quickly, "Kindly remove yourselves before I call administration."

"Come now," the father said, placing a protective hand on each of his children's backs. "We'll try the other school." He steered them firmly out the door, his head held high. The mother gathered up her skirts in a fist and whirled after him, but not before casting a contemptuous glance behind her. To the woman, to me, or to the crowd of spectators that had formed? I couldn't tell. But I could see the turmoil reflected in her dark brown eyes, flashing with anger and resentment. Anger at the fact that the course of her life was inexplicably intertwined with the permanent mask of her skin. Resentment at the fact that this type of encounter was one she was accustomed to.

I crept forward cautiously. The high-heeled woman was evidently there to weed out people that didn't belong in Summit's pristine halls. The door to my classroom was within sight, a beacon of false security. The woman's beady eye latched on to me and she thrust out her arm, hindering my progress.

"Where are your parents?"

The question made my stomach lurch, but I recited quickly: "They're both at work." In reality, they hadn't come because they didn't want to jeopardize my chances.

Her eyes scanned the registration papers I had crumpled in my hand. "Mrs Johnson's class. Down the hall, door to the right. Class starts in ten minutes."

My sigh of relief was hidden, yet immense; an ocean's undercurrent.

Mrs Johnson stood at the helm of the classroom, wielding her ruler with brusque authority. She directed each student to their seat with a swing of her metal instrument, then set to work attacking the chalkboard. Puffs of white dust tricked to the floor with each aggressive swipe of her wrist.

A quick glance around the room told me I already stood out in my shapeless canvas skirt and worn blouse, with the sleeves rolled up so they wouldn't droop down to my knees. I studied the other girls and noted with jealousy their brand-new stockings and the way their hair was smoothed back and held into place with clips that matched their pinafores.

Cut that out, Meiying. I imagined Baba reprimanding me. *It's impractical. How are you supposed to work properly dressed like that? I didn't come to America to have you act like those entitled children.* What was he doing now? Most likely up to his elbows in car grease, a torque wrench tucked under his arm as he slaved away until the sun vanished from the horizon. A wave of shame crashed over me, as I pictured the fathers of the girls in front of me, how they had walked their daughters to school and kissed them goodbye. They probably went to the pictures on Sundays, too. *Oh Baba, why couldn't you be more like them?*

Mrs Johnson began taking roll, and to my horror read every name aloud in a crisp voice. Each student responded, an echoing chorus from a sea of white faces.

"Ashley?"

"Present!" called out a girl with blonde pigtails.

"Gregory?"

"Here."

And so on, until: "Meiying?"

Silence. The boy behind me snorted, and a flush spread across my cheeks.

"Meiying?"

"Here." I raised my hand, my voice barely audible. "But I go by May."

"What kind of a name is that?" I heard behind me.

"Not an American one, that's for sure."

"Why wasn't she sent to Bentley?"

The racket continued until Mrs Johnson had her share of amusement. *Bang!* She struck the nearest desk with the flat of her ruler, and everyone jumped. "Class, I will not tolerate this kind of disruption." Nevertheless, she looked at me curiously, as though I were an animal she was trying to determine the species of. "Meiying—May—is a member of our class. I expect that no one will question the administration's decision to place her here."

Roll call continued, but several glances were thrown my way. *So much for anonymity.*

"Open your books to page four," Mrs Johnson instructed once she'd finished attendance. "We will be starting with the colonization of America. William, please begin."

"Before Christopher Columbus discovered the Americas, people occupying the land lived in untamed and primitive ways..."

"Where are you from, May-yong?" a voice hissed at me. I glanced over to find a girl—Ashley, her name was—leaning across the aisle, her hand planted firmly on my desk. Our skin tones were nearly indistinguishable, and that reassured me. I did belong here, I decided.

"My name is May. I was born here," I said, not understanding what she meant.

She gestured at my face. "When did you have your accident?"

I touched my cheeks. Were they still red? "What do you mean?"

"Your face. It's so broad and flat it looks like you ran into a wall."

"... and once the pilgrims landed safely from their voyage, their arrival was celebrated with a large feast..."

I turned my attention to the reading. A large diagram on the side showed the natives and settlers, gathered around bushels of food. The textbook had described the dinner as a welcoming, but the natives were huddled around their chief, withdrawn like they were foreigners in their own land. The chief gripped his staff, bracing for some unseeable future.

I unpacked my lunch, feeling the scrutinous gaze of my classmates. The sweet smell of soy sauce streamed out when I lifted the lid. Ha cheung. Nai wong bao carefully wrapped in bamboo leaf. I could feel the gasp of repulsion behind me at the globby alien food on my plate.

I forced a smile. "My mom must've packed me the wrong thing by mistake." I stood up and scraped it into the trash can.

My stomach grumbled, perhaps annoyed at my obstinance. I watched wistfully as the others produced their neat lunch tins and milk cartons. If only I could trade places with one of them, chatting absentmindedly and munching on peanut butter sandwiches. Oblivious to the history that had secured them a seat here, and not on the other side of the fence.

But I couldn't see myself as 'one of them'. Perhaps I was more like a peanut butter sandwich instead. Light on the outside and a dark mess on the inside, that somehow sealed the whiteness together. Still, it was the appearance that mattered, wasn't it? Peanut butter sandwiches did not belong in Bentley.

"Why were you ignoring me in class?" demanded a huffy voice. I looked up in surprise to see Ashley, surrounded by a group of her friends. They looked like the drawing of the natives in the textbook, only with bleached skin and complacent expressions. When I didn't respond, she pushed: "How did you get into Summit?"

I thought of the woman in the hallway, and how her eyes had shouted in defiance. Her children were probably eating lunch at Bentley now, on tables scarred with graffiti and slurs. That school could offer them nothing. But maybe there wasn't anything for me here. Why had I gotten by, when they were caught behind that mesh barrier? Did I really belong here, even if you couldn't see the spread of peanut butter from the outside?

"Hello? Can you speak English?" Ashley's face loomed close to mine.

I felt my mouth twist into something between a grimace and a smile, and the rigidity of the morning's ordeal cracked slightly. "I guess I make a good sandwich."

Mama was busy at the stove, stirring a pot thick with jook. The smell of it filled the apartment, already cramped with stuffy sofas and brushstroke paintings. Hearing my entrance, my mother turned and smiled, her eyes creasing. And for that smile I hated her, hated the face and the eyes and the room that was so clearly not American. The shelves of foreign food and the draperies and carpets of foreign cloth. I had a sudden urge to throw the steaming jook out the window, which was propped open with a small Buddhist statue. Siddhartha wouldn't mind—he was probably sick of those wrinkled mandarins people always left him. Maybe he'd also wished for a peanut butter sandwich. White bread with the crusts cut off.

I guess I was standing there for a while, thinking about Siddhartha and his eating habits because suddenly Mama wrapped her arms around me.

"What's wrong, Meiying?"

"Don't call me that," I muttered, burying my head into her qipao.

"Meiying is a beautiful name," she insisted. "It belonged to your grandmother. Now, aren't you going to tell me about your day?"

"Mama," I said, faltering, "Are you sure I should be at Summit? Everyone thinks I should've been sent to Bentley, even my teacher— not that she said it, but—"

"Nonsense. You have a beautiful white face." She lifted up my chin, cupping it with her hands.

The little resolve I had built cascaded down, and I began to cry. Tears shuddered out of my eyes, dripping crookedly across skin that, more and more, resembled a mask.

SOPHIA FELSINGER

Bitter Plums

The first thing I notice is the cold. I blink into awareness slowly, the world around me gradually coming into focus again. Dark wood, a ceiling, a closet, seven pictures on the wall. Our bedroom. I turn and look, the room is empty. Your side of the bed is unmade, the sheets cool when I touch them. I roll over again, look at the clock on my bedside table; it is half past nine and Sunday.

I stretch, get up, leave the warmth of my blankets, exchanging it for cool air and the feeling of wooden floors beneath my feet. I shiver as I make my way to the bathroom to grab my robe, opening the curtains as I walk past the window. My steps are quiet as I leave the bedroom and go downstairs. The kitchen is as empty as the bedroom was. You are not at the table but there is coffee and bread and jam. Plum, my favourite.

I make myself breakfast, two slices of bread, and listen to the birds outside as I eat. My split lip aches with every bite I take but the sweetness of the jam almost washes the pain away.

Afterwards I go upstairs again, showering quickly and then dressing carefully. My side aches a little as I stretch to grab a sweater from the top shelf of my closet, and I end up choosing the grey one instead of the purple I was originally going for.

You call my increasingly dark wardrobe my 'funeral attire', and I conveniently keep forgetting to tell you that it is my colourful clothes that are buried somewhere deep down in the closet, perhaps right next to your tux.

When I am finished dressing, the house is as empty as it was earlier, and I wonder idly where you might have gone to as I take out the cleaning products from beneath the sink. It does not truly matter where you are, only when you will come back. For now, I have the house to myself, and I use the time to clean the bathroom and kitchen. I enjoy cleaning, at least if I let myself see it as something meditative, something to focus on, something that takes my mind off other things. Cleaning is simple, if at times gross and uncomfortable; it is structured clearly and unapologetic. There is no room for errors because there are no errors to be made. Sinks and floors are forgiving; there is no need to be cautious or careful or afraid. One cannot harm anyone or anything while cleaning.

But cleaning also never takes quite as long as I think it will. I am done before midday, and you still have not returned. I could call you to ask where you are, or text you to ask if you are alright but the sun is shining in through the windows, the house is quiet and clean, and my ribs are still sore.

I leave my phone on the kitchen counter and go into the garden instead, bringing a book with me. Our neighbours' garden is empty, the kids are either still asleep or playing inside, and I enjoy the quiet, small mercy it is. It is rare I get a moment like this, all to myself, all alone, and I cherish it, let the seconds tick by, one after the other, unobserved and all for myself.

The book is good, a gift from my sister who has a penchant for crime novels with gruesome descriptions of murder and detailed descriptions of sex, and it takes my mind off the memories of yesterday that try to creep in, as well as the plans I have for today, plans that have been long in the making.

I go back inside again once the sun gets too hot, and putting my book on the kitchen table, I go to the bathroom upstairs. I wash my hands, look up and watch my face turn from neutral and relaxed to horrified as I look in the mirror. I forgot. Today, I forgot. Because I woke up alone, maybe, or because the neighbours' children were still inside and their garden was empty, no one there to see me and my face.

My hands shake a little as I take out the foundation and concealer from my washbag, going through the motions quickly, each stroke and dip practised a hundred times already. The colour on my face that is not supposed to be there is mercifully light, green and yellow today, easier to hide than the predecessors, the blue and purple that hurt to even touch with a brush or sponge.

The only purple on my face is the tinted chapstick I put on afterwards. I have the house to myself. Who will judge? And even if you come back, I had plum jam this morning and the fruits in our garden are almost ripe.

I watch myself apply the makeup, the protection, layer after layer on my skin, evening out the tone, matching the colour to my skin until everything is gone, neatly tucked away in a closet, or hidden underneath a mask, buried by make-up and chapstick.

Even with my face now looking like it should, I do not go out into the garden again, at least not immediately. Instead, I make lunch, cook enough for us both, should you come back today. You have been disappearing every now and then for at least three weeks now, sometimes for a few hours, sometimes for almost the entire day. You rarely provide an explanation or excuse, and I almost wish that your disappearance from this house would be on a weekday in the evening, when you come home hours after you have finished working, because it just was a busy day at the office, honey, you know how it is, they needed me. I had to stay longer, and no, my tie is tied perfectly fine, and that's just wine on the collar. What are you even talking about? Hand me the water, would you.

Only it would not be water; it would be wine or Scotch or whatever you have in that cabinet of yours I never touch and never dust. Not that it is dusty to begin with. Too frequently used.

That daydream disappears while I cook and I focus on other things that are not horrible wishes but rather the sound of children playing outside. Cooking is a process that happens automatically when I am distracted, and when the food is done, the rice cooked and strained, the vegetables mixed in, the children are still screaming and laughing outside, and our house still only has one person in it. There are no crooked ties or badly concealed affairs brought in from the outside, dragged over the doorstep like a dog's carcass, dead and surrounded by flies, dressed up in linen and pretence.

The only person concealing anything in this house is me, yellow and green, you would not even bother. You do not bother, no need to present facts as anything but. There is no hiding, not from you, there is nothing you have tucked into the back of the closet, except for a few empty promises, maybe. You have a mask too but one that almost always falls as soon as you step inside this house, step over the dead dog as if you could not see it, could not smell its foulness, the decay.

My mask is worn everywhere. It is makeup and cloth of just the right length, a smile, some teeth, some hair over my face, sunglasses and a sharp tongue, a laugh at certain times, and eyes that are wide open, taking in non-existent lipstick, perfectly straight ties. Hands that shake but hands that grip, too, and hands that have always refused to touch the dead dog. Only one day, they will have to, and they will have to pick the plums from our tree, too.

Lunch is ready and consumed in silence by me, and me alone, and I put your portion in the fridge, carefully labelled. The plum jam stares accusingly at me, asking questions I do not answer. Where is he, where is your lover, where are you? Where are you going?

Just to the garden, today. Book in hand, birds singing in the tree. I bring a pair of sunglasses and a mirror, just in case. I lie down under our plum tree, and when I roll over on my back, baring my throat and stomach, the most vulnerable places, I see dark leaves above me and purple plums that have been green already; they follow the colour guide in reverse. They are beautiful, not quite ripe yet, and I long to stretch out my arms and touch and pluck and eat. Tonight, or tomorrow. But no later than that, the plums will not keep, unless turned into jam.

Around noon, clouds drift over, obscuring the sun, and I pack my things and go towards the house again. The two youngest of our neighbours' children have already gone inside. Through the window I can see Helen talking to them but the older kid, the one with dark brown hair and a smile that is missing one tooth, is still in the garden, looking at the sky, and then at me.

I smile and wave. He waves back, exposing his teeth, his smile, the gap.

"You missed a spot!"

He points at his face, and I mirror the action, trailing my fingers from underneath my eye to the corner of my mouth.

"When eating plums, you missed a spot. You have some purple here."

He points at his mouth, or rather just to the side of it, and I smile and nod my thanks. He grins back and turns around, walks inside. My hand drops along with my smile, and I wipe the chapstick off my face, away from my cheek where it smudged, and press just this side of too hard and feel again where yellow and green hide, purple not too long ago.

I cover my face as I walk inside, cup my hand around my mouth and nose, breathe like this, my hand now a mask, a shield, something to hide behind for when my hand as it is is not good enough, for when I need to transform into something that is not me and sometimes not even quite there. A dead dog, perhaps. Like this, with my hand cupped over my face I get less air but still just enough, always just enough. I do not reapply the chapstick this time, only some concealer, to be safe.

You finally return in the evening, and at first, you give no explanation as to where you have been the entire day. You just bend down as I greet you, kiss me, your lips so soft against mine, so gentle.

I tell you about my day, and you smile and laugh and joke, and I smile with you. You keep your mask on today, as you do every once in a while, and I listen as you tell me about how you went fishing, met an old friend of yours, coincidentally. Last week you went to the gym; the week before on a long drive; the week before on a run that lasted two hours, and I would wonder where that sudden interest in sports has come from, only that I already know, and the only thing I truly wonder about, the only thing I care about, is how to tell whoever you are going to, running to, fishing with, to stay the hell away from you, away from your hands. How to tell her to lift her own two hands to your face, cradle your face and rip off your mask before it is too late.

I could tie the dead dog to your running shoes as a warning sign but only if it is tonight, because after that, this house will be void of me, and all my masks will be lying on the floor, and whomever you spend your time with will probably not see you again, anyways, come to think of it. It would not do to have an affair as the husband of a runaway bride, especially if it is a bride, a wife, of three years.

Most people would frown upon that, even the tie-crooking ones. It is better for them, especially the tie-crooking ones.

Dinner passes in what passes as a relaxed atmosphere for us. You even notice that I cleaned the kitchen. You smile freely today, tell me about how you saw Elise at the river; she was taking a walk with her children.

"They're getting a divorce," you say, mouth full. "Her and Robert. It's been a long time coming, hasn't it? They never seemed happy, and it's probably better for him, anyways. I expect she'll be taking the kids. What did you put into this? Garlic? You know I don't like that much garlic, darling."

I shrug, do not look up from where my hand is clutching the fork. I take another bite, my eyes avoiding yours. Not now, not today. I do not cower like I used to, back in the beginning, the first year of our marriage when everything unravelled. I do not scream like I did in the second year. I do not walk out or try to do anything at all. I just keep eating. You were in a good mood mere seconds ago; perhaps it will keep.

But your fingers come into view, tip my chin up and I am left looking at you. You have put your fork next to your bowl, tidy, and you are smiling, the barest a hint of a smile, now.

"Are you not going to answer me?"

Your voice is soft; the window behind me is partially open and I can hear the last few birds singing, nestled in our plum tree, tucked away from sight. We are invisible too, at least from the outside, our curtains are drawn, swaying in the breeze. Your voice is soft but your face is not. They can hear, outside, they can hear but they cannot possibly see what is happening inside, the mask has been slipped over the entire house now, no one can see what is happening underneath.

"It is part of the recipe," I say, my voice nowhere near as soft as yours. Softness has no place in this. "You liked it last week, I didn't change anything today. If you don't like it, maybe bring some of the fish you catch, then I can cook that."

Your fingers disappear from my chin, your smile slides right off your face, and the cutlery rattles as your fist lands on the table, making me flinch.

"Julia," you say, calm, always so calm, despite your fist trembling on the tabletop. "Julia, I think it would be better if you held your tongue now."

I open my mouth to answer, say something, anything but you stand up and turn, walk towards that cabinet I never touch, bend down and open it, look at the options. What will it be, which colour, brown, golden, white, red?

I take another bite of my dinner while you are busy choosing your drink and my eyes are drawn to our entrance door, to the dead dog on our floor that only I can see. Its eyes have rolled back in its head, only the whites are visible, and the flies buzzing around it have become louder, a constant hum in the back of my mind.

I have taken care of everything, not just dinner. My bag is packed, my sister is informed, I have money, a plan, somewhere to go. I have a way out of this, and I have the courage to take it, too, for the first time.

Today you choose gold, you straighten, close the cabinet, and I look away from the carcass in our home, the body soon to be a skeleton, and look at you instead. Your mask is gone entirely now, lying somewhere between whiskey and wine, crumpled, and you walk towards me slowly, place your chair next to mine.

I continue eating as you start drinking, slowly, ever so slowly. You are sitting just far enough behind me that I cannot see it when you lift your arm and I tense when your hand lands on my shoulder.

You huff, amused, and your hand starts running up and down my back, slowly and gently. When I am finished eating and want to stand up to put the dishes in the sink, you catch my wrist and tug me down again, pulling me a little closer to you.

"I love you, you know that? I love you. I'll bring you a fish next time, my love."

I nod and turn my face away, just far enough that you cannot see it.

"I love you too," I say, a lie so sweet on my tongue, and you start stroking my back again and start humming, too, a song I do not know. It probably looks like it should, us sitting at the kitchen table, your hand running up and down my back, me half leaning against you, as if there had never been any threats at all, nor any pain. It looks domestic and quiet, peaceful and like two people in love.

The lengths you go to to secure your mask will never fail to astound me.

After dinner, I excuse myself to the bathroom. I shower and wash my face, apply a little makeup, just enough to cover up. I put on leggings and a comfortable T-shirt, clothes as suited for the streets as they are for staying inside and I smile at you as you pass me to go to the bathroom. You smile back and lock the door behind you.

I know how long you take in the bath, I know your routines, and I know I have almost exactly fifteen minutes to disappear. My bag is packed, I grab it from underneath the bed and walk downstairs, turning off the lights as I go.

I have texted my sister already. I do not have to walk far from here to get to her car. Far enough for nosy neighbours not to connect the car and our house, even after they hear of my disappearance.

I pause in the kitchen for a few seconds, take one last look around. I am leaving a lot of things behind; a lot of possessions and memories; three years of marriage and hiding and pain; three years of constantly washed and re-used masks until the tears started to appear. The masks were repaired, sewn together; any holes would be patched up, over and over again.

My fingers are sore after years of holding needle and thread, after years of stitching and patching up but I still walk over to our entrance door, pick up the dead dog that is not truly there. The flies buzz away, disturbed, only to circle me seconds later. The dog is heavy but not as heavy as it looks, and its fur is soft, if matted with blood. I carry it to the sliding door that leads to our garden and step outside, place it on the damp grass. The flies stop buzzing around me and fly away, a swarm taking off into the cold night air. The dog's eyes twitch, turning, looking, the whites returning to where they are supposed to be, and then it gets to its feet slowly, unsteadily.

It is bleeding still; I can see a hint of bone shining from underneath its fur and I grip the straps of my bag tightly as it turns its head to look at me. Then, it turns around, and the carcass moves. The dog is running, away, away, away. Away from the house and who is still inside of it.

I can no longer tie the dog to your running shoes as a warning sign to whom you spend your days with but there are other ways to warn someone. Ways without blood and violence, without pain and anger. I will find a solution; I am sure of that.

With the dog now gone, I finally start walking, making my way across our garden, away from the house. The air is cold; a soft breeze sweeps through the trees, sounding like a whisper, a scream, a cry. The plum tree at the far end of our garden is just a silhouette in front of the dark sky, darker than the night even, hunchbacked and old.

I walk over, one foot in front of the other, taking something away from myself with every step. Inhale, exhale, let go, let go, let go. Piece by piece it all falls away, sheds like old skin, like fur, like a mask torn to shreds—the fear, the pain, the anger, the shame, all that landing on the grass beneath my feet. I let go. The bark is cold as I touch it, damp. The leaves above me rustle, the branches bending low, a few of them almost touching the crown of my head.

Let go. I remove my hand from the bark, running it through my hair. I turn towards the house just in time to see the bedroom lights switch on, illuminating part of the porch from above. I watch your silhouette as you get ready for bed.

The wind picks up. The leaves around me are rustling loudly, and if I close my eyes and tip my head back just so, then it is a roar, a scream. I stare at the bedroom window, can clearly make out your movements, and I recall what you do every day, every night, the rituals you have before going to bed.

It will take another three minutes for you to leave the bedroom, and then perhaps another two before you realise that I am not where I should be.

You will look in the kitchen first, expecting me to be hunched over the table as I so often am, and when you find the kitchen void of my presence, you will check the living room, which will also be dark. No trace of me there, either.

Only then will you think to even look outside, look at the gnarly old plum tree, its leaves swaying in the wind. You will see me, then. The fury will slide off your face, easy and quick as water, and I will watch as your expression grows neutral, like it does every morning, a mask of pleasantness over your features, the mask of a loving husband, a good neighbour, of someone who enjoys fishing and likes his acquaintances' kids. You will walk outside, stride towards me, grab my wrist, your face already turning back to fury, the mask torn to shreds once more because really, who will see? Everyone is asleep.

Your hand will wrap around my wrist, and you will lead the way, drag me back to our house, as if I did not know my own garden, as if I did not know where to go. As if I would run if you let go. I have no doubt that your fingers will bruise when you find me.

For now, I look up, look at the branches above me, the plums barely distinguishable from the leaves in the darkness. I extend my hand, my fingers searching for a plum, finding it more through touch than vision. I pluck it from the tree, testing how soft it is with my fingertips.

I bring it to my mouth, take a bite. The plum is bitter, not sweet, it is not ripe yet. The plum's flesh is hard and slightly sour, and it takes willpower to keep on chewing.

I watch the bedroom window as I eat, taking small bites. I finish the fruit just in time to see the lights flicker out, and as I toss the pit aside, I can see your silhouette approach the stairs, illuminated by the lights in our corridor.

I look at the rectangle of light for another few seconds before I breathe out, slowly, deliberately. Not looking away, I pick another plum from the tree, not testing this one. I need to hurry, now.

Carefully, I walk towards our garden gate, turning my back to the house. I pray I do not slip on the wet grass. I walk towards the gate, one foot in front of the other. The plum is heavy in my hand. My wrist hurts from the last time you grabbed me there; the bruises you left as purple as the fruit I hold.

I reach the gate just as I hear the kitchen door inside the house creak. I open the gate a second later, step out of it, away from the streetlights, away from our house, towards our neighbours' hedge facing the street, tall and green as it is. I walk up to it, step behind it, my body so close to the leaves I can feel their dampness on my skin. I am hiding, and like this, the house's hungry, golden eyes cannot see me.

I wait.

The plum is smooth in my hand, and I run my fingers over it as I hold my breath. You step out on the porch a minute later; I can hear the wood creaking. Carefully, I turn, angle my body in such a way I can see but cannot be seen. The porch light above you is on, moths buzzing around it, and your face is illuminated. I watch, fascinated and terrified, as your expression changes, as one mask gets exchanged for another, and another.

You look furious as you step through the door. Neutral, as soon as you are outside. Three breaths, three passes of my thumb over the plum, three agonising moments. Then your face changes again, neutrality sliding off like water running over a smooth surface, leaving fury behind once more.

Fury, neutrality, fury.

And then—worry.

You look around, your gaze darting past the plum tree, out onto the street where I am standing. Your eyes almost touch me but you cannot see me, not this time. I am not there. You do not see me, only a gnarly old plum tree, dark grass and a hedge that is not exactly a safe space but still, something to hide behind.

I watch as the worry slides off your face, replaced by anger once more, and then fear. No mask, not this time. Your fear is real. I have lifted my hands from metres away and with my disappearance, I ripped your mask off your face. You turn, and the front door closes behind you with a bang.

I watch as the lights in the house turn off, one after the other, living room, kitchen, corridor, bedroom. Darkness.

Once the last light has disappeared, I turn around and walk down the road, the air cool around me, and wet. I take a bite of the plum as I walk. It is softer than the other one, and its juices spill over my chin. My hand holds it tight, the bruises on my wrist as dark as the plum itself. I go, I walk, and I remember how the fury slipped from your face. I breathe, and every breath is another bit of fear trickling away. It is me, letting go, go, go. The plum is soft, ripe. Good. I bring it to my mouth once more, take another bite. The juice spills over my hand, and I smile.

The fruit tastes sweeter than any jam you ever bought.

SARAH HOLM

The Shopkeeper

It had been a completely ordinary day. There were a few customers, a few sales. Completely ordinary, which was mostly why he noticed when the clock failed to strike seven. He knew it was closing hours—he'd just checked his phone before starting to close up the shop. '*How annoying,*' he remembered thinking. Winding that damned thing was always a pain.

When the bell above the door rang, he bit back a sigh, looked up from his counter, and fought to replace his frown with an amicable smile. A glance to the door proved that he had, indeed, remembered to turn the sign around. He wasn't sure what was so hard to understand about the big, bold letters reading '***CLOSED***', but maybe it was his fault for assuming the average client had more than one, half-dead brain cell. Or maybe it was his fault for not locking the door.

"I'm sorry," he said, not sorry at all. "We've just closed. Perhaps you would like to come back tomorrow? We open at 8, close at 7."

Half of the client's face was concealed by the shadow cast by their hoodie, and their hands were shoved deeply into the large pockets. Nevertheless, the shopkeeper noticed their pursed lips.

When they finally spoke, their voice was quiet, but the words were clear, "I would like to see your latest addition to the local history collection."

"I'm afraid it hasn't arrived yet."

"That's fine," they said, voice halting as if reading from a script. It was normal, for a first timer. "I'll have a look at volume 9."

The lines were said, and so began the transaction. It would be late by the time they were finished, which didn't please him in the slightest, but he had a reputation to maintain. Beyond that... All that mattered was the payment.

He lifted the countertop so that the client could follow him and led them to the back of the shop, through the door with a sign that read 'employees only'. Not that signs meant much to his current client.

The back room was cold and dark, even when he turned the lights on. From the corner of his eye, he saw the client tuck their arms further within their pockets. He didn't particularly love the cold, either, but it was necessary for his craft.

"So, do you have an idea of what you want?"

When he turned to face the client, their hoodie was pushed back, revealing dark curls and a smattering of freckles across a girl's face. A very young, very *human* girl. He faltered in his step, a deep frown beginning to form.

He'd never had a human as a client—rather, he'd never had a human as this kind of client. They were ignorant about everything, frightened to look beyond where they felt safe. He felt anger begin its sticky, hot path up his belly and throat. How did she find him, who—

"Something simple. I just need to get away from here, far away." She spoke even clearer now, and the determination on her face would have been admirable, if not for the fear in her dark eyes. She was nothing but a frightened *child*.

"Who told you about this place?"

Her determination faltered, and she took an anxious glance at her surroundings. It seemed she was just beginning to realize how out of depth she was. He could almost pity her.

"A friend," she said, finally. He waited for more, but the explanation, it seemed, was over.

He gave her a long, unimpressed look, to which she responded with a defiant frown. He sighed, feeling the anger fade. There was a first time for everything, he supposed. As long as she paid... He could figure out which one of his clients had betrayed him later.

"Very well. First, let's discuss payment..."

Before he could even finish, the girl had taken her hand out of her pocket. She unfurled her palm, and atop it sat a small pile of perfectly round golden coins, all of them inscribed with the same pattern.

The shopkeeper recoiled immediately. "Where did you get these?" he demanded. Not a moment later, he held up his hand. "Never mind that, I don't want to know. I don't care. Take those coins back to wherever you found them, and *never* come back here." He shoved her hand away, anger boiling deep within his core, wild and untamed.

He'd gone this long without trouble, and he intended to keep it that way. How dare this girl—this *human* girl—show up out of *nowhere,* with something like that stashed in her pockets. She had no idea, no possible *clue* of what she'd gotten herself into.

"Please," the girl said. "If not with this, I'll pay another way. Any other way, *please.*" Her voice cracked on the last syllable, and her eyes were wild with panic. Her resolve had finally crumbled. "I don't want to die, please help me."

The shopkeeper observed her for a long while. He struggled to control his breathing as she wept openly in front of him. It was ridiculous, *absolutely* ridiculous. He had no obligation to her, and the only thing that mattered more to him beyond the shop was his own life—he would certainly lose both if he helped her.

But he knew all too well the feeling of dipping your toes into the yawning abyss that was this world, only to drown in it moments later. He knew what it was like to be a human—insignificant, mortal, and vulnerable. He knew how desperately he had clung to his own survival, however long ago it had been. And he knew that he would not turn away the girl.

"You are a foolish, *foolish* girl," he said quietly. "But I will do as you wish."

There were tears in her eyes, a grateful smile on her lips as she snivelled pathetically. The shopkeeper grimaced.

"Don't thank me. I never want to see you again, and if you tell anyone about this transaction, I have the means and motive with which to make you suffer for the rest of your pathetic, minuscule, mortal life." He sighed deeply and with some satisfaction when the girl shrank back, wide-eyed.

"You may sit there while I work." He pointed to a small stool off to the side of his workbench. She slid onto it after a moment of hesitation, but he paid her no mind, settling down at his own seat.

The clay was cool and malleable beneath his fingers, easily manipulated into the shape he envisioned. He murmured incantations as he went, slowly and carefully, so as to not trip up on any of the words. Even after all this time, he took the utmost care with his creations. It was a lesson his master had drilled into him early on, and probably one of the only ones that had stuck.

Next, came the paints. It was his favourite part—they made all his creations come to life. Normally, he would take a few *days* to complete an order, but under the current circumstances... He'd had to work quickly, efficiently. There was no time for little details, or the stories he would create. He hoped it would not make the end result less lifelike.

Once the paints had dried and the final incantation was spoken, he looked upon his workbench and saw the girl's new self. A beautiful hooked nose, mischievous eyes, and a wide mouth. He'd kept the skin dark, but altered the shade, and as for the rest... Well, that was up to his spells. They were strong, nearly unbreakable, but they needed something to hold on to—something inanimate, as his master had discovered early on. When applied to one's own face. Well, the consequences were never pleasant. And it was better off left at that.

He plucked the ceramic mask up off the table and turned back toward the girl.

In the time it had taken him to complete her request, she seemed to have fallen asleep. He cleared his throat, and within the moment she was awake, rubbing at her eyes. There were tear tracks beneath them.

"Before I give you this, we need to establish some rules. First, you never come back here. When you leave, get as far away as you can and pray they don't follow." When she nodded, he continued, "Second, once you put this mask on, it'll take a while for you to get used to it. Don't take it off until at least a week has passed. Third, don't ever go looking for something you know nothing about again.

Save us the grief of having to clean up after your mess." He paused. "Do you understand?"

"Yes."

The ceramic mask passed from his hands to hers. She looked at it for a long while before turning it over. He placed a hand atop hers. "Don't put it on now. Wait until you're a good few miles away." If anything, he could at least deny he'd helped her if someone—or something—came knocking at his door.

She was quiet for a handful of moments, staring down at the face she cradled in her hands. When she spoke, her voice trembled, "I know you said not to thank you, but... I hope you know that whatever happens to me, I'll be forever thankful for the second chance you've given me." She smiled.

The shopkeeper didn't know how to respond, so he said nothing at all. The girl nodded once, turned on her heel and walked towards the door. As her fingers touched the cool metal, a familiar chime sounded from the front of the shop.

"Stop," he said, very, very quietly. His client turned her head slowly, and he could see from the fear in her eyes that she'd guessed just who had decided to drop in unannounced. He beckoned her closer with one hand and she complied quickly. "Listen to me. Keep quiet and stay here. I'll handle this. If things seem grim. Hide. No one can enter my workshop without my say-so."

She nodded, face white, eyes wide. He hoped she could pull it together long enough for him to work a way out of this mess.

The doorknob felt like ice, and when he stepped outside the safe confines of his workshop it was unbearably hot. He walked up to the counter, plastering a small smile on his face along the way, and faced one of the creatures he'd tried so hard to avoid.

There were few things that phased the shopkeeper anymore. Fewer things still which scared him. But these beings were truly deserving of the moniker monster. They were ruthless, cunning, and older than many knew. He'd heard that their true form could destroy your perception of time and space, but, as far as he knew, no one was lining up to test that theory.

"Shopkeeper," the creature greeted. Its mouth didn't move, open in a permanent grin with rows of large, sharp teeth.

"I'm sorry, but we're closed," he said.

The creature closed its mouth. "And yet, the door is open."

He shrugged. "I forgot."

A laugh rang out in the shop. "Ah, of course, of course. I'm certain you're glad that it was me, and not some thief, that came in."

"Can I help you with something?"

The thing frowned deeply. "Yes, you can. I seemed to have misplaced something—something very important—and I was hoping you could tell me where it is."

"What are you looking for?"

"Are we really going to play this game?" The grin was back. "I don't mind at all. I enjoy watching you squirm, and I think your fear smells wonderful. If I could bottle it up, I would, but, alas, my kind isn't one for long term solutions." It walked towards him, and with each step the shopkeeper felt his nausea rise. It leaned against the counter, nails digging into the carefully lacquered wood. "I like you. We *all* like you; you're a staple of our weird and wonderful community. But you know the terms and conditions of our deals better than anybody." In an instant its hand shot out and grabbed him by the chin. With one strong tug, it pressed their foreheads together and inhaled deeply. "Don't be foolish enough to side with the humans."

He could feel beads of blood form where its nails pressed against his cheeks, and he felt about ready to empty the contents of his stomach. He swallowed the bile down, grimacing at the acidity.

The urge to give up was overwhelming. But if it knew he'd helped the girl for certain, it was just playing with him now. It would never let him go alive, not without a deal. And deals with these monsters were never without dire consequences.

On the other hand, if it somehow believed him...it might let him go. The girl would have her second chance, and he could set up shop somewhere else. His services were needed all over the world; he'd have no problem at all.

"She came in, and I refused to help her."

The grip it had on him tightened abruptly and his jaw creaked under the pressure. "You are about to cross a line, here." When he said nothing, it let go. "Fine. Like master, like apprentice. At least the last one—"

Before it could finish, a voice sounded from behind him, "Stop."

The shopkeeper resisted the urge to scream, he resisted the urge to vomit, and he resisted the urge to kill the girl himself. In front of him, the creature's eyes lit up.

"There she is!" it cheered.

Faster than he could process, it crawled over the counter and grabbed the girl. Its fingers were long and spindly, and while one hand could easily fit around her throat, it used both. All the while, the girl didn't even struggle, eyes fixed on the ceiling above her. "Where are my coins?"

She reached, feebly, into her pocket to produce the golden coins. They fell to the floor. With one, swift movement, it picked them up and swallowed them.

"I would tell you to be more careful next time, but, well." It grinned. "Oh, come, now. No screams? No struggles? I know you want to. You have that look in your eyes, like your life is flashing before you in technicolour. What do you see? Your parents? The lover you never should have left? The dog that died when you were eight? Tell me, please."

The girl's eyes filled with tears, but she did not speak. She'd given up, just like that.

Maybe it was the fact that after consuming the girl's soul and then feasting upon her body, the creature would most certainly turn its sights on him for trying to deceive it. Or maybe it was the fact that the sliver of soul he had left was crying out to him, making his remaining humanity impossible to ignore. Or maybe it was the fact that she would give herself up to an awful, unknowable fate so willingly after fighting so hard to live.

Whatever it was, it didn't matter. Not really. He was running on adrenaline, and if he didn't act now they would both surely suffer the same consequences. He was always one for self-preservation, and not much for grovelling. He would get them both out of this mess.

"You can't hurt her."

Annoyed at the interruption, it turned to him. "Oh?" it said, mockingly. "And why is that?"

He breathed deeply. "She is to be my apprentice." The girl turned her wide eyes towards him, but he ignored her for now. If everything went according to plan, he would have plenty of time to explain.

"What?" It laughed, loud and grating. "Why is this the first time I'm hearing about it, then?"

"It doesn't matter," he said. "I forfeit the right to my immortality, as my master did before me, and her master did before her, and so it has been since the first of us, and so it will be until the last of us."

The creature's grin disappeared slowly. "You can't be serious."

Beneath it, the girl struggled to talk, and so it tightened its grip in warning. "Quiet now, the grown-ups are talking." She gasped, clawing at its hands. The shopkeeper glanced at her quickly, hoping the look he gave her would inspire confidence in his plan, and she quieted soon after. The creature relaxed its hold.

Just to prove it wrong, the shopkeeper removed the plain, black band around his finger, took the girl's hand in his, and closed it around the ring. She was crying again, and her fingers grasped at his own desperately. He patted her hand and nodded before pulling away.

Giving her the ring was more of a symbolic gesture than anything, but it would have to do until they could forge a proper one for her.

The creature lessened its hold on the girl. "Do you even know what you're doing, foolish human?" She didn't respond, glancing between it and the shopkeeper. It smiled widely. "You are trading one deal for another. He'll take your soul, just the same as I."

"She knows just as well as you or me," the shopkeeper said loudly, drawing the creature's attention away from the girl's panicked face.

'Please have faith,' he thought. *'We can both make it out of here intact.'*

"You cannot take that which doesn't exist," he continued. "And since your pact wasn't with me, you can't reclaim a soul that is, for all intents and purposes, mine."

"Our deal was made before yours," it said, seeming amused. "I have first claim."

"I have reason to believe the deals were made at the same time."

The smirk disappeared from the creature's face, its hands releasing the girl entirely. As soon as she was free, she scrambled back as far as she could, fingers massaging the rapidly forming bruises at her throat.

"I grow weary of this back and forth. You know the rules, shopkeeper. A soul that is promised must be delivered, no matter what." It sighed, long and theatrically, before grinning once more. "But I admire your courage. Fine, I'll believe she made two contracts at the same time. Thus, we will divide the soul in half."

The shopkeeper nodded and held out a hand. "It will be so."

Long, cold fingers gripped his own. The creature was grinning even wider, and as the shopkeeper waited for it to say its part, it pulled him forwards.

"Just kidding," it said, eyes wide and wild with bloodlust, before taking its other hand and shoving it deep into his chest.

He could feel it grip his heart, could feel the blood and the broken ribs and torn muscles and damaged lung. But he could also feel his hand on the creature's face not a moment later, and the incantations form upon his lips like they had thousands of times before. And he spoke quickly and without pause and with the utmost care.

One of the first things he had learned as an apprentice was to always, *always* use inanimate materials to form masks. They are to be used as a tool to blend in with the humans, and not as an entirely new identity. There are a variety of spells that can be used to help this process along, such as infusing the masks with their own personalities and stories—something that could be extremely useful for the more reclusive beings. Most importantly, masks can be taken off. Your own face, however...

The creature ripped its hand out of his chest and screamed, flesh and bone morphing rapidly, turning it into something else entirely.

Released from its hold, the shopkeeper slumped onto the counter and touched the sharp edges of his exposed ribcage gingerly. With a grimace, he placed both hands at the cavity and began to heal himself.

Meanwhile, the creature thrashed wildly as it changed, screeches turning quickly into whimpers, then moans, then nothing at all. The shopkeeper looked up and smiled.

On top the pile of blood and flesh and bone stood a rather confused, rather naked, man. A perfect replica of one of his master's favourite masks.

"Hello there," the shopkeeper said. "You must be terribly lost."

Upon seeing the shopkeeper's current state, the monster-turned-man promptly fainted. If it weren't for the perforated lung, the shopkeeper would have laughed. Instead, he returned his concentration back to the mending process.

"Oh, God."

The girl was looking quite faint, and perhaps a fair bit ill. The shopkeeper didn't blame her; once the adrenaline wore off, he was sure to be sick as well.

She looked up, and as if finally noticing that he was, in fact, still alive, rushed towards him.

"I'm so sorry," she said, dropping to her knees. Fresh tears sprang to her eyes, and soon there were streams. The shopkeeper wondered faintly just how much one girl could cry in a day. "I'm so sorry. It should have been me, it should have been me. Oh, God."

Her sobs were loud and, quite frankly, grating. The shopkeeper nudged her with one knee, and she looked up.

"I'm not going to die." At her disbelieving look, he rolled his eyes, then winced. The adrenaline was starting to wear off. Not good. "I have a few strong healing spells up my sleeve, alright? Plus, I'm technically immortal unless I take on an apprentice."

"You *were* lying to that thing, then. You aren't really going to take my...my soul? Or make me your apprentice?"

A wave of pain brought a flush to his face. He spoke through gritted teeth, "Let me...fix this first."

In the time it took him to patch himself up, the creature turned man on the floor of his shop still hadn't woken up. He wasn't sure what to do with it yet, although he felt the best course of action would be to send it back to where it came from. The thing had betrayed a contract; it deserved what it had gotten.

Besides the creature, the girl had followed his instructions and locked the door and closed the blinds. He didn't want any more unannounced guests, not for a long, *long* time.

Afterwards, the girl chose to look around, checking in on him every few minutes. The constant vigilance was annoying, but he couldn't spare any attention to telling her to knock it off. Not when the pain was so intense that he'd blacked out a few times already.

When he was ready to talk, he was breathing heavily from both the mental and physical exertion. He felt ready to pass out again, but he'd promised the girl answers.

"Go on, then. Ask me your questions."

She was quick to jump on the opportunity, "Will more of those things come for me?"

He observed her for a long moment, wondering just how much he should tell her. Human minds were feeble, more than any other being. They couldn't take much of anything that didn't conform to their idea of 'reality'. But... the girl had seen more than most, and she still seemed somewhat sane.

"They have no grounds to, since the one who made the contract with you is... well, for all intents and purposes, dead. Its pact is null and void. They live by certain rules, you know."

She seemed relieved, and he debated whether or not he should leave things at that. But it seemed unreasonably cruel to allow her to go back to her life now, when she might never be safe again.

He sighed quietly, and continued, "I guess it depends more on the deal you made. Just because I got rid of that one doesn't mean another won't come looking for you to hold up your end of the bargain. They're a prideful sort."

The girl shifted in her spot on the ground, averting her eyes. For a while, the shopkeeper thought she wasn't going to speak, but then she cleared her throat and looked up at him.

"I can't go back, can I? To my old life." His silence seemed to be the only answer she needed. She laughed a little. "I guess it doesn't matter much, anyways. I'd already accepted that I was going to have to leave everything behind."

To that, the shopkeeper said nothing.

"Can I ask you another question?" When he nodded, she continued, "Was it lying, when it said you would take my soul? Is that how it works to become an apprentice?"

He felt another sigh begin to build in his chest. The trajectory of this conversation was beginning to lead to topics he didn't really want to get into.

"Not all of it," he said. "Just enough to complete the part of mine I still own. Then, I would be mortal, and you would be immortal."

"And were you being serious, when you said that you were—"

"Look," he interrupted. "Anything that happened before was for my own self-preservation. Before you barrelled into our conversation, I almost had it convinced..." He took a short breath, nostrils flaring, which then quickly turned into a quiet sigh. "I just want you to understand that becoming my apprentice... It isn't easy, and it isn't quick, and, honestly, I'm not even sure it would keep the others from coming after you."

The girl looked down. He saw shame in her face, and fear. Then, she seemed to steel herself; when she met his eyes, there was determination, strength. The fear lingered, in the lines around her mouth, the tremble of her lips, but she'd come to a definitive decision.

"Will you accept me as your apprentice?" ... And there it was.

The shopkeeper kept silent for a long moment. He thought of his master, and how, towards the end, she'd told him that you never have a choice in who you take on as an apprentice, that *they find you*. He wondered if she was laughing at him this very moment, shaking her head like she usually did when something unfortunate happened to him. He wondered if she would approve of this girl, but, then again, she'd approved of *him,* hadn't she?

He sighed, and hoped he wasn't about to make a mistake. "Do you understand what you're asking?"

"I understand the risks."

The shopkeeper held out his hand, and the girl took it. "Then it will be so." He waited for a moment. "You have to repeat the words back to me."

"Oh, uh, it will be so." She looked closely at their hands, and when nothing earth-shattering happened, she frowned. "Is it... done?"

"Yes." He got to his feet, unsteady and lightheaded as the world spun around a few times before righting itself. She may not have felt the pact, but he sure as hell did. Goddamn humans.

"Thank you," she said. When he looked back at her, she was smiling, eyes wet. "I'm sorry, but I don't think I can ever repay you."

"I didn't do any of this for you."

Her smile softened, as if she knew something he didn't. "Thank you anyways."

"Let's just get this place cleaned up before I pass out."

"Alright," she said, and that was that. The shopkeeper was glad; he'd never been one for sentimental moments.

MIA RAMAGE

The Collector's Shop

If asked, I couldn't pinpoint where my childhood had ended and the ugliness had started. Looking back on the winding tunnel of my life, it seemed the ugliness had always been there, curled up in my crib, waiting to make its presence known. I know that this cannot be true, and there was a time that I knew a happy life, but like all tragedies, it comes to the point where any joyous memories are sharpened by the pang of knowing the sweet will soon sour.

What I can tell you definitively is that the pervasive ugliness changed its form the day I stumbled across the Collector's Shop. Perhaps stumbled is not an apt lexical choice here; I doubt there was any chance that I found the shop rather than it found me. Wrapped in my thoughts that harsh December morning, I didn't notice my feet had brought me before a small, crooked, blackened building, only breaking out of my reverie by the perimeter of peace the building granted me. On the bustling streets, crammed with frantic shoppers, the shop stood untouched by the people around me, who moved past without so much as a glance towards it.

Enticed by the serenity, I stepped in, feeling the biting cold subside by the blast of heat as the door opened, and the bell rang out with shining clarity. The door swung shut behind me and trapped me in the bizarre, old-fashioned room. The closing of the door had blocked out any natural light, the grimy windows doing nothing more than filtering the light and distorting it to the heavy brown that seemed to touch every part of the room. The room itself was cluttered; tens of shelves stood in seemingly random angles, swollen with overflowing pieces of paper and small objects that the half-light didn't want to refract for me to depict clearly. All the debris left only a straight path forward to the front of the shop, where the figure stood waiting for me.

The impression of him I will impart to you is the most honest I can give, as his features were unremarkable to me at first. He had greying hair parted down the middle, a short, yet spindly frame, a comical eyeglass balancing off one eye and magnifying its pupil like a squirming black beetle, giving the impression his face was lopsided. What caught my attention the most were his fingers, slender and sharp, drumming over the countertop with anticipation as I stepped forward.

"Hello," I smiled, dipping my head awkwardly to him.

"Hello," he replied, watching me flounder in the middle of his shop. "Is there anything in particular you're looking for?"

I approached his countertop, the only clear space in the shop, with only a rusted till, a shapeless bust, and an erect object cloaked in a mirror. "I'm looking for—" I paused, struggling to come up with a suitable response.

"You don't know," he finished for me. "It's quite alright, quite alright. I often find in this sort of business that's the kind of customer I attract."

"And what business might that be?" I asked, looking around. "I didn't see a sign outside."

The rate at which his fingers drummed the tabletop picked up. "A tricky question, that. Would you like to see for yourself?"

I hesitated, and the air around me stopped moving, tendrils of light creeping back towards me and the sound of the man, or as I came to know him, the Collector, becoming hazy and not dissimilar to the feeling of being underwater. Oh, had I never added my assent to his offer! With that one head movement, everything was brought back into focus again, and I gave my approval for one of his deft fingers to flick the covering off that object, for a screaming silver to brace my eyes.

I flinched away from the object, seeing it to be a mirror, meticulously polished and gleaming smugly, taunting me.

"Look into it."

"I'd really rather not."

"Are you scared of a mirror?"

My smile trembled. "A little, yes."

He wet his lips and pushed the mirror closer to me. "Look into it."

My eyes were drawn downwards, and a slight shudder passed over me at the sight of my own face looking back up at me. There was the ugliness, the poison that had been in my cup with every moment. And in this mirror, every fault seemed magnified; the thinness of my pale lips, the crooked overlap of my teeth, the wrinkles and marks over my face, the bulbous end of my nose, the watery, bloodshot eyes that sat asymmetrical above the broken bridge of my nose.

And then, with another flick of his finger, I saw my nose straighten, the skin smoothen, the teeth shine brilliantly white, every wrong righted in an instant.

I only looked up to see if it was real, see my own happiness reflected in another's face. The Collector was indeed smiling at me, his eyes, like my own, glimmering at the image in front of him. I looked back to the mirror, tears stinging my eyes and rolling down my face when, as I turned back to greet the welcome vision, I saw the mirror image had reverted to its original visage. Only now, the pain of the misshapen truth had been multiplied tenfold, because I had seen true beauty, felt the surge of happiness it carried, knew what it was to have had it and to have lost it. Enraged, I had lunged at the mirror, picking it up and shaking it, hands threatening to crack the sides, as if my anger could bring back the mirage.

The Collector watched the outburst with nothing more than a polite 'o' shape forming on his lips. I set the mirror back down, turning to him in anguish, a shivery, weak-legged sickness overcoming me. "How did you do that?"

"The real question," he said, "is would you like it to be real?"

"You can make that happen?"

He cocked his head, his brow knitting together. "With your permission, of course I can."

I grappled in my bag, pulling out a purse and proffering it to him. "How much?"

"For the procedure? Oh, I won't be taking your money."

The events of what happened in that shop are hazy at best, often only coming back to me in moments of lucidity, but I have always remembered the way I looked at him in that moment, the thought in my head that stood above the rest and proclaimed; *if saints truly are real, this man must be one of them.*

He produced a pen and a piece of paper with a flourish, laying them down flat for me to sign, which I did eagerly, the keen whining need to see what I had seen in the mirror drowning out any potential misgivings. When I had signed, and the paper had been tucked away, he dragged around a small chair and had me sit, handing me the mirror. I looked in it without fear, knowing soon the apparition and the reality would be one and the same.

Taking the mirror from me and facing it away, he asked, "What would you like me to do first?"

I thought deeply, about what ailed me most, and settled on, "The skin. Change my skin."

He gave a small bow which triggered a high-pitched giggle to rise up my throat. "As the lady commands."

My eyesight was pulled inwards as one of his long, curled fingers stretched just above my line of sight and rested on my forehead, tracing lightly over the skin and curving until it rested under my cheekbone.

I felt it come off. All the blemishes, the spots produced by my natural oil, the scar above my eyebrow from a drunken night out, the marks from teenage acne which had never fully healed, the bumps and imperfections I couldn't explain, all of it lifted. But there was something else with it. The wrinkles on my forehead, which I had long abhorred, were peeled away as if they were nothing, and with them the nights of studying that had earned me everything I had wanted, the glorious days spent tanning in the bright, tropical sun, every single memory and part of me that had created those small little lines. The laugh lines that coated my eyes, the corners of my lips, the details created by years of happiness were snatched up and devoured in a few seconds and replaced by a blank canvas.

When his hands lifted from my face, I sat, numbly, watching him handle the skin I had shed as if it were the most delicate thing in the world and arrange it on the empty bust, the shadow of my face now hanging on another head as if it were a mask.

He turned back towards me and smiled. "There. Don't you feel better?"

I placed a trembling hand on my cheek, a smooth silkiness sliding over it, and I nodded.

"What next?"

"Next?"

He picked up the mirror again, this time holding it in front of my face, and I saw creamy, perfect skin, surrounded by jarringly distorted features. He moved the mirror away again. "With potential like yours, don't let it go to waste. What next?"

"My mouth," I begged. "Fix it, please."

He smiled at me, moving his face closer to mine, bringing a finger to my lower lip and parting my mouth slowly. I sucked in at the proximity, and as he began his work I felt him drain off the other times I had been in this position, from my first kiss at nineteen, when I thought I would die from the explosion of emotions, and that same joy mirrored in countless other partners throughout the years. The lips that had first kissed my mother, my father, that had braced the cheeks of my friends, lay limply in the hand of the man before me.

I tried to speak, but he quieted me fervently. "Stay quiet, darling. Those lips need time to settle." Without another word from me, he placed my lips on the bust to join my skin. He looked at his handiwork, satisfaction radiating from him. "Very good. You're shaping up nicely."

I didn't know whether he was speaking to me, or the mask of my face that lay on his desk.

"Teeth next, I think. Don't you?"

Through my new mouth, I managed to say my first word. "Yes."

"Little bit trickier, this one," he said, rolling up his sleeves until they reached his elbow. Without warning, he reached into my mouth, and a scream erupted from me as he set my gums on fire, my mouth awash with the metallic sting of blood as one by one, my teeth were torn from me and rattled on the countertop. He sang merrily between my screams as he counted them, until I fell into silent agony, slimy tendrils hanging from the stumps of my mangled gums.

I looked forlornly at my teeth on the counter like they were fallen friends. The pain of my wisdom teeth growing in, the excitement from having my adult teeth, the words I had spoken with them, the foods I had bitten and sustained myself with, every proclamation of love or happiness sitting before me.

"Don't cry," the Collector warned. "It makes the whole process so much more complicated. Have to work around the tears, you know. Of course, I could always block your tear ducts. Or remove them entirely. Then again, the eyes are a tricky science. Might just leave them till the end, eh?"

I moaned, a deep, guttural sound racked with pain, the kind of sound only the most wretched beings have been accursed with hearing.

He slapped his hand to his forehead, and I saw rivulets of my blood leap from his hand. "Silly me! You'll be wanting your teeth back. Well, not back. You understand I can't do that. Your new teeth, of course." He ran his hand over my mouth lazily, and I started in pain and lurched forward to be sick as something pushed through my gums and thirty sharp little heads began to wriggle through.

"Ah," he said. "I might have mentioned that. See, it's best to let your new teeth grow in. Much healthier for them, you know. But don't fret, don't fret, they're faster growers than their human counterparts. No less painful, but they should be ready in a few minutes."

I clutched my mouth, feeling as though I was giving birth thirty times simultaneously. The sharp ends moved towards each other, a bee sting to my mouth every second.

The Collector had finished arranging my teeth behind my old lips, and in an unparalleled horror I recognised the bare bones of my face he had shaped. I recognised it was far from ugly, and perhaps never had been. He strode over to me with more confidence as I writhed and hissed. "No point waiting around for the teeth to grow out. Shall I do the nose while we wait?"

I prayed and fought for my protests to leave my mouth, but I didn't have control of the new shape and could only make the whimpers of a wounded animal.

"No queries? Right you are, then," he said, and with unreserved glee, settled his thumb and forefinger over the tip of my nose, and tore it clean off.

Blood was pouring out of the hole in the middle of my face where my nose had been, trickling from my mouth, pushing against my sensitive skin. I felt my chest constrict and my heart harden to stone, every breath I had taken through my nose suddenly expendable and pointless. And there I was, choking and gasping for air I couldn't reach and yet somehow, still alive.

He yanked my hair back to examine my ears, and I realised I couldn't feel his breathing on my neck, nor could I see the movement of his chest, because he simply wasn't breathing. Then I realised neither was I.

"I know we didn't discuss your ears, but with a little reshape they really could be something. And you did sign away your face, so really they're mine to take."

Take them he did, and with them he took the sound of my child's first word, the first time anyone said, 'I love you', the music notes that had greeted me, of laughter, every little thing I had heard since birth. He took it all, and when he soothed me as he replaced my nose and ears, I heard nothing. It was as though my ears had been adjusted to a different station, one that no one else but the Collector could control. His voice was as inviting and soft as ever, only now I could understand he was speaking to me in a language not made for humans. When he ran moisture over his lips this time, I noticed the split in his tongue.

"Feels so much better to speak in my native tongues. You don't mind, do you? Obviously you don't, it's your language to speak now too. It's just so liberating to be your true self, I find. Now," he said, snapping from his jaunty demeanour back into a cool detachment as he examined my mutilated face, "not much left for me to do. I have to say, you've been one of my best clients yet. So agreeable. Gold star for you." He pondered, his hand stroking his chin. "I suppose all that's left is the eyes, really. I promised you I'd leave them until the end."

My mouth felt overcrowded with teeth, and even my tongue lying at the base of my mouth caused me immense pain, but I managed to croak out a single, "No."

"No?" he repeated, cocking his eyebrow. "Oh, well, if you insist.

I'm not a monster. Besides, it might do you some good." He leaned forward, his hands on either side of my chair, and his beautiful and terrible eyes met my own, the only part of me left. "I'll let you keep those eyes. I want you to remember my face, and this workshop, and what you signed away of yourself. I want you to remember the life you had before, the beauty, and what you could have kept if you hadn't been so foolish. And especially," he leaned back and swivelled the mirror around to face me, walking to stand by the half-complete mannequin, "I want you to remember this."

My brain was calling out to me to stay seated, but the gleam of the mirror was too strong, and I looked into the face of my lifetime foe. The shriek that tore from my body was enough to make even the Collector jump in his skin. My face, my once perfect face, had been ravaged and destroyed, and yet I could still see a shadow of the face I had once desired in it. Yet that was the worst part; the lips were comically bloated and red, the teeth underneath a bloody snarl as they protruded from my mouth. My tongue was heavy and fat and sat like a leech amongst the running blood, the forked end of it flopping out of my mouth uncontrollably.

My skin was not just smoothened, but taut, pulled against all of my features like an overstretched balloon just waiting to pop. The skin itself was shiny and featureless, devoid of humanity. The cheeks were puffed and intruded into my eyes, and the skin, where not stained by a thick, clotted brown blood, had the look as if it had been coated in a peach plastic. I pulled at the face, hoping to remove the too-thin, crumbling nose the way the Collector had pulled it off so easily, but it wouldn't move. None of my face would move, and I realised, like my heart, it had simply ceased to move with the rest of time.

The Collector looked at me not with pity, but disgust. "Careful. If the wind blows, you'll be stuck with that face. Now, come and look at this little beauty."

Dutifully, I shuffled to where he stood, and if my face could have collapsed at the sight, it would have. My old face had been fashioned into a full mask, upturned in a glorious, human smile. I crooned as I reached out to touch the mask, the most beautiful thing I thought I had ever seen.

"Ah, ah, that's for me to touch, not you. It's mine now, remember?"

He said, and he picked it up lovingly as it floated, paper thin, in his hands. He walked slowly with it, whispering to it as I stumbled, gasping, after him down the rows of shelves.

"Here will do nicely, I think," he said, placing the mask gently amongst the other bits of paper. I looked a bit closer, stumbling back and hitting another shelf, a gargled cry emerging as my skin brushed those pieces of paper. But they weren't papers at all, they were layers of skin, millions of masks of real human faces he had stolen. And somewhere out there, wherever he was about to send me, there would be millions of others like me, No-Faces, whose facades would replicate my own repulsive nature and whose eyes might share an unspeakable and irrevocable regret.

I staggered away, back to the spot where I had walked in this blighted den. The door swung open behind me, the wind tugging and unrelenting in its quest to drag me back to where I had once belonged and was now a nomad.

I clutched onto the door frame, resisting the pull of the real world outside, where sunlight would expose a thousand more horrors the dim room didn't show. "Why have you done this to me?"

He looked at me, bored. "They always want to blame me. You came here because you didn't feel comfortable in your face. You wanted to hide, so I gave you a mask. You can't begrudge me taking the old one. You should have realised if you ask someone to take parts of you, there'll be very little remaining. There is one thing you have left. What's your name, sweetheart?"

I would tell it to you, reader, but it's no longer mine to give.

The Suitor

Meera was caught up in an elaborate fantasy again, this time in front of a lit fire. She almost hadn't noticed the beads of perspiration forming on her forehead as she was consumed by the sounds of batter sizzling on oil.

The doorbell rang and she hastily grabbed the loose end of her *dupatta* and dabbed her forehead with it. The synthetic fabric of her *kurta,* clearly unsuited for bright summer afternoons, strangely prickled her skin. But if anything thirty years of experience had taught her, it was that she had little choice about her clothes after her mother had given a verdict. She quickly untied the knot and let her long hair fall to her waist. In the past month or so, many a prospective suitor that had arrived at their house had complimented her majestic mane. She carefully brushed a single strand of hair in a way that it fell over her forehead and across her eyelid.

Something about meeting people her parents had shortlisted for her to marry, felt surreal. But it was just like all the stories that she had heard from relatives growing up. The family of the boy arrived at the girl's, and the rest, as they said, was left to fate. Her father had assured her that it would be her choice in the end, and she found herself repeating that over and over again, lest she forget.

From a distance, she could faintly hear her father greeting the guests and visualised him holding the door with a wide grin on his face. Witnessing her father greet people with an unhardened expression, was almost like watching humanoid features being painted on a clay sculpture. Her father would then offer the guests a beverage, which would be the cue for her mother to enter the living room. The guests would be subjected to rather obvious remarks about the weather and subsequently, India's performance in the latest cricket match. Then the conversation would be subtly steered into a position from where her father could comfortably pick up on talking about the fact that Meera had been the district topper in her board exams. And then with plastic grins, the entire room would burst into exclamations about how girls were always two steps ahead of boys.

Then it would be her turn to enter the room with a plate full of awkwardly shaped fritters she had carved out of minced vegetables. Her mother had indicated that the taste of the fritters would be a major element in all their secretive assessments.

The one who was supposed to see her today was a professor of History in a renowned college in North Delhi.

"History!?" her mother had exclaimed, puckering her face in a painfully unsubtle manner. But Meera had always admired (sometimes even envied) historians, merely for the fact that they could afford to exist somewhere outside of the realities that haunted the present. Apart from the timelines and words written in fine print, so many things were subjective, so many perspectives were at play. She never really got around to study the subject, mostly because her parents seemed to think that a life in academia was too much of an investment, and simply a knowledgeable mind was too little a return.

This admiration itself served to make her anxious, for she had found that expectations were even more brittle than the fancy ceramic plates her mother saved for serving guests. In all the meetings that her parents had arranged thus far, this was the one she was most hopeful about. Preparing for her grand entrance, she carefully arranged the fritters on a heavily decorated tray, and twisted her lips in a smile in the angle her mother had taught her.

"Meera, come here darling, they want to meet you!" her father's voice called out. She leapt into attention, almost biting the insides of her cheek.

She strode into the living room with mock confidence and placed the tray on the rectangular centre table. Carefully brushing the strand of hair off her face and tucking it behind her ear, she gracefully folded her arms in greeting.

One of the walls in their living room was decorated with a piece of maroon fabric she had embroidered with tiny bits of glass that were iridescent in the warm glow of the afternoon sun. Meera had grown up in this very house and little had changed about this room in all these years. The walls had always been painted in a sober shade of yellow, and the curtains hanging on their window were still an awkward burnt blue that cast a pall over the entire room when it was drawn shut. The wooden table, placed at the heart of the room, was aligned in a way that the longer edge of it faced the chair her father almost always occupied. In the mornings, her mother would wipe the impressions of teacups left without coasters on the table, and films of dust that gathered over the scattered newspapers. Everything was almost the same, except the large canvases that were painted by her, that now hung on the walls perhaps out of necessity to mask the yellow, slowly tarnishing into a shade of ochre. She was almost startled (a little troubled too) at the stark difference in the ambience of the room whenever they had guests over. There were coasters on the centre table, and the chairs were embellished with pieces of white fabric with convoluted designs sewed on them. But most importantly, it was always awkward to witness her father let someone else borrow his throne. With so many people in it the room certainly seemed bigger, sometimes even unrecognisable.

She caught a glimpse of the Professor from the corner of her eye. He was sitting right in between his parents, his gaze fixated downward with the same bashfulness that was otherwise expected from the bride-to-be. He had looked up for a second when she had entered the room but averted his eyes as quickly as fireflies flicker away into the night. He was dressed in a starched blue-collared shirt that was neatly tucked in, and his hair was combed with fastidious care. There were smudges on the thick glasses of his spectacles, that became quite visible in the sunlight. She noticed that his palms were wedged in between his thighs and his spine was slightly hunched. The sight of him reminded her of the time when she sat occupying a small space in between her parents when they were called to school because she had failed her math exam.

Almost everything about him was rather unsurprising, save for the fact that the lower half of his face was covered with a jet black mask.

"Please, do have something." Meera pointed towards the tray on the centre table, as if trying to break into the enigma surrounding the masked man. Having feigned ignorance up until this point, he slightly glanced at her for a moment.

"Of course, did you make them?" he asked, almost straining to bend forward to wrap his fingers around a fritter.

She nodded with a grin, suddenly becoming aware that the dangling earrings that she donned, danced with her animated gestures. Over the next few seconds, Meera witnessed a grown man defeated by the misshapen croquette sitting in his palm. Something in the way he fiddled with it, told her that he was most unwilling to unfasten that mask. She found herself marvelling on the plain piece of cloth that was way too many things at once—the tool of the thief, the harbour of the aggrieved, and the purdah of the ashamed. She wondered which one of these things the hunched professor considered himself to be.

Conversation stirred as the topic of politics surreptitiously entered the room, and Meera was thankful for the awkward silence being lifted. Arguments bounced off each side, like an ill-guided table tennis match, except there could be no winner in this, and discussion would soon take the form of a snake trying to bite its tail. Politics was one subject in an Indian household, that even common ground could not be discussed without loud, eloquent speeches. In between the storm, Meera found herself torn between the two men exchanging heated anecdotes of patriotism, and the two elderly women exchanging tired looks. In the midst of this boisterous camaraderie, she caught a glimpse of the mask being unfastened.

A carmine-tinted laceration cut across his cheek and stretched to the top of his lip. He bit into the croquette cradled in his palms, and before she could even get a thorough look, the mask was back up again.

Meera was suddenly made aware of the rust-coloured *dupatta* draped over her chest that had been sitting untouched all this while. The fabric was placed against the bare skin of her neck, and it was strangely uncomfortable in the heat. Yet, it had been a part of her wardrobe for as long as she could remember, apparently necessary for protecting her modesty. She adjusted it slightly in a way that didn't make her feel that the fabric was trying to throttle her. The burn mark on her hand from hot oil was masked with the long sleeves of her *kurta* and the dull pink of her chapped lips were painted in a vivacious scarlet. And of course, the freckles on her nose were not visible sitting under the solid layer of foundation. Only with this renewed assurance of propriety, did she allow her gaze to linger on her match for just a moment.

She wondered how the ghastly scar had made its way on his visibly docile face. Perhaps it was the result of an accident? Or the result of a gruesome fight? She studied him carefully, but nothing about him even slightly hinted towards a quarrelsome nature.

Meera noticed the Professor's eyes playing all over the room, and wondered if he had caught her name scribbled on the corner of the canvases decorating the room. His eyes fixated on the painting hung right in the centre of the wall facing him. She hadn't been particularly proud of that one, but somehow she had never wanted to sell it. A woman clad in royal attire was the centre of the foot-long frame and she held a flower with withering petals. With her eyes closed shut, the woman had somehow drifted in the aroma of a dying flower perhaps gifted by an admirer. The portrait was of someone she didn't recognise, yet it was one created by her subconscious.

For a few seconds, his unwavering gaze studied the strokes of her brush, and after a while, a softness that was a discernible smile spread to his eyes. He didn't turn towards her to praise the masterful painting as so many had done before. He kept looking at the portrait, and she wondered if he had found more layers to it than she had herself. Witnessing someone closely observe her art, watching them trying to unravel her, was a process she had always found intriguing.

As her father monologued about her achievements as an artist, and old eyes looked at her admiringly, she concluded that very little was required of her in the conversation. Her thoughts drifted again, this time to the moonlit mountains on a crisp winter evening. She was still just a girl when she had accompanied her parents on a vacation to a hill station. Dusk had fallen by the time they made the journey and none of the snow-capped peaks they were eager to witness, were visible at that time. It was a full moon night, and for once she did not have to manoeuvre her way within large crowds. The darkness shrouded everything except for the hush hushed whispers of the few tourists lingering about. There was utter silence and it weirdly felt like she was eavesdropping on a divine conversation not meant for her. She jumped out of her reverie as her mother scrambled all over the place to see if there was any view at all for them. None, she had concluded. They left soon after, and she promised herself to return someday.

Meera never managed to make the trip to a hillside again. But at that moment, a fleeting image of her standing on a moonlit valley, grabbing an arm dressed in blue cotton, made her forget about the slanting rays of the sun that illuminated her living room. Whenever she would turn to look at his face in the night, it would be softly lit with the moonlight, and his eyes would be studying the stars in the sky with the same curiosity he studied her painting with. Even in the soft twilight glow, she'd be able to trace the scar on his face.

No, she'd never be ashamed of the scar, nor any remarks made by nosy passers-by. She would make him believe that there was nothing about him he shouldn't be proud of, just like she had taught herself how to accept all the imperfections about herself. She would remind him night and day how the gash on his face was nothing but a splash of colour to her. After all, she had made a livelihood out of turning blank sheets into objects of fascination. No, she would never let him hide behind the mask again.

"I see you are interested in history as well." The suitor smiled at her, catching her off guard for a moment. He had been studying her paintings set against elaborate *durbars* and monuments all this while.

"Oh well." She cleared her throat. "But I am not as well informed about it as you."

Perhaps this was supposed to be the beginning of a conversation, but he went back into the silent examination. But she was positive that there was a smile behind that mask, even though she wasn't sure if she could see it in his eyes. She desperately wanted to continue the conversation but reminded herself to be patient. 'Perhaps, in the next meeting,' she thought. 'Well, if there is a next meeting,' she hastily corrected.

The wooden frame on which her painting was mounted had a very noticeable fissure on its bottom right corner. She had spotted the frame in a roadside market in Old Delhi. There were delicate carvings on its fine ebony surface that were almost invisible from afar. While trying to mount it on the wall, a corner had chipped off. The idea of hanging a broken showpiece on her drawing room wall had been repulsive to her mother, and in any other meeting, even Meera would have prayed for the guest to not notice her carelessness. But this once, with the man dressed in humble blue, she had known that the painting mattered more than the frame.

She watched him answer questions thrown at him by her parents. For the first time in all her meetings, the answers were not mechanical, as if scripted by someone else. His words were muffled by the mask drawn across his face and he kept feeling the need to tighten the drawstrings behind his ear now and then. He was as timid as she had once been, apparently petrified that his answers about himself could be wrong.

He was thirty-two, just a year older than her, but the number lay more heavily against her than it would ever be for him. At twenty-eight, her parents had started pestering her to settle down, which she tactfully ignored. But at thirty they stopped being fooled by her carefully constructed evasions. On the eve of her thirty-first birthday, her mother had thrown a fit.

Meera was most definitely not against the idea of marriage, even if it was one arranged for her by someone else. She had always been fascinated by the grand wedding ceremonies she had grown up seeing. But somewhere between spending her evenings spinning whimsical tales, and cocky men blindly praising her artwork without any understanding, she had given up on the idea of signing a different surname on her paintings. If it were not for the fact that life to her had been pretty much about meeting deadlines, and uncertainty always looming at the prospect of a missed deadline, she would never have agreed to these meetings.

Eighteen meetings with prospective grooms made the future appear more uncertain than ever. Yet the nineteenth saw her lost in daydreams yet again.

Perhaps weddings were not just about commitments and ownerships. Perhaps somewhere hidden in the small crevices of blind traditions and laws, it was about her palms adorned with intricately woven patterns of *henna*. Perhaps it was also about taking silent strolls with someone after long days of work and discussing art and history. Someone would silently study and marvel at her skilful embroideries and appreciate her otherwise useless knowledge of weaving patterns. Maybe marriage wasn't just about being accepted and rejected by someone else, but also just a little bit about wholeheartedly accepting oneself.

She still yearned for a conversation with the professor, best without the interventions and mindless cackles by senior citizens. She wondered if he had liked the fritter he was eating, for she had somehow lost track.

Two days later Meera was caught up painting a sixteenth-century bazaar, when her father heard back from the suitor. He stealthily entered the room and his voice had a perceptible hint of concern.

"You know professors earn too little?" he scoffed. "Moreover, he was way too awkward wasn't he?"

Meera looked at him, perplexed. But it all made sense to her when she realised that the cold man's cynicism was just to protect her.

The professor had rejected her because she was a little too plump for his liking. She let out a soft chuckle. It had all been her fault. She laughed like she had tasted sour grapes on her tongue. Her fault, for even thinking about unmasking him.

The nineteen meetings seemed like nothing but distant daydreams. But this ludicrous fantasy had left her utterly fatigued. As far as the future was concerned, she was certain about just two things: One, that there would be no twentieth, and the other, that she would take a trip by herself to a hillside, on a moonlit night. Just this much certainty would suffice for now.

Swamp Thing

He couldn't talk with the wolf's head on, but he was still cute enough in his tuxedo. Looking good in a tuxedo doesn't indicate much though—even my sister's boyfriend manages to look like an upstanding human being in one, if you can ignore his tendency to bite. Not to mention that the mask left it up to the imagination whether or not he was suffering from a bad case of acne and didn't make him the social life of the party either.

"Do we...know each other?" I ventured, after being stared at for several long minutes. I gestured vaguely in the air with my glass of fizzy. "I'm told there's a bit of wolf on my grandmother's side."

Those dull glass eyes gazed back at me, expressionless, and I heaved an internal sigh.

"Brilliant." I rolled the word off my tongue, dumping my glass on the table. "Great chat. Should do it again sometime. I gotta run, late for the night dance."

With a fake smile Mother would've framed for the wall, I drifted away from the dining room, heading for the stairs. When I risked a peek through the banister, wolf-boy remained staring at the spot where I'd stood. *Yeesh. Someone came here fresh from the loony bin.* Yet another thing to add to my list of complaints for the mayor when I finally got to meet him on my 21st— please stop inviting nutters to live here when there's a perfectly good asylum five miles up the highway.

Lola sat at her dressing table, in her bathrobe with her hair bundled up in a towel tower, busy admiring her new earrings.

"You're going to make me late for the dance," I complained, sprawling across her bed with a long sigh.

"Don't be a drama queen. You're always late because you never go." Finishing with her earrings, she rose and crossed to her wardrobe, pulling out some of the new dresses she bought earlier this week. "Red or blue?"

"Red. You look ugly in blue." I wrinkled my nose, wondering why she'd even bought a dress in that colour in the first place. Maybe it was the rage at the night balls at the moment.

"Did you talk to him?" she inquired, taking my advice and picking the red.

"Who?" I paused in my attempt to see if I could get into that pretzel position Miss Lovelace had demonstrated at school yoga class.

"Asa." She favoured me with her 'why are you such an idiot' expression, and I scowled, resentful. "Y'know, hot stuff in the wolf mask? His dad's the new groundsman for the dance lawn?"

"Ohhhh, him," I said. "Heck no." I squinted. "Hang on, his name's Asa?" An urge to laugh overcame me and I snorted, struggling to equate such a nice name with someone who came to masque dinners as a wolf. *What a dork.*

"If you made an effort, you'd have a partner for the night dances," Lola said with an arched eyebrow as she unwound her towel and began brushing out her long hair.

"Your hair smells good," I complained, not wanting to dwell on the topic of me spending any more time with wolf-boy. *Please, let me die first.*

"I actually wash it, that's why."

"Ew." I returned to trying to make myself into a human pretzel. Miss Lovelace made it look so easy.

"Just because you've made it to sixteen still taking mud baths in the woods and wearing your shirts backwards doesn't mean we all have," Lola said severely, gathered her lace cardigan, and left for the dance.

As usual, I remained behind on the bed, and achieved human pretzel status at ten thirty, when the dances started. Not that I would know. Everyone knew better than to partner the ruffian Everhart youngest and so I kept my appearances on the dance-grounds non-existent. Lola seemed to think wolf-boy was my second chance, but there was no way I would go anywhere with a guy who wore a wolf's head to dinner.

I took my morning constitutional swim in Blackfriars's lake, a pleasant place full of enough eels, mud and lake-weed to keep sensible people away and my reputation where it belonged—nose deep in dirt. Halfway through my third lap, some idiot decided to wander down and draw pictures in the sand with a stick.

I practised how long I could hold my breath. Annoying as being interrupted was, a bit of practice never hurt when you had a free-diving contest in two weeks that Mother expected you to win. Mother was just jealous because ghosts can't compete in diving competitions.

After breaking my own ten minute record out of sheer spite, I surfaced to find my peace returned to me. Still, the morning was irreparably ruined, and I sulked out of the water to my towel. Dripping wet, I stomped over to where the intruder had drawn on the sand, intending to investigate what had warranted disturbing my peace. Clutching my towel, I struggled to make out the wavy lines. *These weren't created by anyone talented that's for sure.*

Taking a closer look, I discovered that the markings weren't drawings at all and my mouth dropped open.

A couple of sand-flies bit me on the shin.

I didn't notice.

And yet, to say the truth, love and reason keep little company together nowadays.

"That's Shakespeare," I informed the trees, hands on my hips.

"Someone's defacing my lake with Shakespeare."

When I arrived home, I told Lola the exact same thing. She squinted at me, the steam from the hair straightener drawing beads of sweat from her forehead. "So?" she asked. "I'd love it if someone came and wrote Shakespeare for me to find. Romantic."

"Ew!" I yelped, burying my head under a pillow. "Take it back this instant."

"You're a girl," my sister informed me in a long-suffering voice.

"Statistically there's got to be someone in the world who finds grime and ridicule attractive."

"I'm a pretzel," I said firmly, looping my legs around into the pretzel shape. "Your argument is invalid."

She groaned, setting the straightener aside, and left the room. I tended to have that effect on people.

Thoroughly worried by her words, I made sure I spent the day in baggy pants and a backwards shirt, put my hairbrush in the bin and took an expedition to the blackberry thicket in the middle of the woods. By the time the dinner bell summoned me inside and it was time for Lola to get ready for the night dance, I looked like an inhabitant of a trash tip, and felt very proud of myself.

"Don't lie on my bed, you stink," my sister complained, waving her lipstick at me in a manner I found threatening.

"No one wants to write Shakespeare for me now," I said, grinning and settled back in her chair instead.

Lola's only comment took shape as a muffled grunt of distaste as she finished applying the lipstick, and picked up her newly delivered dance shoes.

"Blair's picking me up tonight," she said, pursing her lips in the mirror and making kissing noises. Behind her, I gagged.

"Ew. Are you still dating that loser?"

"He's not a loser!" she snapped, bristling all over like Mr Tiddles when I sprayed him with the garden hose by accident last week. "And you're going to come downstairs and say hello nicely without looking like the Swamp Thing."

"Too bad," I chirped, smiling sweetly back at her. "Nothing swampier than me."

"If he ditches me because of you—"

"Nah, he wouldn't give an eel brain if I fell in a ditch and died. He barely even knows I exist."

Lola muttered something that sounded very much like 'I try very hard to keep it that way.' That persuaded me to feel something that might've been guilt, and I let her drag me down the stairs to the front door. After milling about in the hall for a while, the doorbell rang, and she practically hurled herself out the door onto Blair, who wore his commonplace tuxedo. They proceeded to spend several minutes on the doorstep eating each other's faces off, before setting off for the dance without another word to me.

Thanks for that pointless waste of my pretzel time. Planning to get myself a nice cup of hot chocolate and then play skittles in the hall with Mother's tall china vases, I began to pull the door shut and stopped.

There was a stranger on the path. A tall, slight fellow with a mess of blonde hair that sported a variety of twigs. This choice of hair accessory persuaded me to give him a chance, and I left the door open.

"Can I help you?" I asked in my best polite voice.

"I don't know yet," he said, his voice shy, thick with some foreign accent. He drew a little nearer, avoiding the light from the house, but I could still glimpse enough of him to note that he wore his tuxedo awkwardly, and that the pants had grass stains on the knees, and the jacket was coated in what looked like dog fur.

Not a bad fashion statement.

"Are you…" he paused, as if looking for the right words. "Do you have partner? I have asked around town and all the girls, they have partners."

"Well I don't," I said proudly, puffing out my chest and flipping my hair. "I'm single as a pretzel."

"Oh," he said. "Would you go to dance if you had partner?" His words were stilted, but I got the sense he was trying very hard.

"Duh," I replied, shrugging. "I mean, it's probably bone dull, but I've always wanted to have a look around the dance grounds—wait. Are you offering to take me?"

"Ja," he said, removing one of the twigs from his hair and proceeding to snap it in two.

"OK then." Bouncing off the steps, I pushed the door shut behind me and jogged to join him. Seeming surprised, he stared at me for a few moments, then set off up the driveway. The tall wrought iron fence that lined the dance ground glittered at the end of the main street, and a seed of excitement flowered in my stomach. *I'm going to the dance! I never go to the dance!*

It's totally overrated but like…still.

"You aren't holding my hand." I blurted the words suddenly as we approached the gates to the dance ground and the warden, whose eyes had narrowed at the sight of us.

"No, I am not," he said, blinking baffled indigo eyes at me.

"Hold it," I hissed. "They won't let us in."

The stranger laced his fingers with mine, and I shivered. His hand was freezing and I wouldn't be surprised if mine went numb.

The warden stared at us for a long time, and I offered my best smile. *Another one for Mother to frame.* At last, he moved aside, his heavy armour clunking, and I tugged my new partner into the dance grounds. Thick trees lined the area, surrounded by rings of daisies and red and white toadstools. Lanterns hung from the branches, flickering with fireflies.

"There's no one here," I observed, wrinkling my nose and kicking at a tree root. "Boringgggg."

My companion tilted his head. "That might not be true." He pointed into the branches of the nearest tree. "Pixie nest."

"You're kidding," I breathed, walking over to the tree trunk. "I'm going to look."

"This branch first. I come after."

Little by little, the two of us made our way up the old oak to the nest, where we admired the sleeping baby pixies, and perched on a sturdy branch to talk.

"Lola likes the dance," I said. "She comes with this guy from down the street called Blair. They like biting each other, 'cept they call it kissing."

The stranger laughed.

"I don't get it," I continued after pausing to feel gratified by that response. "There's just a bunch of trees. I don't even know where they are in here. It must be somewhere really far in, but Lola hates trees. She doesn't wander in forests, even for dancing. It doesn't make sense."

He thought about that, and I picked at a patch of dried mud on my cargo pants.

"Maybe," he said after a while, "the night dances take you and your partner where you want to be, ja? She likes parties, so she has party, and we like trees. So trees."

Tossing the scrap of mud into the air, I considered that answer and nodded. "Ja."

My partner blinked, and smiled. "Ja, English girl." A giggle welled up in me, and I swung my legs back and forth, laughing.

"I'm Ciara," I offered after I recovered from my bout of the giggles, and held out a hand.

"Asa," he replied, taking my hand and giving it a firm shake, not seeming to notice how I stared.

This is the lunatic with the wolf mask?

"Wolf," I said faintly.

He ducked his head, blushing. "One of father's hunting trophies. People stare too much. Make them stare at something." Glancing up, he gestured at my mud-coated backwards attire. "Like you. Swamp Thing." A whisper of smile passed over his face.

"I like to swim at Blackfriars's." The words left my lips before I could consider them.

"I know," he said, and I fought off my urge to stare at him some more. *Wolf and Shakespeare?* My good sense informed me that no one would think less of me if I made a run for it now, but for some reason I finished, "Meet me tomorrow? I can show you where the best blackberries are after."

Asa's face shuttered, and he looked away, a sudden heaviness in his eyes. "I do not know," he murmured. "Father does not...like wandering. This morning was luck."

"OK mister wolf-boy, let me tell you a secret: I'm a human lie detector. What's really the problem?"

"It's nothing." He picked at the tree bark. I sidled closer, imitating Blair's facial expression whenever he saw my sister in an attempt to look creepy.

"Tell me," I said. "Or the ghost of Ciara Everhart shall haunt you forever."

Asa laughed, shaking his head at me. "You are not dead, so how can you be ghost?"

"I'll make it happen," I replied staunchly. "Now spill."

Ducking his head, he tugged harder at the tree bark, his cheeks colouring. "I...do not. swim," he whispered.

He can't swim? Unexpected but OK. Rolling with it. "No?" I said.

"Somebody had better fix that."

"I saw you coming home from the dance with Asa every night this week," Lola said, leaning around the doorframe with a happy glint in her eyes. "Got something to tell me?"

I looked up at her, disgruntled that she'd invaded my sanctuary, a place she usually avoided since it was filled with jars of bugs, two lizard cages, my frog, Robert and a fish tank. It also rubbed me the wrong way that she'd caught me. I'd done my level best to keep Asa and my outings a secret to avoid this very encounter.

"Just that dance is a stupid name for a hiking expedition," I said, retrieving two leaves from my hair that were making me itch.

"And Asa?" she pressed, coming inside and inviting herself onto my bed.

"He thinks Growltiger is an endangered species?" I said, not sure what she wanted from me.

"Ciara!" she groaned, burying her face in a pillow. The sight made me wince, knowing I'd be sleeping with her perfume all night. *Ick.*

"Has he kissed you yet?"

The question made me stare at her. An urge to vomit welled up in my stomach. "Uh no? No thank you? Not ever?"

She levelled me with her disappointed look, and I glared back, fighting the urge to smother her with the very pillow she clutched for support.

"Well he does seem to be taming you at least," she sighed.

"Taming—excuse me," I spat, sitting up. "He doesn't think I need taming. He likes swimming in lakes and getting covered in mud and inspecting bugs and climbing trees. We want to go up to Songbird Mount next summer and go hiking."

Lola blinked several times. "You need to get a life, Ciara. And soon. No one will want you."

"I have a life," I snarled, something inside stinging. "And just because you don't want me doesn't mean everyone else won't want me either."

A loaded silence descended over the room. My sister rose, tossing the pillow aside. "Suit yourself." Nose in the air, she stalked out. "Stay in here with your ugly, froggy friends." She slammed the door.

"Well," I said, taking in a shaky breath, my throat feeling thick. Struggling to rally myself, I got to my feet and walked to feed Robert. Dropping his quota of flies into his habitat, I peered through the glass at him. "What do you think?"

I asked him.

"Ribbet," said Robert, staring back with bulging eyes.

Sighing, I crossed to my bedside table, picked up the dial-up phone and twirled until I had the number I wanted.

"Ja, English girl?" Asa said. Somehow he always knew when it was me calling. "We going pond-dipping tomorrow?"

"Can you come get me?" I asked.

"Five minutes," he said, without any further questions. The line gave a disconsolate click as it disconnected.

I tried to force my body into a triumphant pretzel, but I just wasn't feeling it and my legs wouldn't tuck up properly. For the first time in a good six years, I wished Mother was less ghost and more human.

A rock bounced off my window with a pleasant crack, and I slid off the bed and trotted over to push it open. "Hiiiiii," I yelled, waving down at Asa, who'd shown up fully dressed, carting a basket and what appeared to be fishing rods. *He's good, this boy,* I thought, slinging my legs out over the sill. *Who needs a sister anyway?*

"Midnight picnic? Ja?" he called up to me, not all fazed that my route to the ground involved nothing safer than a windowsill, a drainpipe and a dubious ivy vine. Lola would've been screaming and calling the emergency department. Traversing the drainpipe, I dropped to the ground and wiped my hands off on my shirt, creating two pleasant algae stains.

"Sounds capital," I said, feeling better already, accepting my fishing rod and looping my arm in his.

"You good?" he asked, narrowing his eyes at me and I pulled a face. *Couldn't be that obvious, could it? Shame on you, Ciara's face. Try for some emotional obscurity next time.*

"Ciara?"

Oh sneezing pixies. With a groan, I turned and found Lola leaning out of my open bedroom window, make-up plastered face twisted into an expression of some sort. It was probably meant to be sisterly love and remorse, but she mainly just looked constipated.

"What is it?" I yelled walking backwards towards the woods, Asa keeping step with me. "Speak now or forever hold your peace."

"Is that your sister?" he hissed in my ear.

"I know right? Total horror," I agreed, and waited for said horror to reply.

"I just wanted to say—" she began and I buried my face in Asa's shoulder.

"Your heartfelt remorse can die in a pile of manure. Go back to bed."

At my words, my friend choked, and ended up coughing hard into his hand.

"You're giving Asa consumption," I added, patting him on the back and waving a fishing rod at my sister in a threatening manner.

Lola closed her red-painted lips, visible even in the dark and at this great distance. A cricket chirped in the grass at my feet, and I snickered. *Great timing, little guy.*

"You left your cardigan," she ventured. The comment's stupidity didn't warrant an answer, so I folded my arms, waiting for her to get to her point.

"Can I come?" she said at last.

"Nope," I said, detaching a squashed fly meant for Robert from my shirt with a fingernail. "Go back to bed Lola before you say something even more stupid. I'll bring you back a fish if you don't annoy me anymore."

"Please?" she begged, and I found my own jaw threatening to transform me into a goldfish. The prissy airhead seemed dead set on coming, for some inane, incomprehensible-to-a-normal-human-being reason.

"She could come," Asa offered with a shrug, raising the picnic basket. "There's plenty."

"Sand flies, briars, mud, dead fish and the possibility of snakes," I called to Lola.

"I don't care," she said, her voice trembling a little, but she swung her legs out over the sill in a defiant manner. I smacked my forehead with a palm. *Oh kill me now. Hated my guts ten minutes ago, now wants to try night fishing in the forest with me. What an A+ horror.*

"Fine," I growled, throwing up my hands. "Just for heaven's sake, please use the stairs!"

NATHAN STEWARD

Mask

The earliest thing I remember a soldier telling me was to never be first.

"It don't matter what for," he said. "It don't matter if it's just linin' up to piss." I remember I laughed at that, although the resulting glare silenced me quickly. "Nothin' here is worth dying for lad. Nothin'. So don't be a fool, stay at the back, an' live."

I thought of him as a coward. I blinded myself to the cynic's wisdom and believed I was better. The cultural narcissism which pervaded my childhood made me proud. I, like many, had not enlisted to be the second man to shoot.

'Let us go on and win glory for ourselves, or yield it to others.'

These words of Homer were my mantra. Glory, that sweet dream of every desperate boy, clawed at my soul like a cancer, gnawing away at my common sense. I never awoke from that dream, not really, it simply changed—changed into a nightmare. I remembered that old soldier's words then. When the whistle blew and we dragged ourselves through the mud and over the edge of the world—to run through hell, with bullets whispering our names as they hissed past.

I never felt more alone. Even my God deserted me, the voice of consolation I thought ever present was instead replaced by the jeering of shells and those simple colloquial words. They reverberated through me with every waking moment, like some twisted prayer. Soon, Homer was forgotten, for the advice of an unnamed veteran.

Then there arose a moment; ineffable and subtle, yet I believe beautiful, in its own crude fashion.

I let go.

I marched, I charged, I shot my rifle and polished my bayonet like any other Private. But I did not laugh, I did not pray, and whenever my fellows would huddle and exclaim the same, useless questions— "When will the war end?" "When will the post come?" "Do you think I'll be home for Christmas?"—I would stay silent, and think.

I wasn't always good at thinking. I believe my parents hoped for a melancholy genius when they named me Edgar, after Allan Poe, but I disappointed them. I loved my games more than my books, and though they assailed me with the classics, and beat me black and blue with philosophy, I never allowed myself to become what they wanted. I was too happy I suppose. That was my burden—a weighty optimism. How proud they would be to see me now; the secluded nihilist, wrapped within my thoughts as the greatest war of mankind raged in the distance.

That's where I am now, musing to myself, as I trudge at the back of my platoon winding through an abandoned trench. Belgium, I believe, is where I am, Ypres to be exact, although I could be wrong. Not that it mattered when every battlefield was the same. Blood and mud and murder, that was my world now. Names and identities lose all meaning in the desolation of war.

"Chin up Private, Haig wants us on our best form."

I felt a light cuff against my back and straightened, wild-eyed.

Being roused from deep thought within such surroundings was always startling—humanity has great skill at forgetting one's suffering, but much less prowess at actually confronting it.

The man who had spoken watched my awakening with cold bemusement. He had thrown the word 'Private' at me as if he was a General, but I could see only a single tattered chevron on his shoulder. Sometimes that scrap of cloth was all a man needed to survive—physical knowledge of their own fragile superiority. Certainly, it seemed to be helping this particular Lance Corporal, who grinned lopsidedly at me.

"Just a joke old chap, no need to glower."

Seeing I was not going to comment, the man started talking beside me, matching every one of my plodding footfalls with something of a swagger.

"I'm Lance Corporal Summers, but call me Ralph. You know, I saw you a few times back home. My father knew your father, I'm fairly sure they were pals even. Funny isn't it? This entire regiment comes from the same shire, and it just happens they stick us together in a platoon. You know anyone else here?"

In truth, I did recognise this 'Ralph', but had never before noticed him, as I had never before noticed any of my other comrades.

"No."

"You speak!" He laughed at that. "I wondered if I was making an ass of myself in front of a mute. What's your name again?"

"Private Peterson."

"I know that, I mean your real name."

"Edgar."

"Well, Edgar, I've been watching, and don't think I don't know what you're up to."

The look of confusion, edged with fear, that appeared on my face warranted another smile. He leaned in to murmur.

"It's a wise man who stays at the back."

Upon those words, an excruciating whine erupted from the sky, and a shell catapulted into the front of the platoon. I was thrown backward by the impact, and watched, as if paralysed, as men screamed and tore at the shrapnel fragments in their flesh, while others rolled on the ground clutching at invisible injuries. There was a dull ringing in my ears.

Shadows flitted in front of me, barking orders and curses, and then suddenly there was a terrifying noise. It was not the discharge of a gun, the scream of a shell or the sound of Germans.

A man was coughing.

Next he was choking, and another was too. Soon, I could smell it, stabbing at my sinuses, and then it was even visible. A yellow-brown haze, dilating in the darkness of the narrow trench, which snaked its way ever nearer.

I don't have a mask, I thought to myself, closing my crusted eyes.

This is how I die.

Suddenly, I felt myself being grasped and dragged backward into further darkness while a cacophony of screams and hoarse pleas echoed around me. I heard a trap slam shut, and opened my eyes to see absolutely nothing.

Is this... Death?

A scratch and a crack sounded to my left, causing me to snap my head around like a madman.

"Calm yourself old chap, I'm just lighting a match."

Another scratch, and a paltry light crackled into existence; the flame was thrust into the gas of a lamp, and soon the sight was brought into clarity. We were in a large dugout, a dozen soldiers, illuminated by a single lamp clutched by a crouching Ralph who was still grinning, a strange look in his eyes.

"What did I say? Eh?" he muttered to me.

I realised he must have been the one to drag me in there, and opened my mouth to thank him, but then hesitated.

Was I really thankful?

"Hurry up with that bloody lamp!" one of the men hollered from the other side of the dugout.

I saw the lines of Ralph's face tighten in irritation at being spoken to in such a way, yet nevertheless he got up and went over, so that the other two lamps could be lit.

The dugout was large but bare, roughly circular in shape with the rounded edges stretching into shadow. A wooden door—the only exit and entrance to the dugout—was situated to my right. Already, I could see two of the soldiers by the door, frantically scrabbling and patting at the soil at its sides in an effort to insulate it against the gas.

"Where is the Corporal?" a Private asked, his rat-like face bobbing and twisting in an effort to take stock of his surroundings.

"He's here," answered Ralph, who was looking at a dark lump on the floor. I saw him drop down to stare at the Corporal's pale, contorted features.

"He's dead," he added.

At this, a murmur of dissent seemed to trickle through the men in the room.

"I, however, am still alive," Ralph added, "and in the absence of any other authority, will be taking control of this platoon. Is that clear?" He gestured at the badge of Lance Corporal in order to accentuate his proclamation. No objections were sounded, and orders were issued for the men to take stock of their situation and the wounded.

Of the twelve soldiers who had made it into the dugout, only seven survived the next hour. The Corporal and two others were discovered dead almost immediately; the other two took far longer. A man who has never seen the effects of a gas attack could never understand its enormity in the capacity of suffering. It was nigh on forty minutes that we sat there in the dim light, listening to the frantic burbling and spluttery spasms of poisoned throats. To hear the feverish, choked moans of a man who has swallowed gas, is akin to listening to Azrael himself. As soldiers, we all believed ourselves intimately acquainted with the angel of death, but that hour was truly when we were first introduced.

The silence afterward was stark and uncomfortable. The bodies had been deposited into the far edge of the room, and Ralph had given me the instruction to search them and fumble through their equipment for anything of use.

A division of sorts had developed within the dugout. I was at the edge the farthest from the door amongst the dead, while the other six had split into two trios, both conversing and eyeing each other respectively. On the right was Ralph, who talked and debated with the rat-like man from earlier who I had learnt was called Roger, as well as Roger's portly brother, George. If the divide could be seen as class based, then they would undoubtedly be seen as the 'upper' of the dugout society. On the left were three other men who we had learnt had grown up together; a short fellow named Peter, his bulky, perpetually scowling friend Tom and the leader of their group—a rather friendly, good-looking Private whose name was Edward but insisted on being referred to as Eddy.

While I worked, turning out pockets and sifting through packs, these two subsets muttered heatedly to each other. Finally, the leader of the left of the dugout stood up and approached Ralph, smiling easily as he did.

"We were wondering, Sir, what are your orders?"

"Nothing for now, except to sit tight while I evaluate the situation," Ralph replied rather curtly.

"I understand that, Sir, however, I hope you realise that with the gas outside, and us all without a mask, we cannot hope to venture out."

"Of course I do."

"Then, Sir, you must understand the German army is most likely advancing on our position as we speak."

Ralph stood up.

"What would you suggest then, Private?" he said calmly, staring Eddy straight in his eyes.

Unfazed, the soldier continued.

"I believe we should start digging, Sir."

"Digging?"

"Yes Sir, digging with our rifles. If we have no other way out, we must make one."

Ralph snorted derisively, and I noticed Eddy's eyes narrow although his smile did not disappear.

"I have already considered that, Private. Even if we had started digging when we first got here, we would not have the time to construct a tunnel long or stable enough to take us out into a gas-free trench before the Germans arrived."

"Then, Sir, what would you suggest?"

"I would suggest sitting tight while I think, Private."

"And what help would that do?" barked another man from the left, the thickset one called Tom.

"Are you questioning orders?" Ralph said quietly.

I noticed the two brothers sitting behind him gently placing their hands on their rifles. The move did not go unnoticed by the other side.

"Rank means nothin' when we are all going to die anyway," Tom barked, standing up. "I agree with Eddy, we should be at least doin' something."

"Rank means nothing? Let me remind you Private, that rank and order is all humanity has in these times of chaos," Ralph retorted.

The short man, Peter, also stood up to join the others, gazing at Ralph with visible resentment. "We'd need a miracle to get out of here if we just sit around. Do you have a miracle stashed in your sleeve Lance Corporal, Sir?" he said goadingly, sneering at the chevron on Ralph's shoulder.

"I am the Corporal now, boy, and you'll address me as such."

"Boy is it?" Peter let out some very unpleasant laughter, "I'm probably older than you are."

Ralph glanced quickly in my direction to see how I was reacting, opened his mouth and then paused. Slowly, he turned around to stare at me, with the others following likewise.

"Edgar, what is that in your hand?" he said after a moment.

While the interaction was taking place, I had absentmindedly been sorting through the old Corporal's belongings, pulling the items from his pack. Startled at the attention, I glanced down to find a gas mask clutched in my fist.

"It's... It's a mask," I said.

Ralph did not even care that I had forgotten to say 'Sir'. A hungry look had come into his eyes and he advanced toward me.

"You were asking for a miracle, I believe, Private?" he muttered, staring at the mask, before finally snapping his head up. "We have a single chance of life for one man here."

All the men were standing now, aside from me, and had crowded over to gaze at the mask.

"Now, I would rather not pull rank to attempt to take it for myself, and as such we must decide who receives this mask in an orderly, logical fashion," Ralph continued. "Does any man here have a family?"

All the men shook their heads.

"Well then, I suppose lots could always be drawn. We'd just need to find seven items of varying length..."

"Six," I interrupted.

"Six?" Ralph inquired, confused.

"I don't want it."

"You don't bloody want it?" Tom burst out.

"Yes, I don't want it," I repeated calmly. "I would rather somebody else did."

At those words, Ralph clapped his hands with a calculating smile. "Gentlemen, I have a solution. We shall have a vote!"

"A vote?" Tom asked, rather stupidly.

"Yes, a vote. Each one of us will state their case for why they deserve the mask, and we shall vote on whoever needs the opportunity the most."

"But surely," Eddy said, "you must know that everyone will vote for themselves?"

"Of course I do," Ralph replied, before pointing a finger at me. "But Edgar here has already admitted that he does not wish for it."

What Ralph was proposing was starting to sink in.

"And therefore shall be the tipping point—the key arbiter if you will."

"But..." I began, only to be cut off.

"Edgar here knows none of us, nor has he been talking while we have been in this dugout. He is the perfect judge of who deserves the mask—of who deserves life."

Much to my discomfort and worry, the other men actually seemed to be agreeing with him. It seemed ludicrous that the placing of all their fates into my hands was the only thing they were unanimous upon.

A rota was conjured, and after a few minutes of silence, Ralph exclaimed that he was ready to begin. The dugout represented a morbid amphitheatre, as he confidently walked to the centre of the room.

"You already know my name, and you already know that I have distinguished myself in gaining the rank of Lance Corporal..." he began, ignoring the wrinkled noses of the men on the left. "I am a Christian soul, and have only ever tried to do what is best for my comrades and my country. My upbringing was educated, but modest, and I have never pretended to be anything otherwise. While I will admit to not having a family, there is a girl I love, back in England, whom I would wish to marry if I ever return." He paused then, to let a melancholy expression form on his face.

If he was acting, I thought to myself, then he is doing a dastardly good job at it.

"At my heart, I am a peaceful man—an artist even. I hope to write a novel, about the war I mean, about all we have suffered, all we have fought for..." He continued along such lines for another minute or so, before turning to look straight at me.

"I know the importance of what is clasped in your hands. I know what life is, I know its immeasurable value, and thus understand everyone's reluctance to relinquish it. I also, however, understand the importance of democracy—of fairness. If I am not the man who takes that mask, then I swear on my King, and on the great Christian God, that I will protect the chosen recipient, and not allow the mask to be taken by any malicious means. That is all."

He winked at me, unseen by the other men, and then sat himself as the next man, Peter, rose to speak. The wink surprised me, setting my mind reeling, and then, with grim certainty, I understood.

Of course he suggested a vote, in the knowledge I would be the chosen judge. Ralph, for all his poeticisms and perceived humility, was a cunning man. The confidence and composure was not strength of character in the face of death, but instead a faith in my decision. After all, he had saved my life, unbeknownst to the others, and therefore would expect me to return the favour. And why shouldn't I? Why would I doom the man who saved me? An educated individual, pious and reasonable—if perhaps a little prideful—who had shown me kindness.

I would be a fool not to choose him.

After that realisation, I paid little attention to the others and their speeches. Most were rather tedious and clumsy, with men scrambling for reasons that their lives had been worthwhile, for reasons why they would achieve the most in a world where they might be shot next week.

The only other notable person was the handsome one they called Eddy, who sauntered up with even more confidence than Ralph. His speech lacked in substance, but showed him to be a good, moral man, and more importantly—a humorous one. It seemed incredible, but even in that hellish place, he managed to make most of the men laugh.

The last man to give his speech was the rat-like Roger. He faltered with his words, never able to take his eyes off the mask in my hands.

"... And... I... I have a sick mother. I want... no, I need... to return. To look after her, to..."

An uproar greeted his words.

"He's lying!" bellowed Tom.

"His bloody brother has already spoken and didn't mention no sick mother!" shouted Peter.

Roger blushed and I noticed a bead of sweat cutting a clean line down his filthy face. Then, without any warning, he violently jerked forward and snatched the mask from my hands, turning to make for the door.

Tom roared incomprehensibly and charged at Roger, throwing the smaller man to the ground before beating him over and over with his cinder-block fists.

Shouts were erupting throughout the dugout, yet no one moved forward to intervene until, like a harbinger of anarchy, a single shot rang out. George, whether out of fear of loss of the mask, or love for his brother, had aimed his rifle at Tom's large head and fired.

A scream of outrage spilled from Peter, as we all watched the gigantic figure collapse. A large patch of reddened soil inflated underneath Tom's skull, while I could do nothing but stare at the gaping pit in his helmet.

George however, like some deranged elephant, threw down his gun and stumbled over. He grabbed the mask, not even pausing to look at the mangled face of his brother.

Storming toward the door, he desperately clawed at the soil blocking the edges which he himself had helped fill-in. Both Ralph and Peter charged toward him, with Ralph spinning the fat soldier around only to scream futile threats of a court martial in his face. Peter, however, had other ideas of justice, and without any delay, thrust his bayonet into George's belly. Ralph turned to him in astonishment and fury, only to back away quickly from a consecutive bayonet slash which carved through his jacket, leaving a shallow yet bloody cut.

"Are you mad!?" he cried, holding his palm to the wound, collapsing at the edge.

"No," Peter spat. "I want to bloody live."

He turned back around to the pitiful sight of George, sobbing and blubbering on the ground, and lifted his bayonet once again to finish him off.

A gunshot fractured the dugout.

Panting, his face drawn and pulsating with adrenaline, Ralph limped over to the door, his officer's pistol smoking. He looked down at George, who was still rolling and whimpering on the ground, ignorant of the body of Peter beside him.

"I'm sorry, Private."

Another crack and a blast of smoke and the fat soldier was silent.

I could only watch, as Ralph discarded his gun and bent down to yank the mask from George's dripping fingers. He turned back around and hobbled to the centre of the room, one hand clasping the slash on his chest, the other triumphantly gripping the mask. A smile, blissful and dreamy, wreathed Ralph's face as he looked upon me, still frozen at the end of the dugout. He lifted the mask like it was a toast and opened his mouth to speak.

But I would never know what he wished to say.

A smidgeon of steel peeked out from Ralph's jugular, winking at me in the lamplight, before it was quickly withdrawn to make way for gushing crimson.

Eddy, amiable, amusing Eddy, had been watching the entire spectacle unfold forgotten in the corner. Almost comically, he sidestepped the blood like he was afraid to stain his boots, and plucked the mask from Ralph with languid grace. Without even looking at me, he made his way to the doorway and pulled the carcasses of Peter and George out of the way, pausing only when he heard a rustle behind him.

He span around, grinning, the mask which had taken so many lives dangling like a pendulum from his fingers.

"Now this is a surprise. Edgar, what are you doing over there?"

Almost unknowingly, I had picked up George's rifle which he had thrown down earlier, and was now levelling it straight at Eddy's face. A thousand thoughts were spiralling inside me, an anthem which coursed through my entire body, deafening me to Eddy's words.

Yet I did not shake.

I had been trained for this, after all.

"Edgar, we both know you don't want this. Look at all this waste— this death. Why create any more? When you could just rest," Eddy murmured, an understanding smile peaking at his lips.

With methodical precision I flicked back the bolt and squinted down the iron sight at the man in front of me.

Eddy's smirk was starting to droop.

"You don't have it in you," he said finally.

I however, wasn't listening to him. All I could hear, was that old soldier's words.

"Nothin' here is worth dying for lad"
"So don't be a fool"
"An' live."

Dear Mother,

   I hope you and father and little Daisy are well, I know it has been many months since my last letter. It has been a strange past few days for me—I suppose you could say I have had a revelation of sorts.

   My regiment was ambushed you see, and a gas was unleashed upon us. I couldn't even begin to explain why, but I was the only man amidst fifty who had in his possession a mask. It is impossible perhaps for you to understand that moment, alone in the darkness of the mist, as I staggered onward blindly past my choking comrades. That mask was my saviour, and now my lucky charm. I carry it everywhere I go, as a reminder of what I went through. To think, out of all those brave men, it was me whom the Lord chose to survive—well, it's astounding. I felt terrible, yet at once liberated. The mask showed me that there is purpose in survival, a beautiful purpose, and it is my duty to make my way back to you all in England—to live my life.

   I believe I have found my calling. Amidst the suffering of this war, I have discovered the eerie beauty of poetry. I know I have not always risen to the expectations you and father placed upon me—I know I disappointed you both—and I am sorry.

   I have however changed, and no longer resist my natural calling as an artist. I believe I shall make you proud, and look forward to my return home.
   Best wishes,
   Edgar

P.S. I have enclosed a poem I recently penned. It's a bit of nonsense really, and I'm not too fond of the title, but I hope you enjoy it nonetheless.

The Battle of Sin
The seven sins of old met deep in the dark
Before them stood life's faded spark,
Greed lunged first, desperate and alone,
Wrath inflamed, instead took it for his own.

MASK

Greed's brother-in-sin reared his bulbous head,
Gluttony, in all his glory, shot Wrath dead,
Envy slashed Pride, then leapt into the fray
Wounding Gluttony, to steal life away.

Pride in his fury, killed both with ease
Then turned triumphant, clasping life's keys,
Lust, ever forgotten, stabbed him from behind
And made to leave, victorious and blind.

Sloth, the observer, took the final shot,
And left with the life which he had sought,
For if one talks of the battle of sin,
Then know it is the least impressive who shall win.

Fear of the Mask

Thomas refused to wear the gas mask. The knock on the door rattled through the thin walls of the house and pierced my mind with an overwhelming frustration. Groaning with impatience, I hauled myself up from the antique rocking chair and dragged my legs towards the hall. Composing myself, I swung the door open, its rusty hinges shrieking in protest. Thomas' face was streaked with tears that glistened like streams of moonlight and his lower lip trembled uncontrollably. Somehow all my annoyance dissipated and I knelt down before him in the doorway.

"Did you forget to bring your gas mask to school again, Thomas?"

He lifted his face up to mine where I could see my own reflection in his huge, pale blue eyes.

"Mummy... my teacher sent me... back home to... get it." Between each word was an exaggerated sob that seemed to shake his whole body violently. Sighing wearily, I stood up, ushering Thomas through the door and following after him. The house was awfully dark—a layer of thick, constant, tangible shadow enveloped every available space. Rather fitting, I thought, as it seemed to reflect the mood in every household since the war had started. All the windows and shutters had been painstakingly taped shut as an anti-gas sealant measure, casting the house into gloom. Rays of sunlight occasionally sliced through the gaps in the shutters and carved their way through the darkness. I guided Thomas to the living room and sat him down on the sofa, kneeling in front of him. He had recovered significantly and was now able to speak more fluently and therefore was determined to put up a fight.

"Mummy, I don't like the gas mask! I can't breathe and it's so smelly and I can't see!"

"Thomas..." I tried to interrupt but now that his flow of speech was in motion he refused to stop. "I think it's going to make me blind—it's so misty and I can't see! Every time I try to breathe the rubber sucks part of my face away!" With that, he broke down into howling sobs, soaking my blouse until it was drenched. Hushing him tenderly, I rocked him back and forth, patting his head gently. As his breaths gradually became more even, I prepared myself to persuade him.

"Thomas," I said, as sternly as I could manage, "these gas masks are very important—they may save our lives one day." He was already shaking his head firmly in stubborn refusal. "You even have a special mask." I continued, picking up his gas mask to emphasise my point. "Look! It's a Mickey Mouse mask for small children like you! That's not so scary is it?"

In desperation I held it up in front of him, with its red rubber pieces and bright eyepiece rims. Honestly, I was unsure as to whether it was less or actually more scary than my own plain black gas mask. The sight of the ghastly thing only made him wail louder.

"OK then, Thomas." I ploughed on in my futile mission to convince him. "The government says that we should practise wearing our masks every day. We're going to put them on for 15 minutes each evening before bed. And we'll do it together, OK?" Thomas looked up at me and an ember of hope sparked within me.

"Every day?!" he whispered.

Had I done it? Had I persuaded him?

"Yes, every day Thomas," I replied, a smile starting to creep across my face. A sudden bout of wails erupted from him, so loud it seemed incomprehensible that such sounds could come from so small a being.

"Daddy wouldn't make me do this! I want Daddy!"

A wave of painful longing washed over me, drowning out all of the remaining fragments of my hopes and warm memories.

"Daddy is fighting in the war, Thomas." I forced the dreaded words through gritted teeth and squeezed my eyes shut against the image of Edward that flashed before my eyes. "He might be away for some time but he would be really proud of you if you put the gas mask on."

"Daddy... would be... proud... of me?" Thomas asked, with a childish innocence that melted through the aching bleakness.

"Yes, Thomas. Do it for Daddy, okay?" With slow reluctance, he began to bob his head up and down. "Shall we head back to school with this then?" I asked with a smile, holding up the gas mask. There was something intimidatingly chilling about its appearance—an odd eeriness to it. I could see the fear in his eyes at the sight of the mask, but then he quickly nodded and looked away. I stood up to place the gas mask in its cardboard box and draped the long string strap over Thomas' shoulder. Standing rigidly, he looked oddly soldier-like, with his arms stiffly held at his side. I suddenly saw Edward there, standing in his new uniform, boots polished until they were shining. It was my turn to look away and I picked up my own cardboard box containing my gas mask.

"Shall we go?" I said brightly, with a false cheerfulness that ate away at my conscience and made me cringe inside. Thomas nodded absentmindedly.

The war had made the world seem like a different planet. I no longer thought of the clouds as bringing rain and life, but rather they were an army of darkness, soldiers storming towards an ominous abyss of shadow. The tension in the air was stifling, as if it was bursting with thousands of secrets eager to spill onto the streets. It was nearing the end of winter, but there was still a crisp chill to the air that stung at my skin and burned my throat as I breathed in. Thomas' school was just around the corner and we neared the entrance within minutes. "Ready?" I asked.

"Ready," he replied, gnawing at his bottom lip apprehensively. Swinging open the door to reception, I signed Thomas in and was about to turn to leave when the receptionist called out to me.

"Oh, Mrs Walbridge!"

"Please, call me Penny." I interrupted hastily. The sound of my last name only made me miss Edward even more than I already did.

"Penny," she continued, flushing with embarrassment, "I think you ought to stay today." She gestured to the side in order to speak to me privately and out of Thomas' hearing range. He was rather preoccupied with the abacus in the play area anyway. "I understand that Thomas has had some difficulty with the gas mask, am I right?" she continued in a hushed voice that tickled my ear. Oh no, not the gas masks again I thought to myself.

"Yes, but we've brought it in now and I'll make sure he brings it to school every day." I replied quickly, eager for the conversation to end. I wasn't sure how much more of this gas mask business I could take without screaming.

"Oh yes, that's good," the receptionist remarked. "But the children are going to have a gas mask drill today."

Dread filled me like molten lead and I felt unable to move my legs. There was no way that this was going to end well. "I really don't think that's the best idea..."

"I know that Thomas is very nervous around the gas masks but I think this is certainly necessary for his safety and Miss Hendy, that is Thomas' teacher, insists that he learns to become comfortable with this."

"Surely it would be better to let us sort this out ourselves. I mean, you can't force this on him, he's only six years old for goodness' sake!" In my hot frustration I found myself, rather confusingly, defending Thomas. Footsteps echoed down the hallway and a teacher marched down the corridor, her high heels clicking constantly against the polished floor.

"Miss Hendy," I said, with a respectful nod in her direction.

"Ah, Mrs Walbridge," she said with a strained smile that stretched her red lipstick across her weathered face. "How lovely to see you. And is Thomas here now?" Upon hearing his name, Thomas popped his head around the corner from the play area and ran towards me, wrapping his arms tightly around my legs. "Are you ready to come to class now, Thomas?" she asked. Thomas made no response, chewing on the end of his sleeve ravenously. "Mrs Walbridge, I think it would be best for you to come this way."

I nodded grudgingly and followed Miss Hendy, Thomas trotting cautiously in front of me. Upon entering the rowdy classroom, I sat at the back with Thomas and waited for Miss Hendy to calm the children.

"OK, Thomas." I began hesitantly, not sure how he would take this. "Remember how we agreed to try the gas masks on? Remember how we're going to make Daddy proud?" Thomas bobbed his head up and down. I hated having to do this to him. I could already sense his steadily growing panic. "Well, today, we're going to make Daddy even more proud. We're going to try wearing the mask in the lesson with all the other kids too!" I forced the enthusiasm into my voice, trying not to sound as patronising as I felt.

"You mean, we have to put them on?"

"Yes, Thomas," I answered firmly, determined for this to work.

"And this would make Daddy proud of me?"

I nodded fervently, not trusting myself to speak.

"OK, then," he said with such wavering uncertainty that it almost persuaded me to scrap the whole thing and leave. Miss Hendy had settled the class and was now giving instruction.

"So, class, today we're going to have our first gas mask drill in order to help us to get used to them. Isn't that exciting?" The reaction of the children was surprisingly varied. The majority of the class were practically bouncing in childish excitement, thrilled by the prospect of games and fun—any way to escape from the ordinary dullness of the usual school day. But some of the children were absolutely terrified. Thomas, however, contained his tears and bit his bottom lip hard, desperately attempting to control his instant panic.

"Everyone quiet! Quiet! I said QUIET!" Miss Hendy commanded severely, trying to settle the class back down. For a teacher of such young children, she really didn't seem to be very understanding or compassionate. "Right, now can everyone take out their gas masks and place them on the desk," she continued once a hushed silence had settled in the classroom.

A loud cluttering and chatter erupted suddenly as children pulled their masks out from their cardboard boxes. The commotion dissipated just as abruptly as Miss Hendy held up her hand for quiet. "Now, I want everyone to listen carefully." She eyed the class, surveying each child to check that they were listening. Oddly, I felt that I was part of the class, back in school and being scolded by my own first grade teacher. The memory made me smile, despite the fact that my mischief had long been abandoned.

Satisfied with her observation, Miss Hendy continued "I know many of you already know how to do this but I just want to clarify." She picked up her own gas mask to demonstrate. "First, hold your breath." She spoke slowly, as if in slow motion, with an emphasis on each syllable of every word. "Then hold the mask in front of your face with your thumbs inside the straps. Thrust your chin well forward into the mask and pull the straps over your head as far as they will go." At this point, her voice was considerably muffled due to the barrier of the mask. She proceeded nonetheless. "Finally, run your finger around the face piece taking care that the straps are not twisted. Does everyone understand? Any questions?"

Standing there in her high heels and wearing a terrifying gas mask appeared strangely comic and I had to compress a bubble of laughter that rose up in my throat. No one said a word but a couple more children started to cry, sniffling audibly. Miss Hendy pulled off the gas mask and smoothed out her straggly, dishevelled hair.

"Right then," she said as there were no questions. "Your turn."

I turned to Thomas and offered a comforting smile. I wasn't sure what much else I could do. "Ready then?" I asked. He shook his head in protest, any previous bravery having vanished. But I shook my own head and held up the mask. "We've got to try putting it on Thomas. At least once. Hold your breath now, OK?" I don't think I even needed to instruct him—he was already holding his breath in terror. Carefully, I pulled the straps over his head, his fragile body jerking backwards as I tried to keep the straps from twisting. As soon as the mask was on, real panic set in.

"Mummy? Mummy I can't see you! Everything's going cloudy— I'm going blind!" Thomas was shrieking, his genuine fear crackling in the air. "I can't breathe, I can't breathe, I can't breathe!"

"Thomas honey, calm down, I'm right here." I tried to hold him but he squirmed out of my grasp, desperately trying to rip the mask off. Every time he breathed out the rubber washer under his chin flipped up and hit his face, further fuelling his panic. His shrieks had escalated to a steady stream of screams that pierced my ears painfully. Kneeling down, I ripped the mask off his face and held him close, hushing him gently. His face was wet with a mixture of tears and cold sweat. Gradually, his screams were reduced to shuddering whimpers, until eventually he fell quiet, exhausted by his draining outburst. The utter silence in the air was like an alarm sounding in my ears as I suddenly became conscious of the stares that penetrated through my skin. I raised my head slowly to look around the class. The children were petrified. Miss Hendy looked furious.

"Come this way with me please, Mrs Walbridge." I had never heard such coldness in the undertone of her condescending command. Obediently, I took Thomas gently in my arms and carried him out the door. "I don't know what you've said to that child but you must teach him some discipline!" Miss Hendy was marching in front of me, her back to my face, even as she was speaking, as if she couldn't even bear to look at me in her disgust. "If not for his own good," she continued, "then at least for the safety of others. Do you have any idea the damage that your scene has just caused?! I'll never get those children comfortable with the masks now."

"Miss Hendy..." Suddenly she turned swiftly on her heel and I almost crashed straight into her.

"Just go," she interrupted, leaning forwards into my face. I could feel her breath down my neck and spittle that sprayed onto my cheeks. "You've done enough. Make sure Thomas brings his mask tomorrow—today was the third time that he forgot!" With that she stormed past me and headed back to her class. I swallowed down the many furious comments that threatened to spill from my lips. I knew it would do no good to express my anger.

After the short walk home, it dawned upon me the seriousness of Thomas' refusal to wear the gas mask. One day it could cost him his life. And if that happened, I knew I would never be able to forgive myself. There was always going to be something that I could have done more, some way I could have tried harder. I had to share the burden. Picking up a pen and a piece of paper with an envelope and, having settled comfortably into the rocking chair, I began my letter to Edward.

An hour later and my page was still blank, with nothing but the words '*Dearest Edward*' inscribed at the top. Somehow, spilling my worries onto the paper wasn't as easy as I thought it would have been. Sharing this burden was selfish and unfair of me—Edward didn't need even more to worry about. Nevertheless, I knew I had to tell him and forced my pen into action, writing about the danger of Thomas' refusal to wear the gas mask and my endless exasperation in trying to convince him. But most of the letter was about how much I missed and loved him, how I yearned for him to come home. I forced myself to end the letter, before my tears soaked the paper and smudged the ink—some words were already unreadable.

"Are you ready to go, Thomas?" I called. "It's time for school now." Thomas rushed around the corner and caught me completely off guard: he was wearing the gas mask. I could hear his fast, shallow, panicked breaths through the barrier of the mask. "Thomas? Thomas are you all right?"

"Mummy, I think I feel sick," he groaned. "I need to take it off!"

Alarmed, I quickly pulled the mask off his face and wrapped my arms around him.

"I tried, Mummy. I tried to be brave but I just can't!" he whimpered miserably. "I've let Daddy down!" The sorrowful misery in his voice made my heart ache and I hushed him softly.

"No, Thomas, Daddy would be so proud of you for trying. You managed to put it on all by yourself. We'll keep putting the mask on every day but only for a little while, OK? Only a few seconds to start with. Does that sound good?"

Nodding promptly, he wiped his nose on the sleeve of my shirt and I rolled my eyes in amusement, genuinely impressed by his courage. "We better be off to school now," I said, keeping an eye on the clock. "Let's not forget your gas mask this time!"

As I was heading back home from the school, after dropping Thomas off, I noticed the posters stuck up on the walls, scattered everywhere around the buildings. They depicted a gas mask and the caption read *'Hitler will send no warning—so always carry your gas mask!'* My hand automatically went to the cardboard box that was slung around my shoulder and I lifted my head to look around the street. The neighbourhood was oddly empty, as it had been for the past few months since the war started. Those who were about had turned up their jacket collars and wore long gloves with their hands in their pockets to stop open skin being hit by gas if there was an attack. There was something awkwardly cold about this that made me feel like an outsider in an unfriendly territory. There was an air raid warden patrolling the end of the street in his gas mask, wearing a steel helmet and heavy overalls. He was holding a gas rattle, which was actually, rather comically, usually found in the hands of supporters at football matches. Despite this amusing coincidence, the gas mask looked terrifyingly alien and made the warden appear dehumanised. I quickly walked past him and turned the corner into the house.

Weeks passed in a blur of monochromatic tones and Thomas made no progress. I still had not heard back from Edward and my worry was eating away at my sanity. Every night I heard the inevitable 'Put that light out!' or 'Cover that window!' from an air warden to some poor householder who had forgotten to turn off the lamps or draw their curtains. I was constantly straining my ears for the potential sound of the gas rattle, warning of a gas attack or a drill. I still had no idea what to do with Thomas if that situation ever occurred as it was bound to. The days seemed to disappear into a black hole of darkness, slowly spreading into every aspect of our lives.

It was a Wednesday when I heard a knock on the door. I thought Thomas had returned from school. It was the telegraph boy. They were nicknamed *'Angels of Death'* because they only ever delivered news if a soldier was missing or killed in action. The look on his face told me the news instantly. I could barely feel the envelope between my fingers as I took out the telegram. I already knew what it would read:

THE SECRETARY OF WAR DESIRES TO EXPRESS HIS DEEPEST REGRET THAT YOUR HUSBAND PRIVATE EDWARD WALBRIDGE WAS KILLED IN ACTION SEVENTEENTH FEBRUARY. CONFIRMING LETTER TO FOLLOW.

THE ADJUTANT GENERAL

"I'm sorry," the boy mumbled, after having seen my face fall in dread. I nodded distantly and closed the door as he turned away sombrely. There had to be a mistake, I thought as I sank to the floor with my back against the front door. I had dreamed about this happening. I had expected a hot, fiery pain to scald and burn me with a scorching agony. What I felt was so much worse. A cold, icy numbness crept through my body as if ice was solidifying in my veins. I felt hollow and empty; I was frozen in place, unable to move. Tears streamed down my cheeks silently—no sobs racked my body as I thought they would. A deep ache consumed me with a torturous anguish that refused to subside. The world around me shattered, as if I had been living in a crystal dome that had only just collapsed around me. Edward was gone. I don't know how long I sat there before a knock on the door scattered my distant thoughts.

"Mummy? Are you home?" In silence, he waited for a reply but even as I mouthed the words, no sound came out. "Mummy, you forgot to pick me up today so Bobby's mum walked me home. Can you open the door now?"

Bobby? Oh yes, Thomas' best friend.

"Mummy, are you there?"

Finally regaining control of my limbs, I heaved myself up from the floor, staggering against the wall. Wiping my eyes and trying to compose myself, I braced myself to tell Thomas the news. How could I do this without breaking his heart? Without breaking my own all over again?

"Thomas, how was school?" I exclaimed as I opened the door, my voice sounding unnaturally cheerful and disgustingly forced.

"It was... OK, I guess." He could already detect that something was wrong.

"Come on in," I said hurrying him through the door, eager to hide us from view.

"What's wrong, Mummy? Something is wrong..."

"Nothing dear, noth—" I stopped myself mid-sentence. It would do no good to lie to him. I knew it would only make this more difficult. My throat suddenly felt desert-dry and I licked my parched lips. "Come sit down Thomas." He sat down on the sofa and I knelt in front of him. "I just got a letter." I began hesitantly, unsure as to how to phrase it. Thomas nodded but confusion was written all across his face.

"It said..." My throat closed up and I had to stop speaking to keep from choking. "It said..." I had to finish the sentence now or I knew that I never would. "It said... that Daddy won't be coming back." The words rushed out all in one breath, like a gentle breeze that somehow seemed to carry all the sorrows in the world.

"You mean, I won't see Daddy again?" Thomas' puzzlement gradually turned to understanding as I nodded slowly. "Why? Where did he go?" His expression spiralled into a frenzy of bewilderment.

"He's dead," I whispered. I could find no other way to say the words. "Daddy's in heaven now." The shock of saying the words out loud was like a slap on the face and I felt as if all the air had been knocked out of me. All of a sudden, a flood of emotion poured through me, flooding my cold numbness and replacing it with waves and surges of an aching pain. I became distantly aware of Thomas' howling sobs as he clung to my arms, gripping me so hard—the physical pain was trivial, nothing compared to the torment of grief.

Exactly one week later, there was a knock on the door.

"Morning Ma'am." said the postman, standing on the front step as I opened the door. I smiled tiredly in response, my eyes swollen and puffy from days of weeping. If the postman noted how awful I looked, he politely made no attempt to remark on it. "A parcel for you Ma'am," he said cheerfully, handing me a box wrapped in rough brown paper and turning away as I nodded my thanks. Looking down at the parcel, I froze, my whole body stiffening in shock. There was a letter. It was in Edward's handwriting. Regaining mobility in seconds, I slammed the door shut and raced to the living room.

"Thomas! Come here! Now!" I called in fractured commands as I tore open the letter frantically in nervous apprehension. I had to force myself not to skim read the letter in my fervour, savouring every handwritten word. It read:

My dearest Penny,

My dear, if you are reading this letter you most likely would have received the telegram informing you of my death. I wanted to send you one last message before it is too late. I have been drafted to the front and know that I will not make it home to you and to Thomas. Words cannot express my love for you and the emptiness I feel without you here. Concerning Thomas' stubbornness, I have sent this letter along with something that I believe will help. Anyway, I won't be needing it anymore. I will always love you. Remember that.

With all my love,
Edward

Biting my fist to keep from sobbing, I skimmed down the page to the next paragraph, this time addressed to Thomas:

Thomas, my dear boy,

Know that I will always be proud of you in everything you do—no father could ever be more blessed with such a brave and wonderful son. While I am away, take care of your mother for me and be strong. I have a gift for you and hope that it will help you overcome your fear of the mask. It was mine. Wear it to remember me. I love you to the moon and back, son.

Daddy

"Yes Mummy?" Thomas interrupted my thoughts and I looked up at him. For some reason I was beaming, my glowing smile stretching from ear to ear. I patted my lap, gesturing for him to come and sit down as I read out the letter to him. "Did you hear that Thomas? Daddy left you a present!"

"But it's not my birthday, Mummy," Thomas protested in such innocent confusion.

"Why don't you go on and open it anyway?" I said, reaching for the box and placing it in his lap. Slowly, he tore the brown paper away from the box and lifted the flaps to see what it contained. Horrified, I beheld the sight of a gas mask—as alien and dehumanising as all the others that I had seen. Anxiously I turned to see Thomas' expression. He looked strangely mature, with a look of understanding and recognition on his face.

"So this was Daddy's gas mask?" he asked.

"Yes Thomas."

"And he said that I can wear this? For him?" I nodded, nervous to see his response. Suddenly, a broad grin illuminated his face and it was as if the sun had emerged from after a storm.

"I'll wear it!" he declared proudly. "I'll wear it for Daddy!"

"Yes," I said, "for Daddy."

Watching Thomas confidently standing there in Edward's gas mask, I wondered whether it masked his fear or showed he had overcome his fear of the mask.

The Trojan Horse

My older brother's handsome, reassuring face smiles down at me from billboards, up at me from my phone screen, is handed to me as I leave the train station by masked leafleteers on my way to St Agatha's Church Hall. They've airbrushed him, removed the skin imperfections and de-aged him; he could be an advert for shampoo and toothpaste and razor blades all at once. It's his face, but not his face. I crumple up the flyer and bin it, resisting the urge to snatch the stack of remaining flyers from the volunteers and do the same with them. But as Monday's events demonstrated, I'm too much of a coward and I love my brother too much to hurt him. And if I'm honest, what I was truly angry at was seeing video of my own face plastered across my social media, beaming and laughing whilst behind it I shrivelled.

On Monday night, I relapsed after nearly a year's sobriety. I drank for most of Tuesday, too. I had a zoom call with my sponsor yesterday and I'm getting myself back on track. Today is a new day.

It began when my sister face-timed me a week ago, fuming that I had 'pulled out' out of the magazine piece the following Monday. The connection was terrible but I could make out her characteristic glower in the blocky orange mosaic of her face on my phone screen. I explained patiently that I could hardly pull out of something I hadn't agreed to in the first place.

"Dan needs your support," she fumed. "Whatever you have, reschedule it. Try not to be so bloody selfish for a change."

Like most conversations with family, the call consisted of much character assassination in both directions. As a barrister, Allison was exceptionally well-practised at this.

"I have the 'dentist' then," I lied, using my code for AA meetings. I don't like lying. One of the big epiphanies I've had in recent years of therapy is that I, like many others, have spent most of my life living in a way that is not aligned to who I truly am and the values I hold dear. After years of hiding behind a fake, people-pleasing persona–with all the misery and self-hatred that's brought me—I've finally managed to construct a sense of who I am and what I stand for; and I have pledged to live by that come hell or high water. Going to the house to tell fibs for this magazine piece threatened to compromise what I'd worked hard to build.

"Skip it this once. I'm sure you'll survive another week."

For a moment, I considered telling her the truth, that I could not support our brother in this. But it would get back to him, and I don't think I could stomach upsetting him like that. So I made up a lie. I had chosen my AA meetings as they're a sensitive area that people usually don't like to intrude upon. Not Allison.

"I'm sorry," I lied again. "I just can't make it. Besides, he doesn't need me. Or you. He's ahead in the polls, he's going to win." In seven days my brother would be the MP for Buckley & Aldersham, magazine piece or not.

In truth, the magazine interview was completely unnecessary. There was already strong public support for Dan's campaign, which was putting front and centre the preservation of the local environment.

Buckley & Aldersham is as green as it is middle class. The idea for the magazine feature was Sunil's, Dan's Campaign PR Chief, a bundle of writhing nerves contained within a Superdry hoodie. When my brother's rival Maggie Huttlestone accused him of being a 'carpet-bagger' who had 'swooped in from his riverside duplex in Richmond' as part of a 'cynical power grab', Sunil shit himself and arranged the interview with a local magazine. It was ostensibly to be a feature piece on us three siblings and our late father, a bootstrap working class success story who had owned a string of pubs in Buckley & Aldersham. But the article was a Trojan Horse, intended to smuggle in a puff piece on Dan. Its purpose was to showcase his connection to the area (in which he'd been born and spent over half his life) and to give him an extra publicity nudge ahead of that week's polling day. A pointless waste of time, but everyone was now fully sold on the idea. Sunil because he considered it a 'critical counter-riposte' to the Huttlestone Campaign. Dan because he saw Sunil as some sort of divine oracle and would bathe in sludge if Sunil thought it would 'play well'. Allison because of her drive to gain ever-more proximity to power and to have her photo in a glossy magazine. The magazine editor because he because he was packing serious wood for Dan and his environmental pledges.

And naturally, everyone expected me to be there, like the good little brother I am.

"It's just *photos,*" Allison assured me. "You won't be interviewed or anything. Dan and I will be handling the story. Just sit there and look pretty. It'll scan badly if you're not there."

She tried adding pressure, tried appealing to reason, tried stroking my ego, I still said no. So she lost her cool.

"What a selfish little man. Do I have to remind you of all the things Dan's done for you?"

My sister loves Dan almost as much as she hates me. I hung up as she launched a volley of abuse down the line, the swarm of pixels convulsing angrily on screen. It felt good. The thing is, I'm not even sure if she really believed I had to be there. For Allison, bending people into submission until they break to her will is one of her happiest pastimes.

And given the resistance I always put up, I'm one of her preferred species of game. For the rest of the day I ignored the barrage of WhatsApp messages pinging angrily away on my phone. Later that evening, Dan phoned me up. We had a lovely catch-up and at the end of the call he asked me if I would be free on Monday for the magazine interview but no worries if not. I somehow found myself saying yes of course, and was there anything in particular I should be wearing?

The magazine piece was taking place at our old family house; now Allison's family house. As instructed, I had taken a COVID-test before I showed up, sanitising on entry whilst the masked magazine crew brought in black trunks containing lighting equipment. The interior of the house was all varnished oak surfaces and *objets d'art*. The kitchen was sleek and spot-lit with glinting chromatic appliances. Beautiful, inauthentic. When we were kids there was a scummy carpet where the glistening floorboards now lie, and the kitchen walls and ceiling were stained yellow from the deep-fat fryer. Allison had done the place up, filling it with buttoned leather armchairs and oil paintings. There was a genuine log fireplace in the lounge, and the house now looked like a Lord & Lady's residence, or where a barrister of considerably greater wealth and influence than my sister might have lived. Dan was in the study with Sunil, running over the social media 'assets' for his campaign on the latter's Macbook.

"Mark," Dan greeted me as I entered, shaking hands and hugging me as Sunil scarpered off with his Macbook. "Thank you so much for coming. I am *so* sorry for being such a dreadful egomaniac." He was wearing a jersey and jeans, a calculatedly casual look.

I laughed and dismissed his concerns, telling him it was my pleasure. When Dan talks to you, you have this feeling that you're the only person in the room he truly wants to be talking to. Everything else, everyone else, fades away.

"They got rid of our bunk I see," he said with a smile as we left the study and went downstairs, his arm around my shoulders.

When we were little, Dan and I used to share a bunk bed in what was now Allison's study, even though Dan was four years older than me. As the eldest, Allison had her own room, a box room with My Little Pony wallpaper that would eventually grow obscured with Metallica posters and photos of her and her friends on school trips abroad. Dan got the top bunk. We shared our toys and comics. Before I had my own allowance, he used to let me have his duplicate football stickers that he couldn't trade off at school. I never loved football like he and my dad did, but I tried to. When I was ten he showed me a *Mayfair* magazine he'd traded with a friend at school for a bottle of cheap gin he'd stolen from our parents' drinks cabinet. Under the covers, I saw my first images of naked women by torchlight. We went to the same secondary school together where Dan was a prefect and an athlete. He had no interest in actual politics as a teenager, but even then people had a sense that was where he might end up—in his leaving Yearbook he was voted 'Most Likely To Be Prime Minister'. He was one of those students who was popular both with the teachers and with his peers. He got good grades and was the star of both the football and the athletics team. I, on the other hand was a nobody, not even held in enough contempt to be bullied with any regularity. A C-student. Where my brother had won a scholarship our father had to pay fees for me—something he would remind me of regularly on the drive home from parents' evenings or when I came home with a dismal report. I wasn't my father's favourite. When he laid into me though, Dan would leap to my defence. Allison would observe from the sidelines in silent, smug judgement, perking up and smirking when my dad would gesture her way to show me what a positive example looks like. She was top of her year at her girls' school. We went to the boys' school of the same name, though our single-sex regime didn't stand in the way of Dan getting female attention. From his GCSE years, there was always a band of girls in the uniform of another school waiting opposite the school gates for Dan and his clique to come out. You could watch them dissolve into smiles and giggles as the two groups merged and headed out into town, backpacks slung over their shoulders. If Dan ever saw me walking home while he was with them, he would never ignore me as you'd expect some brothers to do. He'd always wave to me from across the street, or sometimes, after a quick check for traffic, would jog across the road and catch up with me for a quick chat. The boys and girls in his group would stand there waiting for him to return. A couple of times he took me with them when they went to the cinema. Unsurprisingly, he was chosen Head Boy in his final year. Gradually, I began to benefit from his stardom, tagging along with him to the odd house party or pub visit. I was still an outcast and a weirdo, but I began to watch my brother and learn to mimic his mannerisms, the way he put his hand on people's shoulder and laughed with gusto at their jokes, the types of witticisms he made. I became a bit less of a nobody, although my identity was very much 'Dan Fletcher's little brother'. Even after he left for university, the teachers would see me as little more than a faint echo of Dan. Unfavourable comparisons to him were a favourite weapon of theirs to wield against me, for all the good it did. In his final year, on top of being Head Boy, Dan also won his House cup. It was a resounding success with which to end his secondary school career. He didn't get into Oxford or Cambridge as had been hoped by many of the teachers, and so didn't get his name embossed in gold on the walls of our assembly hall. But his name was carved ethereally into the collective memory of the school, as one of the Great Boys of its history. He was less of a star at university, though he did well enough, completing a degree in Economics and gaining some modest recognition on the sports teams there. He surprised everyone by going to Sandhurst after graduation. He served in Afghanistan in the Household Cavalry Regiment, leaving the Army four years later with the rank of Captain and having been awarded the Distinguished Service Cross. He worked in public affairs institutions for a few years before eventually entering politics, where he was now standing for election as the MP for his hometown of Buckley & Aldersham. And barring a miracle from God, he would win.

The make-up artist lightly powdered my face while Dan charmed the magazine crew. Allison arrived from putting on her own face and came down dressed in a smart lilac suit with a large dragonfly brooch on the lapel.

"You're not late for once," she observed, giving me a peck on the cheek. Masks off, the three of us entered the lounge. They took photos of us seated on the burgundy settee which they'd positioned to have the fire crackling in the background (and Allison's published novel standing prominently on the mantelpiece). It took about an hour in various poses. Some dignified and serious, some silly—pulling faces, pretending to have a pillow fight with one of the cushions. Evidently, they wanted to recapture a sense of us playing together as children, letting our hair down, being a family. A more accurate photo might have had Allison punching me in the arm to get me off the TV so she could watch her programme, with Dan pilfering liquor from one of Dad's pubs to split with his mates. But I guess that wouldn't quite capture the 'messaging' Sunil was going for. After the lounge photos they decided they wanted some 'natural' shots, so they staged one batch in the kitchen where Dan was making us tea while we all had a jolly laugh about something, and another in the garden of us all playing frisbee with Allison's Labrador (Sunil, afraid of dogs, remained safely inside watching through the conservatory doors, endorsing the decision to get the dog involved as an 'excellent shout from an optics standpoint').

By the end of the shoot, my cheeks were aching from hours of fake grinning and I wanted to collapse into a heap. Dan and Allison had a much easier time of things, either because they were genuinely enjoying themselves or because they find it much easier than me to slip in and out of social masquerades. Both of them had jobs that required them to change visage suddenly, to move seamlessly from charming to assertive to impassioned to tearful.

"Exhausting," Dan remarked jovially, but he didn't look remotely tired.

Allison made us all some coffee, and contrary to her assurances that no questions would be asked, questions were asked. To Allison, lying is a morally neutral tool to be deployed as expedient. Much of the questioning was directed at Dan about his campaign pledge to ensure Buckley Park was granted national heritage status and thus protection from the encroaching real estate developers. There was much fawning and obsequiousness. Naturally, Allison and I were asked about our own support for Dan's campaign and somebody had the *genius* idea to film short video clips of us 'for the website' that could also be repurposed for Dan's campaign. The prospect delighted Allison, and Sunil practically came on the spot at the promise of the additional 'collateral' that could be proliferated across social media.

"I'm not sure," I found myself saying, as Allison brought the coffee into the lounge. All eyes turned on me, and my sister froze with the tray in her hand.

"Not sure about what?" Carla, the interviewer, asked.

"About doing the video segments." I shifted uncomfortably on the settee. "I thought we were just doing photographs. I didn't know we were talking about the campaign."

"It wasn't the plan," Allison fibbed, handing out the coffees. "But it's a great idea, isn't it?" she asked the room, eliciting a babble of assent.

"I don't know," I said, feeling the warmth of the fire against my neck. "I don't know if I'm comfortable."

"Rubbish," Allison snapped, putting the empty tray down on the table as Carla and the photographer exchanged uncomfortable glances.

"It's fine," Carla said. "Absolutely not a problem if you're not comfortable, we're happy to just go with Dan and Allison if you're both still keen?"

"No, it's *not* fine," Allison said hotly.

"Allison," Dan said from his standing place at the window, a note of warning in his voice. "If he doesn't want to do it, he doesn't have to do it. Mark, it's fine. It's not important."

"Yes, it *is* important, Dan. All the things you've done for him. We had to drag him here kicking and screaming, and now he can't be arsed to say a few bloody words for his own brother's campaign?" She shot me a savage look. "Go on, what's your excuse this time?"

I felt my brow turn damp. A couple of crew members made themselves scarce. I didn't have an excuse. How was I supposed to explain to them my reluctance to support my brother, a loving family man who was running on a ticket to keep our county green and abundant with wildlife? A man who'd saved my life after my attempted overdose when I was twenty-one; who had stayed with me every day in the hospital until I had recovered, and who'd never once thought to shame me for it. I still remember waking up not knowing where I was, and the sudden sense of relief when I felt Dan's hand on my shoulder. And now here I was, with the camera lens staring into me from one angle and my sister's glare skewering me from another, as she waited for me to speak in my defence. Even Dan, my only advocate, couldn't hide an expression of curiosity on his face as to why his brother writhed so at the prospect of a few warm words. I looked down at my shoes, wordless.

There's a saying misattributed to the Japanese that every person has three faces: the first face, you show to the world. The second face, you show to your close friends and your family. The third face, you never show anyone. I know this third face, I feel it within myself, the one that that has unflinchingly surveyed the most depraved of my sexual fantasies, the most violent of my urges, the ugliest of my prejudices. The face I had long striven to keep veiled. But this third face is ever searching for opportunities to escape, to slip free of its guards and reveal itself to others, if only for a heartbeat.

When I was fourteen and Dan was in his final year of sixth form, my dad took us both to a football game. Dan was in his final year of sixth form at the time. It was our team playing in the semi-finals of a major national tournament—the farthest we'd ever gotten after a surprise streak of victories. We turned up in style, wearing the kit and our faces painted in their colours, red and white. We fitted in well amongst the scarves and banners and other faces smeared in war paint. We chanted the team anthem, booed when the opposing team stepped onto the pitch and lost our minds when our team did the same. It was the first time I felt the raw, tribal energy of football, the sense that this was not just a game, but that we were warring armies and everything counted upon our victory. Even with my limited interest in the game, I felt my blood rise when we scored our first goal and my entire world erupted in screams and cheers.

A fat shirtless man with the team's logo tattooed on his chest hugged me. It was exhilarating. If our team won, we would get through to the final—a once in a lifetime event. We were 1-1 as the game inched into its last few minutes of added time. Hands were clasped to faces on both sides; the tension was excruciating.

And then everything went wrong. A misunderstanding between the linesman, the referee and the players on an offside call caused our team to stall, thinking that play had been stopped, while the other team continued on to score their winning goal. It had been a bad decision, poorly handled, and it caused an uproar on our side. Fingers were pointed by our players as they surrounded the referee. Fans were spilling out onto the pitch, and all around me our united tribe had melted into an ocean of rage. The fat man who hugged me had turned red and was screaming so hard I thought he'd burst. Seats were wrenched from their brackets and fights broke out.

"Go. Now," my dad urged. We headed for the exits but were not the only ones doing so. I lost my dad and Dan in the crowds that were bottlenecking our escape. I was sure it was only a matter of time before I would be trampled underfoot. Not far from where I was standing, part of the stadium wall gave in and I heard screams. I managed to force my way out, and found myself in the middle of a warzone, where fans in red and fans in blue were at each other's throats. I prayed that Dan and my dad were ok. I found my dad first and was alarmed at how frightened he looked. Neither of us knew where Dan was. We searched, and when we found him I wish we hadn't. He had gotten into a brawl with three black men from the opposing side, who were now surrounding him. Ignoring my dad's command to stay put, I screamed Dan's name as we both ran closer, but he didn't hear. Then, two fans from our side grabbed a hold of two of the men accosting Dan. Dan wriggled free of the grasp of the third, and knocked him to the ground. For a moment, I was relieved. But I felt my stomach turn as I saw Dan bring his foot up into the air, and bring it down upon the man's head once, and then a second time, and then a third. My dad caught Dan's arms and pulled him away just in time to prevent the fourth blow. The man now lay on his back, his face coated in blood and his eye beginning to swell. His lips moved slowly as though he were murmuring in his sleep. But what truly terrified me was not his face, but Dan's.

The boy my dad was pulling back was not Dan, the handsome Head Boy of our school. His face, red with our team colours, was contorted by murderous rage, his eyes bulged demonically, spit sprayed from his mouth as he shrieked, "Fucking kill you! Black fucking cunt! I'll cut your fucking throat!" He screamed like that until my dad pulled him far away and gave him a slap around the face before we fled the carnage. No one spoke in the car journey home.

At home, we went to bed and for once Dan and I said nothing to each other as we lay in our bunks. Eventually I stopped trembling and slipped in and out of a broken, jagged sleep, where all I saw was Dan's livid eyes and his bared teeth, and in my dreams I heard the crack as the man's skull fractured. The next day at breakfast, everything was normal and no one ever brought up what had happened the evening before.

Had I seen Dan's true face that day, the one no one was supposed to see? Or had I witnessed the momentary possession of a frightened teenage boy placed in the throes of a terrifying and traumatic situation? I'll never know. But in the years that followed, I caught more glimpses of that face. Many times late into the night after Dan and I had been drinking heavily, he would make a passing remark on a race, a religion, a sexual identity.

If ever I reacted in discomfort or uncertainty, Dan would laugh and tell me he had just been joshing, and the subject would change. He could slip on that smile quick as a magician conjuring a dove from thin air, and make it disappear just as quickly.

Nor will I ever forget Dan's stag party, when a drunken row erupted between him and one of his old army friends. Nobody loved Dan like his army friends; they spoke with admiration and respect for the heroism he'd shown during a fourteen-hour firefight in Kandahar as they awaited air support. They were more loyal than brothers. But on that night, the gentle but sullen giant called Callum got into a quarrel with Dan. I can't remember what started it—something trivial—but I remember as Callum stormed off out of the venue, he stuck his sweaty, bleary-eyed face in my own, and said something that terrified me.

"Your brother is a fucking *murderer*. Remember that." And he left.

Was there any truth in what he said? Had something happened in Afghanistan, or were these the bitter, drunken ramblings of a man who bore a grudge against my brother? I doubt I'll ever know the truth of the matter—Callum died a few years later and Dan's other army buddies would never betray his loyalty, no matter what he'd done. But I never forgot what Callum had said that night. And something about the cool way Dan had watched his comrade storm out that night, the ghost of a smirk on his lips, had given me the chills. Once again, I glimpsed something that did not fit with the brother who used to gift me his shiny football stickers. It was as though I had gained access to a crack in his charming, polished exterior and seen something ugly within that I now know must be kept away from any kind of power at all costs.

I considered for a moment telling the truth to everyone gathered in the lounge. *You promised to live up to your values, never to compromise on who you are or what you stood for. Well? Here's your moment.* My throat went dry as I looked from face to face, squirming for what felt like an eternity. Dan's curious look turned to one of concern, Allison's eyes narrowed. *Tell them the truth.*

I nearly did. So nearly.

But then Dan laid his hand on my shoulder and I choked on the words.

"Of course I'll do it," I croaked, eventually. "Sorry. I'm being stupid."

"Mark, you don't have to if you're not comfortable," Dan said softly.

"Don't be daft," I whispered, as I put my hand over his. "I've got you, bro."

And so the cameras rolled and I gave Dan and his campaign my full-throated endorsement, urging the public to cast their votes in favour of my big brother, the only candidate who would protect our beloved park and ensure Buckley & Aldersham remained a green and happy place for all to live.

I went home a few hours later feeling sick. That evening, I bought a litre of vodka from the Tesco Metro near my flat and drank till I passed out around five in the morning. When I awoke the next morning, my news feed was filled with ads of my own face, cheerfully exhorting to the world that my brother was a man to be trusted and to whom they should hand political power this Thursday. I vomited in the toilet, and went to the shop to get some beer.

I screwed up. Some say there's no shame in it, but I disagree. I am ashamed. But shame does not have to be permanent. This week has not been a good week, but today is a new day, and I will choose to make it a good one. I arrive at St Agatha's Church Hall and under the gaze of the many faces of my older brother I enter by the sign that reads POLLING STATION. Volunteers in the courtyard are handing out flyers and interviewing people; vote for Dan Fletcher, I'm told. It doesn't matter.

He'll win. He was ahead anyway, and the magazine feature and the associated social media campaign had given him the decisive lead he needed. Sunil had written excitedly to thank me for my role in the proceedings. I didn't reply.

Voters in masks are sanitising outside, going in one at a time. With a squirt of gel I cleanse my hands and as I enter the hall they cross out 'Mark Fletcher' on their list. No one asks if I'm a relative of the candidate. My face covering is stifling, and once inside the privacy of the booth, I pull down my mask and allow myself to breathe freely. My face feels reborn in its nakedness to the cool, clear air. I open up the ballot paper, and with the little pencil I place a cross beside Maggie Huttlestone's name. Pulling the mask back over my face, I drop the ballot paper in the box and leave the church. The weather is beautiful and I decide to take a nice long walk in Buckley Park, alone with my thoughts.

An Ephemeral Quality

My earliest memories are of thread.

For hours I would sit on the floor of my mother's atelier collecting the cuttings that lay discarded throughout the workshop, picking up each one and inspecting it carefully in my pudgy little fingers. Purple ones were my favourite. Whenever I found one I would put it in my pocket for safe keeping. It didn't matter that she would have given me all the purple thread I wanted, if I'd asked; it was a treasure hunt of my very own, and I collected tiny victories like pebbles on a beach.

Even then I understood that my mother's work was very special. The busiest times were near Hallowe'en, of course, and just before the Winter Solstice Parade. I watched as she transformed boring old grownups into sorcerers, mermaids, tree spirits, jungle queens. Under my mother's touch her clients grew tall and proud and wise. They *became,* until the costume wasn't a costume at all. It was them.

I remember our last day in that town, the one in the south of England where I was born. The workshop floor was covered in threads the colour of autumn leaves—vivid reds and golds and dusty browns. It was just before the Solstice Parade. The woman who stood in the center of the fitting platform was dark-skinned and gold-edged, and my mother had dressed her in the gown and matching headdress of a firebird. The headdress was made up of golden feathers and it came down over her face in swirls of red and gold leather. I could only just see her eyes. They looked like deep pools of hot chocolate. When she moved, the feathers rustled like the crackling of a campfire.

The firebird woman looked so powerful and brave that I was a little afraid of her. Not my mother, though—she wasn't afraid of anything, not even when smoke started to rise from the fabric where she touched the dress. I picked up the delicate threads from the floor, all the different reds and oranges and golds together, and then hid while my mother finished.

The costume shop was always cold because the heating was always broken, but that day it got too hot too quickly. I thought my mother started to look a little worried, but I knew that couldn't be right. She was probably just excited to go see the parade with me.

The woman handed my mother some money. Her hand left charred black streaks on the wooden door on her way out. After she was gone my mother played with the rings on her fingers and said maybe we should stay home that night.

Later there was a fire at the parade, a big one. It was in the papers the next morning; three people were killed, including a little girl only a little older than me. Mother told me we needed to pack quickly. I could still smell smoke on the air as the bus took us away.

The phone rings. I stare at it warily before taking it from its cradle on the overcrowded desk.

"Harlan Atelier," I say.

"Hello, is this Eleanor?"

"No Madam, this is—"

"I'm looking for Eleanor Harlan Atelier."

I take a breath. "This is Eleanor Harlan's Atelier, Madam, but—"

"Great. Put me on the phone with her."

My fingers tighten against the bakelite phone. "I'm afraid she's not here, Mrs..." The voice sounds vaguely familiar, but it could be any one of several malnourished Louboutin-wearing housewives.

"When do you expect her? It's very important."

There's a clock ticking on the wall. When this place was alive with movement I never noticed it, but now each passing second rings out like a gavel.

"She won't be coming back," I say. "She's dead."

The first time I said those words out loud I felt dirty inside, like

I'd made a racist comment or made fun of someone for being in a wheelchair. Now, though, I've said them so many times that they've lost all meaning. Sorry, my mum's not here. She's gone out for lunch. She's having a cigarette. She's dead.

"Oh." The phone is silent. "Who are you?"

"Ezrabet. Her daughter."

"The scrappy one?"

"There's just the one, Madam."

The woman sighs with all the restraint of a southern screen starlet. "She was letting out the waist on a dress for me. I need it by Friday."

I remember what my therapist said about controlling my anger, and I imagine a soft curtain coming down as I breathe deeply.

"Your name, please?"

"Dawn Woodruff."

I put the receiver down on the desk. My arm aches from holding it. I locate Dawn Woodruff's heinously sequinned cry for help on the rack of completed alterations.

"Your dress is ready, Madam. You can come pick it up any time this week."

After I hang up I go back to my scattered piles of forms, notes, and administrative jobs-in-progress, shoving down my annoyance and my jet lag. I'm numb and exhausted but I keep signing, printing, scanning, and tallying numbers because watching one column of figures flicker by after another is easier than what I'll have to do next: go through her things. Unpack her life.

The bell over the door jingles. I tell myself again that I'll take it down, knowing that I won't until the entire place is in boxes. I stifle a groan, nearly, and look up.

A man is standing in the doorway—my mum's age, maybe, maybe a little younger. I can't tell. He looks like one of those cliché fantasies of a sexy librarian, gold-rimmed glasses and messy mousey hair touched with grey and smelling of coffee and vanilla aftershave. I glare at him suspiciously.

"Hi. Sorry, hello. I was hoping you could help me with something."

"I'm sorry, Sir, we're not taking any new clients at the moment. In fact, we're going to be closing permanently." But he's already digging into his ridiculous leather man-purse. His glasses slip down his nose and he pushes them up with one hand.

"Yes of course, sorry, I'll only be a moment." Before I can say anything else he pulls something black and compact out of his bag. He holds it out to me.

It's not what I expected.

The fabric is so dark that at first I think it's velvet, but it turns out to be soft-brushed leather. The shape is simple, but elegant—sweeping lines around almond-shaped cutouts for the eyes, tilted up at the corners. A slight pull in the fabric at each side suggests laughter. A thick satin ribbon extends from one side of the mask.

"I have the other one," he says, as I take the mask from him. He digs around in his man-purse again and pulls out a matching satin ribbon. "It came apart a while ago. I've had it a long time though, it held up pretty well."

I hold the mask carefully and run my thumb over the soft leather. There's something startlingly intimate about the motion. The piece is well crafted, the stitching strong but unobtrusive. I turn it over in my hands and whatever Sexy Librarian is yammering about dies in my ears.

It's one of hers.

My mother's signature is in the corner along the bottom seam, glistening in silver ink. It doesn't seem like her style—unadorned, almost utilitarian—but it's the same signature as the one on the dance costume she made me when I was five. She stopped making costumes not long after that, directing her talent instead to hemming tattered Levis and graduation dresses.

"Sure. I'll fix it," I hear myself say. My voice sounds like it's coming from underwater.

"Great!" The man beams like a puppy. He looks around the workshop. "I heard about Eleanor."

The world comes back with a roar.

"There will be a funeral. I don't know when yet. There's a mailing list." I point to the clipboard hanging from a hook beside the door. Then I toss the mask onto the table. The man winces.

"Right. So can I come pick up the mask tomorrow, maybe?"

"Sure. Tomorrow's fine." My words are all hard edges and right angles. I go back to the pile of papers and scan the top one. I read it three times and still have no idea what it says.

"Thanks." He shifts awkwardly. "I guess I'll see you, Ezrabet."

He pulls open the door and disappears into the street. The bell has fallen silent by the time it occurs to me to wonder how he knew my name.

That evening I let myself into my mother's apartment, where I'm staying while in town. I try not to spend a lot of time there; it feels like one of those reconstructionist museums, or a moment frozen in time. My mum's antique sewing machine is still there, the one she learned on before buying a more efficient one for the costume shop. Its black curves and gold motifs make it look like a vintage Cadillac among tractors. The walls smell like cigarettes and there's food in the kitchen slowly sailing past its use-by date, and a strip of police tape still clinging to the door frame. I can't handle sleeping in either my mum's room or my old one, so I sleep on the sofa in the living room. It's more threadbare than I remembered. The mirror against the wall is the same though, a great gilded baroque thing that she picked up at a rubbish market when I was twelve. I remember thinking that the mirror and the sewing machine should run off together, leaving behind the rest of this trailer trash hole.

I know I should eat something but I haven't had any appetite since I arrived, so instead I make a pot of tea and empty my bag onto the kitchen counter. The black mask tumbles out of the debris. It looks even darker here in the dim lighting. I find some stray needles and thread in a kitchen drawer and begin reattaching the ribbon to the little lining strip. My mother could have done it better, but when I'm done it doesn't look too bad and holds securely. I run my finger over the silver signature. It feels like something left behind from another life—a time when she was an artist who saw so much beauty in the world, before she started drinking, before she started running from something deep inside herself. A time when we were happy.

The leather is cool against my fingers and again I'm struck by that inviting sense of intimacy, that warm seductive promise. I remember, for the first time in years, the flutter of a firebird's dress. Sooty streaks on the doorframe. The smell of ashes in the air.

I go to the mirror and hold the mask up against my face. My straw-coloured hair escapes around the edges and stubborn freckles spill across my nose. When I was young I was convinced that one day I'd grow into a great beauty like her. It never happened.

The satin ribbons are smooth and weightless. I pull them behind my head and knot them together. The mask slips a little and I tug it back so that I can see properly.

The world looks the same. In the mirror, my head tilts curiously to one side and the creases at the eyes suggest an amusing secret. My hair looks darker, somehow, and healthier, and as I step up to the mirror I realize that I can't see my freckles anymore. I lift a hand to my face and it's only when I see the slender seamstress' fingers that I realize I'm looking at my mother.

I rip off the mask. It catches on my hair, washed out and cracking at the ends, and my stupid freckles are stark against the sudden flush. Maybe I need a proper meal after all.

The mask sits in my hand—simple, unadorned leather kissed in silver ink. I glance uneasily at the mirror once more before shoving the mask back into my handbag.

Being in the workshop is easier than being in the apartment. The street outside hums reassuringly and the tension in my chest settles down patiently into the waiting room of my brain.

Dawn Woodruff picks up her dress and gets snippy when I don't fold it properly. She makes me glad I left this suffocating country behind. I long for my bright apartment in Chicago—it's an absolute matchbox with only a double hot plate to cook on, but the windows are tall and look out over Millennium Park. It made the world seem so full of possibility. Once.

The bell over the door chimes.

The man with the purse walks in, glancing around the chaotic atelier. It's taking on the feel of a gutted animal; thin white clothes racks stand empty amidst raw bare patches and the carnage of stray cuttings. He steps around a half-full cardboard box and picks his way to the desk.

"Hey Ezrabet," he says, and my eyes narrow. Yesterday I'd never seen this man before in my life.

"I didn't tell you my name," I say.

"Right." He tugs awkwardly on his bag. "Sorry, I should have... I'm Brady. I was friends with your mum."

I'm not convinced. "My mother doesn't have friends." Not for a long time. If she did she wouldn't have died alone on a bathroom floor. The thought hits me so hard that I gasp for breath. I cover it with a cough.

"It's been a while," he admits. He studies my face for a moment, and it makes me want to slap him. "Do you have the... is it ready?"

"What?"

"The mask."

It's sitting in my bag under the desk. I want to throw it at him and tell him to get out of my shop. I want to tell him that he's a liar, because if he was really my mother's friend he would have been there. I want him to leave and never come back.

But I also want to see her again.

"Not yet. Tomorrow." I wonder if he knows I'm lying. "I've been busy."

"Of course." He pushes his glasses up the bridge of his nose. "Are you busy now?"

I look at him questioningly. The truth is I'd kill to get out of this room, but I'm not going to tell him that.

"I hear the place across the street has good coffee. Do you want to go sit down for a while and talk?"

"We don't have anything to talk about." I can hear the bitterness in my voice and I hate myself for it. I wonder how long I've been like this.

He sighs. "Oh Ezrabet..."

"What do you want?" I spit the words out like chicken bones. "What are you doing here?"

"I miss her." He says it in a rush. Then he shrugs and pushes his glasses up again. "I never got to say goodbye."

This time I study his face. His temples are going grey and there are lines around his eyes, but he looks like a lost little boy. He tugs on his bag strap and begins to turn away.

I sigh long and hard and force my teeth to unclench.

"I never got to say goodbye either."

The cafe across the road is typical of the upscale trash I see all over Chicago—exposed Edison bulbs shedding watery light on empty shipping crates that probably cost a fortune on Etsy. I maneuver between university students to a table while Brady waits in line. The chairs are mismatched skeletons of wood and flannel upholstery. I settle into one and before long he returns with a black coffee for me and something with cream and sprinkles for himself.

I look at the concoction distastefully. "What in the nine hells is that?"

"It's a... caramel soy mochachino." He bites down a grin.

"That's disgusting."

"Hush and drink your tar."

I take a sip. It's hot and violently bitter. I hope he goes to the bathroom soon so I can put some sugar in it.

"So," he says. "How long are you staying?"

I shrug noncommittally and drink my tar. "Don't know. Not long. I have to get back to work."

"Oh? What are you doing?"

"I work for a dance company."

"You're dancing?" His eyes light up with excitement, and something almost like pride. I want to ask him what on earth he has to be so happy about.

"No, I'm an admin assistant."

"Oh." He looks down at his drink.

The familiar rush of shame digs into my spine. No, I didn't make it. No, I wasn't good enough. "It's fine, though. I get free tickets and stuff." I shrug again. The other shoulder this time. It's hot in here.

"Well, that's good." He sips his drink. It leaves a line of cream on his lip and he wipes it off with the back of his hand.

"Were you really friends with my mum?"

A little smile flickers across his face. "For a long time. We met when we were six and she... she... punched a bully in the face for me." He flushes and hides behind his obnoxious drink.

I take another sip of my coffee. It's horrible. "Do you need to go to the bathroom or anything?"

"Huh?"

"Never mind. So what happened?"

"We got into a fight. After the, um, the Solstice Parade." He doesn't meet my eyes. "I kept track of her over the years, made sure both of you were OK. I thought about reaching out after you went to Chicago, but it didn't seem like the right time. Then, well..." He pushes back his glasses. "I guess there's never really a right time."

"Maybe if you had she'd be alive right now." The words come out before I can stop them. His face cracks just before he turns away.

"You think I don't know that?" he says quietly.

I want to say I'm sorry. I want to say I didn't mean it, that I'm the one who should have been there. I don't say any of those things. I stand and pick up my bag, the one with the mask at the bottom.

"Thanks for the coffee," I say, and push my way through the tables, hoping that if I run fast enough I can outrun myself.

When I get back to the apartment, the cardboard boxes I ordered are leaning up against the doorframe. I haul them inside in two armfuls and set them against the wall in the living room. They stare at me accusingly.

I stall by making a cup of tea. Then I go to the hall closet, where she left some boxes of old junk, and pull them down. The closet smells like her.

There's a clunky black Polaroid camera, the kind that was big in the 80s and 90s. Some design template books, and a newspaper cutout from the town we lived in when I was a kid. I'm in it—a grainy, pudgy baby in my mother's arms. She's smiling. Her dark hair goes down past her waist.

Behind us is the shopfront of her first place, the one that sold the beautiful costumes. The article's headline is *Unlikely Artisan Finds Niche Market in Small Town.*

I set the article aside. Underneath is a tattered flyer in burgundy and gold.

UNMASKED
Samhain Night Masquerade Ball
Come as you truly are!
Sophia Loren Cultural Centre, 31st October, 1989, 7pm

Below the words is a drawing of a masquerade mask made of oak leaves. Roses heavy with thorns climb up the edges.

Come as you truly are. I wonder how many people danced in my mother's creations that night. There's a photo, too, faded and scuffed with time and neglect. My mum's in it, maybe my age, wearing a white masquerade mask. Someone's got their arm around her. I peer closer and realize that it's Brady—except this version of Brady is a stone-cold fox. His mask is black. They look happy.

I dig around in the boxes some more. There's a surprising amount of shoes, T-straps and button-up Victorian boots and Marilyn pumps. An elaborate fur coat, and guiltily I think of the harsh winters in Chicago. While rummaging around, I get stabbed by a stray sewing needle more than once. My finger leaves a smear of blood on the cardboard.

A ribbon pokes out of the chaos. It's thick satin and snowy white. I pull on it, but it's caught on something deeper in the box. I tug gently, shifting the refuse around with my other hand until it comes loose.

Dangling at the end of the ribbon is a white mask.

I stare at it for a moment, watching it spin, then carefully free the ribbon on the other side. At first glance it looks like a twin to the black, but they're not quite the same. This leather is slick, rather than the soft brushed fabric of the black one, and the corners of the eyes are smooth. Instead the leather pulls gently in between them, contrasting the amusement of the black mask with its own faint hint of tragedy. I turn it over and see the familiar signature in silver ink. For a moment I'm tempted to lift it to my face, but a sudden, inexplicable fear catches at me, like a bramble thorn. I set it aside instead.

Standing over the mess of junk, the mirror glitters from the second-hand sun off the building next door. The gold around the edges takes on a melted, ephemeral quality. I take the black mask out of my bag and another guilty flush creeps up as I remember Brady's face, the pain in his eyes. Then I step over to the mirror.

What I see is wholly uninspiring: eyes red from exhaustion, unwashed clothes that have long since lost any prestige, their labels scuffed by time and abuse. They look too big for me, like I've shrunk inside of them since arriving. The mask hums in my fingers.

I lift it to my eyes.

Seeing her isn't jarring, like I thought it might be. It's like stepping into sunlight. The mother in the mirror appraises me curiously. She looks healthier than I've seen her in a long time. I wonder what she must think of me, her arrogant wayward failure of a daughter.

"I tried," I whisper. "I tried to become someone you could be proud of." As I say it I realize that's part of the story, but not all of it. I went to Chicago because I was running away from what we'd become, from the silence that clung like something rotting and long forgotten. From looking into her eyes and never knowing how much of her was truly awake.

This version of her is different, though. She looks like the strong, confident woman from the costume shop, the one I'd watched pin scarlet feathers to a golden gown so long ago.

I reach out and meet her fingertips in the mirror—long, elegant fingers that always seemed to hold so much poetry. Only the thinnest membrane of glass lies in between.

"Why did you leave me?"

You left. For a heartstopping moment, the words seem to be coming from her. Then I realize they came from my own thoughts, the ones I try so hard to push down. *You left. You went to Chicago and left her all alone when you* knew *she was sick.*

I stare at my mother's wide eyes in the mirror. I see fear in them, and a buried memory bubbles up: making a flippant comment at nine years old; being shoved hard against a wall so fast that I didn't realize it was happening until my head smacked against the plaster. It's one of the memories I fought to keep buried, but this time I notice something different, something new—the shock in her eyes, and the fear. She was as surprised as I was. I remember, now, her releasing me quickly and running away. I remember wondering what on earth she was running from.

"You should have told me. You should have asked for help. I would have come back." But even as I say it, I wonder if it's true.

My mother says nothing.

"You pushed me away. You push everyone away." The familiar anger flares up. Its claws reach for my throat, equal parts painful and seductive. "You could have tried to get better. You could have gotten real help instead of finding it at the bottom of a bottle." The venom in my voice startles me.

Still she says nothing, just watches with that half-smile around her eyes. I step closer. Our noses are almost touching.

"You took the coward's way out."

You left. You weren't there. You abandoned her.

The anger is roaring like a hungry dragon and I try to imagine the curtain coming down, like my therapist says, but it's timid and insubstantial. The dragon waves it away like mist.

"Why don't you say something?" I ask. My mother lifts her chin proudly and defiance flickers behind the mask. "What does it matter now, anyway? You're gone and you're never coming back, you'll never have to look at the screwed up waste of space you left behind..." I am horrified to find that I'm crying. My voice breaks and the leather grows sticky against my skin.

"Say something!" I slam my hand against the glass. Her hand meets mine, like a high five. Like she thinks it's all a joke. "Tell me how much I disappointed you." I'm so angry that my vision is turning white. "Tell me that I wasn't able to save you." *You should have been there.* I'm having trouble forming words now, and I don't know whether it's from the lump in my throat or the fury or both. I can't see straight. I slam my hand against the glass again. It rattles violently.

"You left me all alone!"

Once more and, in the space between one heartbeat and another, the mirror shatters. I tear off the mask and sink to the ground, sobbing in shame and terror amidst the broken glass.

Brady and I sit in the coffee house. It was my idea, this time. He has one of those absurd candy bar drinks and I've ordered a mocha. I glare at him with steely eyes, daring him to say anything.

"Thank you for fixing this," he says, when I hand him the mask. "It's nice to... to have something of her."

"Sure," I say. The white one's in between us on the table. I'm not sure why I brought it. Because of that photo, I guess, that one of him and my mum. "The masks..." I hesitate, uncertain how to phrase my question. But he understands.

"The black one," he says, "makes others see you as you want to be seen."

I stare at him. "No it doesn't."

He shrugs wearily. "It wasn't intentional. I don't think it ever was, really. It's something that just sort of... came out of her. I was having a hard time with... I didn't have a lot of confidence back then, and she was trying to help."

"But—" I stop, fighting the truth, trying not to look at it too closely.

"Why? What did you see?"

I meet his eyes, and his expression softens. He knows. This doesn't aggravate me the way I expected it to.

"And the white?"

"The white shows you as you truly are." He smiles self-consciously. "I was never brave enough to wear it."

I sip my mocha. It's not bad. We sit in silence for a minute.

"I'm going back to Chicago at the end of the week." I don't know what that's supposed to mean to him. We just met.

After a moment he says, "OK."

"The coffee's better there."

He doesn't say anything.

"I could give you my email. If you want. I mean, if you ever need to talk or something."

He looks up and a moment of joy flashes in his eyes, like the sun peeking out from behind the clouds. He looks like the guy in the photo then, the one who was so happy just to be near her. I want to ask what happened between them but I figure maybe he'll tell me one day, in his own time.

I pick up the white mask. Once again I'm pricked by that bramble thorn of trepidation, but I shrug it off. I lift it to my face and tie the ribbons behind my head.

Brady searches my face. Looking for her, maybe. I lean forward onto my hand and tilt my chin up, voguing to hide my nerves. Putting on the mask feels like taking something off, like stripping down a layer of skin. I'm about to remove it when he nods, once, in satisfaction.

"You're stronger than her," he says. "You'll be OK."

I smile and undo the ribbon. "You too, you know." I put the mask down on the table and notice, at the join where the ribbon meets the leather, a loose white thread. It slips out from underneath a stitch, just a short stray piece. I tuck it into my pocket—a tiny victory, like a pebble on a beach.

The Domino Effect

The girl was sitting on the bare concrete floor, her back pressed hard against the wall of the underpass as though it might collapse without her support. She was in her late teens; stick thin and scruffy, though she might have been pretty with a wash and some clean clothes. A faded, pink rucksack was clutched loosely in one hand. Overhead, an old fluorescent tube in its filthy Perspex housing flickered erratically, bathing the grimy walls in a dim yellow glow.

The girl paid no attention to her surroundings but simply stared vacantly at the opposite wall with empty, unseeing eyes. The sound of footsteps echoed starkly through the empty underpass. A young man stopped in front of her. He wore blue jeans and a black fleece zipped tight to keep out the early evening chill. He was in his mid-twenties; slim and fair-haired with a pleasant open face.

"Are you OK?"

The girl said nothing, but her fingers tightened protectively around the strap of her rucksack.

"Are you OK?"

"Leave me alone."

The young man hesitated and then crouched down to face her. He frowned as he saw the livid purple bruise around her left eye.

"Listen. I know a place where you can get some hot food and a clean bed if you want. It's safe. Nobody will ask you any questions."

The girl jumped to her feet, the rucksack held defensively in front of her.

"Stay away from me," she shouted. "I'm not going anywhere with you, you perv. If you come any closer, I'll scream." Her voice was firm but the fingers holding the rucksack trembled.

"OK. OK." The young man stepped back and put up his hands. He smiled with the easy charm that comes naturally to young men blessed with good looks. "It's all right. Don't worry. Nobody's going to take you anywhere you don't want to go. I just thought you could use a friend, that's all."

"Well I don't. I'm fine as I am, so leave me alone."

The girl hugged the rucksack closer and the two young people stared at each other for a moment as if in some odd Mexican stand-off.

It was the young man who felt the need to break the silence. "How did you get the bruise?"

She shrugged. "Someone gave it to me." She offered no other explanation.

The young man hesitated for a moment then reached into his pocket and pulled out a brown leather wallet. He extracted a crisp ten pound note.

"Here. Take this."

She stared longingly at the note, but made no move to take it. She looked him up and down slowly as if seeing him for the first time.

"I don't do stuff for money."

The young man reached out his hand and his eyes held hers for a moment. "You don't have to do anything. It's a gift. Just promise me you'll spend it on something to eat and not drugs."

The girl reached out cautiously and took the note.

"I don't do drugs." There was a defiant tone to her voice.

"Good." He put the wallet away. "What's your name?"

She looked at him again as if deciding whether to answer. "Domino," she said at length.

"Wow! Great name. Well listen, Domino. Try O'Neills, the chip shop on Westgate. They'll still be open and they do good portions."

He looked briefly along the gloomy underpass. "And don't stay here. It's not the best place to be at night. Try the bus station. It's got a coffee stall and it's well lit. If you sit on one of the benches like you're waiting for the night bus, nobody's going to bother you."

He hesitated, and for a moment she thought he was going to say something else, but he just smiled.

"Look after yourself, Domino." He turned and continued down the dimly lit passage. The girl's eyes stayed on him as he walked away. He had reached the end of the underpass when she called out.

"Why are you helping me?"

He turned and smiled again, the easy charm back on his face.

"Everybody needs a friend now and then."

"So why should I trust you?"

He hesitated and then shrugged. "Just ask people about Jimmy Blue." And then he was gone.

He was right about O'Neills. The portions were cheap and filling. The girl finished her chips and dropped the tray in a waste bin. Not many people bothered to use it; the floor was littered with cigarette butts, drinks cans and sweet wrappers. A sudden gust of wind disturbed the litter and she hunched tightly in her thin cotton jacket. She turned and headed to the bus station. It was as he had described it; a bit shabby maybe, but large and well lit with just enough activity to make her feel safe. She was thirsty after her supper so she headed to the small coffee bar which provided the caffeine to keep the night bus drivers awake. She ordered a hot chocolate and then waited as the tired looking woman behind the counter bustled away to make it.

"Has Jimmy Blue been in?"

The woman, as small and skinny as the girl herself, looked up from the drinks machine.

"You've just missed him, love. He's taken a couple of guys to the shelter."

"The shelter?"

"Yes. The homeless shelter on Southway. Jimmy set it up. He spends most of his spare time there trying to help people from the streets."

She brought the chocolate across and settled herself against the counter, glad of a chance to chat.

"Jimmy found an abandoned church hall a couple of years ago

and set up a kitchen and a few beds. He begs out-of-date food from the supermarkets and gets donations from anywhere he can. The shelter's not official; more like a squat kind of thing. The council turn a blind eye because they don't have the resources to do the job themselves."

She leaned across conspiratorially.

"Word is that Jimmy was on the streets himself a few years back before a friend helped him out. Now he says he has to pay back that friendship. Oh, he's a saint, he is."

She prepared herself for a full description of Jimmy's saintly characteristics and looked a little disappointed when the girl paid for her drink and headed to a nearby bench. She sipped her chocolate slowly and looked thoughtful, as if she was coming to some sort of decision.

It was eight o'clock the following evening and the girl was just beginning to think she'd got it wrong when she heard footsteps echoing down the underpass and she saw the young man.

"Hello, Domino. How are things?"

She smiled. "Better, thanks."

He looked enquiringly at her. "The offer's still open. A bed and a hot meal?"

She looked up. "Thanks. I'd like that."

He broke into a broad grin. It made him look even younger.

"Good. Come with me."

He led her to a small car. She recognised it as a Mini Cooper S; the sporty version. It was worth a few bob. Her ex-boyfriend was a mechanic in a very dodgy garage, and cars had been the one subject he was happy to talk about. The Mini was covered in mud. Even the number plates were completely obscured. The young man shrugged apologetically.

"I keep meaning to take it to the car wash, but I always seem to find something else more important to spend my money on."

He pulled out his keys and then paused.

"I looked up your name, you know. It's really interesting. Did you know *Domino* used to refer to a disguise that people wore at old masquerades? How cool is that?"

He turned to look at her with an open and disarming smile. She returned his gaze with a cool, appraising look of her own. Then he opened the door and she slid in beside him. The inside was clean and tidy. He put the heating on and the girl settled back in the warm seat listing to the hum of the fan. Next to her, the pleasant young man put the car into gear and pulled smoothly away.

Well, that went well, he thought to himself. He was sure that nobody had seen them, and with the number plates obscured, nobody could identify the car. Funny her being called Domino when he was the one masquerading. He stopped at the lights and smiled to himself as he saw a tall middle-aged man talking earnestly to a woman on a park bench. He was there every night; good old Jimmy Blue. Still doing his best to help every pathetic down-and-out he met. The young man really didn't know why he bothered. They were all scum. Useless rejects that deserved everything they got. Like the girl next to him. They contributed nothing and they wouldn't be missed. A thought occurred to him that almost made him laugh out loud. He hadn't even had to lie about his name. He'd never actually claimed to be Jimmy Blue; the stupid tart had just assumed it. He felt the weight of the knife in his jacket pocket and glanced briefly at the girl next to him, his mind already focused on the exhilarating pleasure the next few hours would bring.

Alongside him, the girl suppressed a smile. So *Domino* meant mask, eh? How appropriate. She'd never even thought about the stupid name before she made it up. It was just the first thing that popped into her head when he asked her. She stared out of the passenger window. The make-up around her eye was beginning to fade and she didn't want the young man to see that the bruise was fake. She'd been surprised when she saw him. From what she'd heard, she'd thought this Jimmy Blue character would be older. No matter; the soft do-gooder deserved everything he got. She reckoned he had about a hundred pounds in his wallet. Once she got the cash card and the PIN number, she'd have easy access to more. The car was worth about fifteen thousand. She'd only get a fraction of that selling it to her ex of course, but even so it would be worth a couple of grand. She had to stifle a grin as a thought occurred to her. She hadn't even had to lie about being homeless; the soft chump had just assumed it. She felt for the Taser in her rucksack and began to plan out her next steps.

SIMHA HADDAD

Fun and Games

We are pretty, aren't we? Beautiful, in fact. Stunning, ethereal swans. We are real life, no-filter-needed masterpieces like in the painting that hangs over James' foyer where the swans gaze at themselves in the lake where their upside down reflections look like elephants. Dali daydreams on Louboutin stilts.

The snaking line of waiting diners, chic in their expensively effortless Los Angeleno finest does not protest when we are ushered in before them. There is a hierarchy of these things here. Like in heaven. Like in hell. First are gods then come angels then righteous mortals and then mortal sinners. In LA, our status falls somewhere in the angel category, and the others in the line, well, we try not to think about them.

Our status is evident even through our face masks, which are made of sparkly sheer mesh so that you can still see our mouths. That's why the seating host tells the busboys to set up a brand new table for us 'right away' in the middle of the packed rooftop restaurant when we realize I accidentally made our reservation for three days from now instead of for today like I was supposed to do. Yet another inconvenience of the pandemic besides the face masks is that businesses never seem to answer the phone anymore, so I had to make the reservations online. I was a little drunk when I did it, and Fleur and I were dancing by the pool, so I wasn't really paying attention to the date on my phone screen. It doesn't matter, though. It's actually funny.

We are seated and we strip off our sheer masks to reapply lipstick and take our selfies before we look at the menus. Soft natural light is the best lighting for photos, even better than ring lights. We are moments away from sunset, a time that photographers call the golden hour. A photo taken during the golden hour will yield an image of us with flawless skin, romantic color tones, and, if taken at just the right angle, an eye twinkle that creates the illusion that our skulls are filled with diamonds. The sunlight photo light drenches the rooftop patio, and we know we have to act fast before it ends in a few minutes.

The restaurant manager offers to take a group shot of the five of us, only it is more like a plea than an offer. We accept, of course. We never refuse content for our channels and pages. This is the other reason the host did not care whether we had a reservation or not. It pays to be famous. Not very famous. Not God famous. Not Marilyn Monroe can't step out of the house without being attacked by a mob of fans famous. But a little famous. Famous enough for hundreds of thousands of people to watch our channels to see how we did our makeup tonight. Famous enough to make sundrenched tables appear out of thin air. Famous enough to always be surrounded by a room full of whispers. Famous enough to matter.

Diners secretly take photos of us from behind their menus. We flash smiles at each other for their benefit. Lovely fifty-thousand-dollar white veneered smiles that glisten under the last dregs of golden hour sunlight. As we smile and laugh and joke and perform we can see ourselves through the phone lenses of these strangers because we have seen ourselves from every angle thousands of times and so we are always aware of ourselves as if we are watching us with prism eyes, our millions of rainbow refractions forever dancing before us wherever we go, so we know that the secret photos they take of us will come out great.

To everyone in the restaurant, it looks like we are having fun, but right now the fun is still work. Our work is make-believe. To make them believe. We are acting for them, and a little for us too. For them, this moment as we glisten under the fading sun is a small taste of what our real playtime looks like. It is a polished imitation for their benefit of the life they wish they had so that for a small moment they can feel that they too are living it, this life of forever-playtime. It is our job to show them a truth that is only a half-truth, to keep up the facade of a lifetime of fun and games when really the real fun and games happen when no one else is looking. The pretend play is work, and we work hard. Very hard. Soon we will play for real, and the real playtime will be for us, not for them.

James runs his hand through his long pink-blonde wig and his wrist begins to twitch. Leanna keeps her hands in her lap, and I know they are shaking too. As are Fleur's. As are Harriet's. As are mine. Golden hour is waning.

This is good because shielded by the night-time darkness we will be able to let loose. To reveal ourselves to ourselves. To play. In the dark, our other masks will come off and we will be able to sink our fangs into the flesh of the real playtime we have lusted after all day long. Our bodies vibrate in the anticipation of our evening, but also with an undercurrent of fear because soon the strangers will ask if they can have photos with us. They won't be able to sneak them anymore. Without the sun, they will need to use flash.

Flash is harsher than sunlight. Much harsher. Flash turns our colored contact lenses into devil-red embers in our eye sockets. Flash produces photos with white-hot flares on our faces. Flash accentuates the bumpy blemishes and reveals the rough skin under our generously applied layers of foundation. We hate these photos. They intrude on our fun, exposing us from under the security of our night blanket turning us from swans to elephants in the time it takes to say, 'I'm a big fan'. We hate these photos, but we will always say yes to taking them because we are not famous enough to say no to more content because all content, even bad content, is what keeps us relevant.

We take fifteen-second videos of the pink sunset for our Instagram stories as the dangerous, sexy whisper of darkness caresses the makeup on our cheeks, the glitter on our bare shoulders, the skin on our thighs. Night is here.

Are you ready to order?

Drinks. We need drinks first. Bubbles. Bottles and bottles of pink bubbles. Bubbles to give us night vision. Bubbles to tickle our brains.

Bubbles to stop the shakes.

"Is this a special occasion?"

Fleur shrugs. "Tuesday."

We all laugh.

Bubbles are the elixir, the magic, the cure. We sip and sip and sip and finally, our hands have steadied and the flash photos that momentarily blind us are fun to take and the darkness that embraces us now is an old friend and we are happy, so happy as the jokes come faster and the laughter gets louder and the food towers in front of us look great in the photos, and it is as if we have soaked up the sun from golden hour like solar-powered lights that are now activated in the darkness to shine our very own spotlight on us, only us, and we are illuminated again in a flattering way and the rest of the restaurant is just a room of moths fluttering around us, and we can let loose because we don't care about the opinions of moths, all thanks to the champagne.

We make potions adding shots of tequila and little pink pills into our bubbling glasses, and the restaurant glows brighter and words get said but no one hears them, really, and it is funny, all so funny, so incredibly hilarious and wonderful and it is such a relief to be able to see in the dark and for everything not to matter.

I am so relieved that I am almost crying with laughter while reaching for a shrimp from one of the food towers in the middle of the table, so I barely notice a chair being pulled up in the space between my chair and Leanna's, but when I turn to my left he is there, a stranger who is not strange to us because we have seen him many times on TV so we know it is OK. He belongs. He orders more potion, and we sip more together, and he fits so perfectly that introductions are not needed. They never are. No one ever introduces themselves in the middle of a game. It would ruin the flow.

When the bill comes, we are floating high so I barely notice it, just like I had barely noticed the Unstrange Stranger joining us unannounced. Just like I barely notice Leanna's face when she sees the total on the bill and asks if she can Venmo me for the rest later because she did not bring enough cash and her credit cards are maxed out. Just like I barely notice the relief in her body when the Unstrange Stranger hands the waiter his credit card and says, 'it's on me', or that he pulls my chair out for me and no one else, or that he walks close enough for his shirtsleeve to always be grazing my bare arm, or that he stands with his electric-hot hand on the small of my back when the seating host takes one last flash photo of all of us as a group outside the restaurant that we will have to edit later but will definitely post because our new friend is more famous than us and it will look amazing.

None of us bothers with our masks now and no one told us to put them back on and even if they had, we wouldn't have heard them and it doesn't matter because what good is a mesh mask, really?

Someone ordered an SUV and it is waiting across the street. We call the driver to tell him to turn around and meet us in front of the restaurant but he does not answer, so I jump into the street to call out to him and wave him over so that he will see us, but really it is because Fleur is filming a story for her Instagram and I want my ass to be in it in because it looks great in this dress. Someone gasps and a car honks and five hot fingers wrap themselves around my wrist and the Unstrange Stranger pulls me back just in time for the black Mercedes racing towards me to just miss me.

Careful. His voice is smooth with a bite like chili chocolate. A man handling a foolish woman. We both laugh. He holds me facing him with his arms unyielding around my waist. He looks almost as good as he does on TV. I ignore the painful prickle in my nose from his acid sweat and focus instead on the layer of his sweet cologne and let that work its way to a shiver in between my legs.

Fleur gets a photo of us like this, holding each other like true lovers in the middle of the road with blurry car lights all around us. We all take turns looking at it and applauding and cheering because it is perfect, and I can't wait to post it later. He lets me go but keeps hold of my wrist.

The SUV pulls around to us and the Unstrange Stranger and I sit in the back, back row while everyone files in, and then we are all dancing and maybe something goes up my nose, but I don't really know, and Fleur and Harriet kiss, and then we are at the house high up in the hills and the restaurant we just came from is a little twinkling star-diamond way down there at the bottom of the hill amidst all the other twinkling star-diamond buildings. It feels so good to be home and to kick off my heels by the marble double staircase under the expensive copy of Dali's *Swans Reflecting Elephants*.

The house is technically James' but we all kind of live here because we never really leave and when we do it is almost always together. It is so natural for us to be here that no one asked where we were going next after dinner. The clubs are closed because of the virus, so this is the only place we would naturally go.

Music comes on through the Bluetooth by the limestone fireplace outside by the pool, so we make sloppy drinks in the kitchen that someone else will clean up tomorrow and dance our way through the house to the music in the garden like children following the Pied Piper's song, only in our case the Pied Piper is Lady Gaga. We dance, and sing along, and undress in unison, and when we jump naked into the pool that has scum on the top because no one remembered to hire a new pool cleaner after Harriet fired the last one over something to do with olives, no one really remembers but she is James' sister so she can fire whomever she pleases. It is the hundredth time we have done this so that no one is actually interested in anyone's nudity but rather focused on their own, sucking in stomachs to impress our new guest who is not really new because he is the hundredth guest just like him who has come to this house and jumped naked into the scum-lined pool with us.

I touch the pool's black bottom with the ball of my foot and linger there for a moment in the quiet water that is probably cold but I am too drunk to feel, letting puffs of air escape my mouth in globes that travel up through the pool's blackness to the surface of the water where it is too dark for us to see the scum rim properly. I wonder whether these air globes will pop right away when they get to the top, or if they will stay there for a while, trapped under the scum, waiting to die.

I push off with my foot and come up for air when Fleur pushes my head under again. She is freakishly strong. She lets go and I bob for a moment, just for show, and then come up again, laughing with everyone. While I'm still laughing, she pushes me down again and everyone's laughter is muffled with my ears underwater.

She holds me for a long time and my lungs start to burn white-hot like the flares on our faces from the flash photos the fans take of us and I think how cooling the water would feel if I breathed it in deep into my hot lungs and I am going dizzy and I am about to open my mouth to let in the cold water to put out the fire in my lungs when Fleur wraps her fingers around my hair and pulls me up out of the water gasping. Everyone is laughing and applauding and when I stop coughing my heart is racing and I am laughing too and taking another long sip of my drink from the side of the pool.

Time skips now between point A and point B, the tape of film that is my memory snipped in random places by the substance in my blood so that I go from naked in the pool to naked in Leanna's bedroom with the Unstrange Stranger, wet and dripping on the two-inch carpet floor and on each other as we push and pull and tease and laugh and kiss. He throws me on the bed, and I kick him off of me. I jump on his back and he smashes me against the wall. A framed photo falls and breaks and we laugh hysterically. Nothing hurts, thanks to the potions.

In a moment of brute tenderness, he comes up behind me and runs his hands over my breasts and I suddenly am desperate for a glass of water.

I go towards the door, still laughing uncontrollably so that I can't even speak, and he grabs me from behind again, but this time he wraps his big arm around my throat. He asks me where I'm going and I can't answer because he is choking me and I try to move but he calls me feisty and thinks it's fun and he doesn't know, I think he doesn't know, that he is killing me. For no reason at all, I zero in on the shit stain on the tufted headboard from when one of us had anal and wiped it there but then never cleaned it even though Leanna sleeps there every night.

Images take over my mind's eye without my consent, flashing clips of moments not forgotten but long pushed down, way down, to where the bubbles cannot reach. I am thinking of people I have not spoken to in years. My family. My mother warning my sister and me not to play too roughly. "It's all fun and games until someone loses an eye," she would say. Ridiculous, I would think. How could a plastic fairy wand accidentally take out an eye? So, I carried on playing even harder than before our mother's warning, and I never lost an eye and my sister never lost an eye but maybe, I think, maybe

I lost the ability to see. To see the shit stain on the tufted headboard, to see the scum on the surface of the pool, to see the look on Leanna's face when the bill approaches the table. Or maybe I saw it all along and chose not to see, which is its own kind of blindness.

I try to gasp for air, but I can't and I can see what it will be like tomorrow after I am dead. I can see it crystal clear like the blue California sky over the sparkling sea tomorrow when they dump my body somewhere off the side of someone's yacht, maybe James' or Harriet's. I can see Fleur with one hand on her champagne glass and one on my body that will be zipped up tight in a Balenciaga gown bag. She will need help pushing me over the edge so they will all help her and I know they won't really notice what they are doing because the potions will have kicked in and there will be the splash of my body hitting the choppy ocean surface, but they won't hear the splash over the yacht's motor and then they will all start laughing at the unheard jokes and I know their asses will look so good in the photos that they will take as their bubbly, manic laughter rises higher and higher into the setting sun.

KATHERINE HAYNES

Dreams of Impossible Cowslips

"So," said Marcus Summervale, "what do you think?"

Ivy Donovan was about to open her mouth and tell him that she found the title of the book he was working on 'pretentious', but then thought better of it and said, "It's interesting. Grabs the attention."

"Yes, that's what I was going for. Something like *Snow Falling on Cedars* or *The Unbearable Lightness of Being*. A title which makes you *think*; a Booker title."

"How far have you got?" asked Ivy.

"I've sketched out the first five chapters and written the first two. I'll read them to you, if you like."

"Of course," murmured Ivy. "I'd love to hear them."

She and Marcus had been dating for four months and she was still a little in awe of him; a man who was a writer. Before they had started going out she hadn't read any of his books. Having been presented with a signed copy of his short stories on their second date, however, she had felt herself drawn into his imaginary world. Alas, it wasn't a world she could always make sense of. She appreciated that he must be very clever, but struggled to make sense of his longer sentences, stopping every once in a while to look up a word she wasn't familiar with.

Marcus wasn't at all her kind of writer. Ivy described his work as 'cerebral' because she didn't understand it. If he asked her what she thought, she would praise the dreamlike quality of his prose.

She had come to realise that she found his work incomprehensible.

Still in love with him, however, she wouldn't have hurt his feelings for the world by telling him so. She was beginning to feel afraid that if he found out, discovered she was a fraud, he would admire her less, and felt the time was not long off before he would declare her boring. It would be awful if he came to resent their relationship, if he thought her stupid.

"I've been working with a mask," he told her, having come to the end of his reading.

"Working with what?" she said, thinking she might have misheard him.

"A mask," said Marcus. "When I put it on, it makes me feel different; free. It gives me the liberty to write what I want, not to edit myself, to rein myself in. With my other books, I've had a kind of censor in my head, telling me not to use an offensive word, or an incident which might upset a friend if they recognised themselves in one of my characters. Now I don't have to worry about all that. It's like having thrown open the door of a prison."

Ivy hid a smile at his exaggerated language. She couldn't tell the difference between his 'new' writing and his 'old'. On the title page of his manuscript, he had crossed out his name and written Maskus instead.

Away from his study, Marcus was attentive and thoughtful. He made a fuss of Ivy, gave her little presents, made her laugh. She had no complaints about his performance in the bedroom; it was just when he became a 'writer' that she felt a gulf opening between them.

Marcus sent his early chapters to his agent and life suddenly became very busy. While Marcus was writing, Ivy answered the phone, replied to email, sent texts. She all but became his secretary.

There was a lunch at which she finally met his agent, Felicity Hubbard. While Marcus was at the bar getting in a round of drinks, Felicity, who was a dark-haired woman in her forties—large-framed glasses perched on her rather long nose—leant forward and said, "You must look after him."

"I beg your pardon?"

"You must nurse Marcus through this. Don't let him be worried about anything, bothered by bills, shopping, that sort of thing. This book is going to be a work of genius and he must be allowed to write it. Nothing must upset or distract him."

If she had ever been going to confess that she didn't understand Marcus, that it might be best if they broke up and he found himself a new love, now would have been the moment. Ivy could see herself disappearing. Nobody would be interested in her for herself. She would always be Marcus's girlfriend or fiancée or wife. Well, she could live with that, couldn't she? It wouldn't be so bad to bathe in his reflected glory; be the moon to his sun.

Although well aware that she wasn't right for him, that the two of them weren't well suited, she decided to go along with Felicity's plans. Perhaps she and Marcus would get married once the book was published. After that would come children and she would be involved with them and have less to do with her husband's work. He would be able to afford to employ a proper secretary then.

At night, though, she lay awake after Marcus was asleep and worried about what the future might bring. Was it something lacking in herself which made her incapable of appreciating his work? Sensing that he was on the verge of becoming rich and famous, Ivy determined not to mention her doubts and allowed herself to be swept along in his wake.

Once or twice, she had crept to the door of his study and opened it a little way to watch him at work. The room was an attractive one, with French windows opening onto the garden and Ivy wished she could have made it into a kind of drawing room or sitting room for herself. She could imagine having friends in here for coffee in the morning or tea in the afternoon. She would serve dainty cakes from bone china, gilt-edged plates. On dark, dull afternoons this would be the ideal spot to curl up with a book. Not one of those written by Marcus, she hastily reminded herself.

Marcus sat at a small table placed against the wall. The table had spindly legs and was only large enough to hold his laptop. The mask he wore was made of shiny, golden plastic and covered the upper part of his face. It was shaped like half a sun with rays emerging from its semicircle. "Is it the sun setting or the sun rising, do you think?" he had asked Ivy, his tone light and mocking. "It's the sun rising, of course," she had said, knowing that this was what he wanted to hear; that his star was in the ascendant. A black and white photograph of 'Maskus' in his study taken by one of the Sunday newspapers made the mask look as if it were made of metal; bronze, ancient, something far more worthy of a serious writer.

She was in the background, of course, when the magazines sent people to conduct interviews. One very young, haughty girl treated her like a servant, as if she were there just to make the tea and hand round the biscuits. Ivy felt a small surge of joy when Marcus slipped his arm about her and said, "Ivy is my muse. I couldn't have done this without her." The girl, who had been hanging on his every word until this moment—eager and excited—scowled, clearly jealous.

"He's mine," thought Ivy. "I'm lucky to have him, to be with him."

She began to dream of a time in which they became a golden couple; he the esteemed and celebrated novelist; she the quiet, beautiful, slightly mysterious wife, who was his inspiration.

Wife. Marcus hadn't yet asked her to marry him, but she was sure he would. Once the book had burst upon the world to win every literary prize, Marcus would take her out to a secluded little dinner—just the two of them—and she would leave the restaurant with an engagement ring on her finger. In her mind's eye she saw a golden gem; a tiger's-eye, perhaps, or a yellow topaz.

Ivy began to feel a little superior to her friends and neighbours, even to members of her family. At work, she began to feel distant from her colleagues. This was her old life, which was soon to be over. The large department store in which she stood behind a counter three days a week and smiled, was polite to people she had never met before and would never see again, where she took money, processed card payments and wrapped exquisite little gifts in boxes tied with cream-coloured ribbon would know her no more. Her future lay in other shops, where the books of Marcus Summervale would line the shelves, be piled upon tables and displayed in windows. She saw a future in which she would accompany him to libraries and schools where he would read his work to a rapt audience.

Again she wondered if they would have children of their own. Brilliant offspring to follow in their father's footsteps. Ivy made more of an effort to be attractive to Marcus. She had her hair cut in a flattering style, paid attention to her nails and make-up, tried to eat well, to exercise and to update her wardrobe.

At last, the book was done. *Dreams of Impossible Cowslips* was published. Marcus appeared on television, looking nervous and boyish. Ivy sat on the edge of the sofa, eyes glued to the screen as he was being interviewed, going through an agony of shyness on his behalf. Unconsciously, she twisted the material of her skirt between her hands and bit her lip. She was glad when the segment of the programme featuring Marcus finished. Radio interviews were less stressful.

"Isn't it beautiful?" Marcus had said, handing her a copy of the book. Indeed, it was handsomely produced, with an embossed cover, shining with gold-edged cowslips.

"Oh, Marcus, you must be so proud!"

Now would come the dreaded time when she would actually have to read the book, try to make sense of it, tell Marcus what she thought of it.

"Look!" he said, turning the leaves. Ivy saw her name on a page. He had dedicated the book to her.

"Darling," she said, "darling."

Overwhelmed, she kissed him. It was easier than putting her feelings into words.

The book was not a success. Despite all the hype and the promising reviews *Dreams of Impossible Cowslips* didn't sell. Ivy was dismayed that its publication seemed to have made people realise there were earlier books by Marcus Summervale. She saw volumes of his work in nearly every charity shop. *Dreams of Impossible Cowslips* was remaindered. Stacks of copies gathered dust in the discount shops. No one Ivy knew said they had read it.

She herself had struggled through long, meandering paragraphs, baffled by why the heroine loved the hero, puzzled as to why the field they met in never seemed to change. Was it a ghost? Were they ghosts? Was the whole thing some dream of one of the characters?

Ivy learned the odd little phrase here and there, so she could quote Marcus's own words to him, but the book's poor reception caused him to take both her hands in his and say, "Please, darling, don't."

All the hopes and plans Ivy had harboured came to nothing. She continued to smile brightly at customers, to eat lunch in the staff canteen, to catch the train home. Days when she wasn't working and weekends were spent at the house Marcus had been left by his late father.

"It's disappointing, I know, but people will come round in time. They'll realise it's good—"

"Good! I wanted it to be more than good. I wanted it to be... immortal."

It was inevitable that Marcus should feel low following the reaction to what he had hoped would prove to be his masterpiece, but Ivy was determined to try and cheer him up, to get him writing again.

"What are you going to do next?" she asked.

"Nothing. I'll never write another word."

"Marcus, don't be silly. You're a writer. It doesn't matter about publishers and reviewers and all that. It's the writing itself that matters. That's what you've always told me. *Dreams of Impossible Cowslips* may be unappreciated, but it'll become a classic, you'll be famous—"

"I want to be famous now!"

There. He had said it. For all his fine words about the writing's being the only thing that mattered, for all his posing and posturing, wearing the mask, what it really boiled down to was that he wanted celebrity.

"Did you hope to be rich, too?" said Ivy coldly.

Marcus laughed, somewhat bitterly.

"Well, it would have been nice to move away from this dump!"

His beautiful house! Was that how he really thought of it? Ivy had come to love this place. How little they understood one another, after all.

"Don't be sad, darling. Begin another book. Start it tomorrow morning."

"I can't!"

"Of course you can. I have faith in you."

Marcus looked at her with a strange expression on his face and Ivy seemed to shrivel up inside, as if he had seen through her lie. After all, she couldn't even begin to comprehend what his work was about. She had just been along for the ride, using him as her meal ticket.

"Perhaps you're right," he said, "after all, I've nobody to disturb me. No visitors, no phone calls. It's all gone very quiet lately, hasn't it?"

Ivy licked her lips.

"Yes, just for the moment. Your next book will do well. I know it will. All the interviews will start again. It'll all come back. Just you wait and see."

"Perhaps you're right," said Marcus again.

He held her gently, kissed her. Kissed her on the mouth and on the hair.

That had been on a Saturday night. Ivy had climbed into bed with him, clung to him like her namesake, then, drowsy after wine and lovemaking, she had fallen asleep.

Ivy woke to find herself alone. The room was bright and she realised it must be well into the morning.

"Marcus?"

Ivy got up, used the bathroom, padded downstairs in her bare feet. Marcus wasn't in the kitchen and there was no smell of coffee brewing. Yawning, she went from room to room. The door of the study was open and papers moved in a draught from the French windows, which stood open to the garden. Ivy walked out over steps and flagstones and dew-spangled grass to find Marcus.

The sun-shaped mask lay discarded on the path. Marcus had hanged himself from a tree.

Although he hadn't asked her to marry him and she hadn't been his wife, Marcus left everything to Ivy and everybody treated her as his widow.

On the day of the funeral, she winced when someone told her how well she looked in black. She was aware of getting out of the car, of having someone steer her gently by the elbow as she made her way through the churchyard.

It was a horrible place. The churchyard seemed to stretch for miles. It was square and flat, with no levels and very few big, elaborate tombs. Gravestones stood in row upon row in the bleak landscape, grey beneath grey sky. The only flowers were the ones standing in vases or urns; the only trees were sparse and distant. Ivy would have hated to be buried here.

The church was cold and Ivy shivered in her good coat. She knelt and stood and sat as she was directed to, sang the hymns. Had Marcus been religious? She had no faith herself and they had never spoken about God or what they believed in. "His sun has set, anyway," Ivy thought to herself, wondering what had become of the mask. Maskus. Mask us. Didn't we *all* wear masks? Hadn't she been playing at being the writer's muse? She wondered idly how much money Marcus had left her. Would she be able to give up her part-time job? At least she could leave the flat she rented and move into his house. Some good had come of his death, after all. She was still young; other lovers might come into her life.

She felt nothing as Marcus's coffin glided away and a red curtain slid across, signifying that it was gone. Where would he have wanted his ashes to be scattered? Again, it was something they had never discussed.

It was almost a relief when the service was over. Ivy felt a little lighter as she stood, could scarcely understand why some of the congregation were crying softly.

Felicity approached her and said in a stage whisper, "You will be his literary executor. We must see if there are any stories or other manuscripts which haven't been published. You'll need to collect his letters, or diaries he may have kept."

"Why?" said Ivy. "What's the point?"

"It sounds harsh, heartless, but there's nothing like death—suicide in particular—to boost an artist's sales. Take it from me, there will be tremendous interest in Marcus. He'll be famous. You'll make a lot of money."

Ivy backed away from her.

"Oh," said Felicity, "I know you don't want to hear this now, but once you've stopped grieving you'll see that this is good business sense. Marcus wanted fame, didn't he? You can do that for him, keep his name alive, keep his memory green, further his career, albeit posthumously."

"Shut up!" hissed Ivy. "Just shut up!"

She turned away from the other woman, shocked to realise that Felicity was right and that she, Ivy, would do all she could to secure her future. She would make as much money out of Marcus as possible. She was excited at the idea and appalled to find herself so materialistic, so very, very wicked.

They emerged from the church, blinking as they left the porch. Ivy couldn't understand why there was a little clutch of people blocking her path, pointing and exclaiming.

"Excuse me," she said and they parted to make way for her.

The grass which had been growing scantily around the gravestones, and in which not so much as a daisy had been visible, was now studded and smothered with cowslips.

"It's impossible," gasped Ivy, "impossible!"

She and the others looked at one another in wonder. At some future date, they would come up with a logical explanation for this 'freak of nature' but just at that moment they felt the touch of the uncanny.

As she walked back to the waiting limousine, Ivy could see yellow flowers to the left and the right of her, crowding along the borders of the pathway, packed tightly around the memorials to the dead, and she felt she was destined to see them in her mind's eye for the rest of her life, that her dreams would be haunted always by visions of impossible cowslips.

We, the Dead

Don't overthink it.

That is the first and only rule. Let your arms go limp, drop your head, and stumble forward absentmindedly. Moaning helps. Be aimless but vicious. Remember that once you smell the scent of human brains, there can be no turning back. There can be no rest until that brain is in your mouth.

I, personally, have not eaten human brains. My wife did. She never told me how they tasted. Maybe I don't want to know. I want to be clear, we're not zombies. We just pretend to be. Anyway, this all began about a year ago.

Back then we lived on the fifth floor overlooking Division Street. When we listed our place on airbnb that one time, we were quick to point out its proximity to the Red Line, the Jewel grocery store, the lake, and less quick to point out our very loud Swedish neighbors (since killed off (RIP)).

I was a graphic designer for General Mills. Mostly my work focused on puzzles and mazes for the backs of cereal boxes like Cocoa Puffs and Cinnamon Toast Crunch. The trick was to make the mazes fun but not too complicated. A kid should start the day with a sense of accomplishment, I felt. Anyway, I lost that job when kids started being eaten. No kids equals no cereal and no cereal equals no demand for cereal puzzles.

My wife Kacie was working as a Meeting Planner for the American Dental Association. It paid fairly well and she seemed to like some of the people she worked with, but it wasn't her dream job. Every third day, the door would close with a slam followed by a, "That's it. That. Is. It."

Then the keys would rattle across the counter and a diatribe about work would commence. "Are you listening to me?" she would ask so loud I could hear her through my noise-cancelling headphones.

But the keys and Kacie would always be gone the next morning. Anyway, *the outbreak.*

Theories differ on how it started. Some people say it started with contaminated water. Some say it was a mass terrorist attack gone-awry (or gone exactly according to plan). I should have followed the news more closely. Conflicting reports gave me a headache.

If there were to be zombies, I thought they would come all at once and probably at night, which would have been more dramatic I suppose. Don't get me wrong, there's been definite drama. Everyone that I know, even the most bleeding-heart pacifists, bought at least one gun, some even managed to get a hold of flamethrowers. But as the living population plummeted and every day echoed cries of, "OK, this is not normal," it became normal. You just learned to live with the fact that we were in the zombie apocalypse wasteland we used to joke and make movies about.

When everything started really going down the tubes, most of the city fled to the country, out to where there were more chainsaws per capita. I don't blame them. The country was the quickest to fortify and eventually it was hard to make it out there without the country firing back at you.

After the city emptied, Kacie and I really started to feel isolated.

Kacie's parents lived near Rockville, not too far away, but Kacie wasn't exactly on speaking terms with her mom after some pretty uncool political comments and, apparently, the zombie apocalypse wasn't going to change that. Meanwhile my entire family were early goners. I'm sure they made it quick and polite. Somewhere out there was my undead Dad, still in his socks and crocs. I tried not to imagine it.

Long story short, we were holed up in our apartment, biding time, looting the local Jewel, flicking through old Instagram photos and pretending they were new, and just trying to live our lives.

On the day they came for us, I heard a scream from the street below. Outside, a woman was trying to beat back a zombie with her free hand while digging into her purse with the other. From the purse she managed to pull a small handgun and shoot the zombie in the face. She missed every subsequent shot until her ammo was spent. I couldn't bear to watch the rest. The flimsy venetian blinds creaked as I twisted them closed.

After about a minute, despite myself, I peeked through the plastic.

As one might expect, the woman was being devoured. I sighed, not wanting to look anymore.

But there was another problem.

Rarely, if ever, was a zombie alone. Sometimes zombies came in small groups that Kacie jokingly referred to as 'book clubs'. Book clubs were lethal, but a manageable kind of lethal. I had seen a few book clubs on looting runs and evaded them with only a few nightmares and mild recurring panic attacks. But what I had never seen before was what Kacie called 'sororities'. Sororities, which could number thirty zombies or more, meant certain death/undeath.

Below, stumbling around the corner from Wells and onto Division, was a sorority.

My wife was in the shower singing 'Spice Up Your Life'.

"Kacie!"

"Uh-uh?"

I banged on the door.

"Kacie!"

"I just got in here!"

The door was unlocked and I walked in. I saw my wife's silhouette through the opaque shower curtain, steam pluming above like the chimney of an old coal train. My wife always took insanely hot showers. So hot in fact that there was rarely any hot water left for me. We had had this discussion many times before. She always ignored me. But whatever. Now was not the time.

I threw back the curtain. Kacie turned around, slightly surprised.

Water cascaded down her face and she couldn't see my terrified expression through her matted hair. A small mischievous smile curled the side of her mouth.

"Oooh, welcome to the shower, babe."

She pushed back her hair and wiped her eyes free of soap. I

turned off the water.

"What?" she said with the force of a Naomi Osaka forehand. Her expression soured. "Is this about the water temp? I literally just got in here."

"No. It's not about that."

There was a chorus of moaning undead from the street level. I stepped into the shower and closed the curtain, my bare feet immediately scorched by the pool of scalding water.

"Ow! How can anyone shower in water this hot?"

Kacie grunted, locked and loaded for an argument.

"It relaxes me."

"Do you have like mutant skin?"

"Mutant skin?"

"This has got to be unhealthy on some level."

"I didn't ask you to come in here! I would never just barge in on my naked wife showering!"

Her logic confused me.

"*Your* naked wife?"

Kacie snorted out a laugh. Sometimes our marriage was like the bomb squad; cut one comment and the tension would defuse, cut another and everything would blow up.

Luckily, I'd cut the right chord.

Kacie put her hands on my shoulders and made her sexy face which involved both a pout and a single eyebrow raise.

"We can share the hot water you know?"

For a second I forgot what I came into the shower for. Was it for this?

A loud screeching came from somewhere near the front of the apartment complex.

Oh, *that's* what it was.

The thought of approaching zombies cooled off our otherwise steamy encounter. I stepped out of the shower and ran to the front door, checking the bolt locks and sliding over our makeshift barricade. In the process, I scratched the floor terribly.

Sudden guilt and embarrassment rushed through my veins. *Our landlord would fine us, guests would see the scratch and judge us, Kacie would complain with every entrance, especially when she came home from work unhappy.* These were the lingering thoughts of an old life. I was surprised I still felt them, especially now that no one cared anymore.

Kacie darted out of the shower with a towel on and ran for the bedroom.

"I think they—" I yelled back to her, then realizing my volume, softened to a yell-whisper. "I think they broke through the downstairs barricade."

Kacie leaned out of the bedroom as she fumbled with the top button of her jeans. A red light flashed over the room. The alarm I had wired over the apartment foyer must have been tripped. I was no electrician and I felt a sudden flash of pride. 'It actually worked!' I thought.

There was moaning from the stairwell.

Kacie had thrown a shirt over her head but didn't have time to get both arms successfully through her sleeves. She was frantic, rummaging through drawers, looking for something. In all my years knowing her, Kacie was never frantic.

Suddenly, I was terrified.

There was banging at our door.

Kacie threw up her arms and let them fall limp against her thighs. She shook her head and tousled her hair. The twisted wad of wet curls made her look deranged.

"I can't believe this."

Kacie walked into the bedroom and sat on the mattress.

"I can't believe we're going to die."

"Shouldn't we..."

The beginning of my sentence just hung there awkwardly.

It was a sorority. We didn't have a gun. Or a flamethrower. Or an escape. But we were smarter than this! How could it end so pathetically? So painfully?

Kacie knew what I knew. She knew it as she looked out of our fifth story window.

"I don't want to jump. I don't want to die that way. I'll see how bad it is once they start trying to eat me and then I'll make a decision."

The barricade shook with force.

Kacie kicked at the loose clothes she had pulled from the drawers in her frantic state. She picked up two masks from the ground and snorted out a laugh.

Both were zombie masks I bought as a joke, a prank I was going to pull after my friend Imran invited us over for a dinner party. I thought we should show up at his front door wearing the masks and give him a good spook. But I chickened out. The outbreak was still pretty fresh at that point and the prank was ultimately too dark for me.

But I kept the masks. After Imran's dinner party, Kacie and I went home and got into bed. It had been a fun, bottomless party and Kacie crawled up to me with one of the zombie masks on.

"If a horde of zombies come, we should just bend in," she slurred.

"Bend?" I said laughing.

"B-lend. Blend in. Like they did in that scene from *Shaun of the Dead*. You remember that?"

I agreed it was a good idea. We practised our best zombie moans that night.

Now, a sober Kacie was throwing me one of the masks.

"I can't think of anything else," she said as she wiped tears out of her eyes. Then she put hers on. It was grotesque and awful and I wondered if I'd ever see her real face again.

I followed suit, breathing in the mildewy rubber.

"So what's the plan?" I asked.

"Be dead."

The door to the apartment broke. The bureau barricade fell over. The horde climbed over the wreckage and my wife and I just stood there wearing zombie masks. We just stood there.

Kacie moaned and pretended to be after something. For a second I was frightened by just how much she had committed to her performance in the face of such horror.

Zombies entered the bedroom. And I just stood there, resigning myself to what was once an absurd but now completely normal death.

I moaned.

And the horde nudged into me and stumbled aimlessly and I just stood there not caring anymore about anything.

The next twenty-four hours unfolded in a surreal non-state. I moaned and doddered along with the sorority as we scavenged through the empty streets for humans. If there was screaming or eating or decaying, I didn't pay attention to it. I just followed.

There wasn't much time to think about Kacie. I was aware of her there next to me and tried to stay close. But every time there was a flicker of worry, or the desire to ask her a question or see her face, I felt as though the scent of my brain was showing. I don't know. I couldn't think. We both couldn't.

More time passed. How much I don't know. The sorority joined another sorority and then another. We drifted from place to place. Without escape, our diets became pretty gross. Don't think. Don't think.

The only corner of my mind I allowed for thought was just trying to stagger close enough to Kacie, the only zombie in the obviously fake zombie mask. Despite the mask, Kacie was a brilliant zombie. She showed no signs of thought, her moaning was guttural, her stumbling uncanny. I couldn't wonder about how she did these things, or what she was thinking of our situation in general.

But at some point I couldn't resist a single small thought. As much as I tried to bat it away, the thought gnawed at me: Was Kacie still... *Kacie*?

But it was impossible to ask her anything. We were stuck. If I started to think any more about it, the other zombies would pounce. Don't think. Don't think.

Anyway, a year has passed.

Of all the places we saw, of all the things we did, I'm embarrassed to admit I don't remember any of them. We must have left the city and made it deep into the rural countryside, past smoldering strip-malls and vacant houses. More and more commonly, humans were scarce.

But today, as we hobbled outside of an abandoned donut shop, a man in black cowboy hat came flying at us on a white motorcycle. Around the tires were large chains, used for riding on snow I assumed. But it wasn't winter, dummy, so it must have been for some other reason. As soon as he started riding over the bodies of the zombies in front of us did I put two and two together. Here was a human jazzing for some zombie whoop-ass.

Soon enough, with a loud "Yee-haw!" the man on the motorcycle turned to reveal a small sidecar in which rode a skinny little girl in a trucker's hat, spraying the horde with shotgun blast after shotgun blast.

I had gotten used to seeing this kind of thing. Especially the implications it brought with it. To be afraid of dying was to think. And I couldn't care less about myself anymore.

But as they rode away, the girl delivered a final random shot. Next to me, I sensed a woman zombie fall.

That is when I heard a noise that had not registered in my brain for a long time: a scream of life.

I turned to see that on the ground next to me lay a woman wearing a zombie mask over her face. She was grabbing her stomach where the shotgun blast had taken a piece of her with it.

"Take it off! Please take it off!" she cried.

Pain and instinct took over and I stopped my staggering and bent down and touched the face, touched the rubbery fake blood, and I moaned as I pulled it off.

Underneath was Kacie.

"Not mine. Yours dummy. I want to see your face."

I trembled as I lifted my mask. As soon as I did, a look came over her. A look of recognition maybe, or regret, or love. She looked like she wanted to say to something. But the words never came and the rosiness left her cheeks and she was gone.

I never thought I'd have it in me to know someone as well as I knew Kacie. My memory isn't very good, I jumble up stories most of the time, forget who I was with, how much time I put in the parking meter. But with Kacie, it was like I had a whole other brain.

And I remember meeting her. I had mentioned to my cousin Frances that I needed to get rid of a couch. She told me that her friend from college was in need of one.

"Do you mind if I ask her? She lives not too far, in Lincoln Park."

So my cousin's friend from college and her roommate Kacie came over. Without introducing herself, Kacie looked at the couch and said, "Sweet couch dude."

Sweet couch dude.

As she lay there bleeding, I bent down and sensed the other zombies coming towards me. They knew the dead was living, that the woman lying on the ground beneath me was human.

What if I hadn't said anything about the couch to my cousin? It wasn't an important detail in the conversation. I remember I didn't even know why I mentioned it. I was just going to get my neighbor to help me move it to the curb. And what if my cousin hadn't remembered to let her friend know? And what if my cousin's friend's roommate didn't decide to come with her? How was it that the love of my life needed a couch right when I was giving one away? How and why and how?

They were closing in.

I had watched Kacie. Watched her become so many things. Listened as she untangled life, both hers and my own.

So I bent down and bit my wife. I bit into her face to let the others know she was not dead. She could never be.

Tonight, when the time is right, I will bury my wife. And in the morning I will walk on, my arms limp and my head hung, as I begin again my search for the living.

TONY HUNTER-CRAIG

Masks of Respectability

I blame the Patels for getting me into this fix. If they'd made it more difficult to nick stuff from their corner shop I wouldn't have gone in there in the first place and seen the advert in their window.

Assistant Private Investigator wanted, it said. Flexible hours. No experience necessary. Driving licence and some knowledge of digital cameras required.

So, it's all because I fancied a Mars bar that afternoon that I'm sitting in a farmhouse style kitchen straight out of House and Home magazine, waiting for Mr Grimshaw to come back and kill me.

I'm not sure how he's going to do it but, judging by the amount of plastic sheeting he's spread on the floor around me, it's going to be messy. He said he'd be back in a few minutes. Needed to get another roll of gaffer tape from the garage, he said. He's already used up one roll taping me to this chair.

In the meantime, apart from admiring the Shaker style units and reclaimed flagstone floor in his designer kitchen, I've been mulling over the events that brought me here and, more significantly, why he's going to murder me just because I saw him run over a dog. I can't ask him. I've got about a yard of tape wrapped around my chops.

Not being the most reliable type of person, I was a stranger to steady employment before Rockford Surveillance took me on, but the owner wasn't fussy. He said I had an instantly forgettable face and was completely unremarkable. Ideal qualities for the job. The office was two rooms above the Patel's shop and I think he filched the name from some old TV detective show.

I spent the next couple of years following cheating husbands and wayward wives, sitting in a clapped-out Fiat Uno with a camera at the ready. I was paid a per diem pittance and the assignments were boring but I soon found a way to supplement my meagre income.

Most of Rockford's clientele were reasonably wealthy middle class professionals living in the upmarket suburbs of the city. BMWs, Jaguars and big detached mock Tudor houses or barn conversions were the norm. They provided a rich source of improprieties.

The first time I decided to do a bit of freelancing was more out of sympathy than avarice. I'd been keeping an eye on a bloke whose wife reckoned was having an affair. He had all the appearances of a model husband, but she was right. I clocked him coming out of a hotel one afternoon with a stunning brunette. To make sure it wasn't just a one-off I decided to keep up the surveillance for another few days. One morning, while I was waiting to check if he stopped off for a quickie on the way to work, his wife followed him out of the house. 180 pounds of shapeless dressing gown capped with dirty blonde hair, yelling her head off while managing to keep a cigarette stuck to her lower lip. He got into his car without a word as she stood there glowering, hands on broad hips, shouting at him like an overweight drill sergeant.

I decided he deserved an out. As soon as he parked up, I pulled into an adjoining slot and approached him. I spilled the beans and offered to let him delete all the photos from my camera if he gave me a grand in cash. I would report back to my boss that there was no evidence of an affair. We did the deal as soon as the banks opened and he was as grateful for his good fortune as I was for my small one.

After that I quickly learned that a heck of a lot of well-to-do people wore a mask of respectability to hide their true characters, and I discovered they were willing to pay to keep their masks from slipping.

I always chose my targets carefully. Individuals with a reputation to uphold. People in positions of responsibility. Outwardly upright citizens who would be horrified if their indiscretions were revealed.

It's surprising what you find out when you observe someone closely for a few days. I uncovered all manner of misdemeanours, from the manager of a lower division football club who was placing bets against his own team, to a county councillor who was up-skirting women on escalators.

I never demanded ridiculous sums of money. Enough to make it worth my time and effort but easily affordable for my 'clients'. Five thousand was the most I ever asked for, and avoiding embarrassment is a powerful motivation to pay off a blackmailer.

Mr Grimshaw was different from my usual clients in that I came across him quite by accident.

I'd been shadowing a trophy wife whose old man had become suspicious. She was dead easy to tail either in her flashy red sports car or tottering around on killer heels.

On that particular evening, September 4th, I'd followed her car to Brampton Woods, a seldom visited local nature reserve. It definitely looked fishy to me so I switched my dash cam on and filmed her as she bumped along a rough dirt road to a parking area.

She pulled up alongside the only other vehicle, a late model Mercedes G-wagon with a personalized number plate. I slotted the Uno between two overhanging trees at the side of the track and started snapping away.

She climbed into the Merc and the two of them were soon at it. I could see the G-wagon rocking on its suspension and the windows misting up. As soon as the light began to fade I decided to leave them to it and reversed until I found a place wide enough to do a three-pointer.

It was on the way back down the track that I first encountered Grimshaw. His silver Range Rover shot out of a firebreak right in front of me. He seemed to be in a hurry but once clear of the woodland he slowed down a bit and I caught up with him as we both headed back towards the city.

We reached the suburbs and that's when he hit the dog. I can't say he was at fault, the stupid mutt ran out into the road, its owner nowhere in sight. However, Grimshaw didn't even slow down. It was like he didn't know he'd run the thing over, or didn't care. The dog looked extremely dead so I didn't bother stopping either, but I knew that you had to inform the authorities if you ran over an animal, and I guessed that wasn't going to happen.

I checked my dash cam. It was still recording. Sensing an opportunity, I followed the silver Range Rover to its destination, a standard issue detached mock Tudor on a pleasant tree-lined avenue.

Early the next morning I went back and got my first good look at Grimshaw. Middle aged, wiry, clean shaven with thinning hair, expensive suit and briefcase. I followed him to a modern dental surgery where I found out his name from the plaque next to the door. I confirmed it with the receptionist when I went inside to make enquiries about the price of fillings.

He was the ideal mark. Wealthy with an image to protect. I was sure he had plenty of dog lovers on his patient list.

A letter would be the best method of initial contact I decided after a few days' contemplation, so I wrote a simple note by hand to avoid leaving any clues on my laptop if anything went wrong:

'I followed you from Brampton Woods on September 4th. I know what you did and have it on video. The evidence is for sale for £2000. If you are interested, message me on this number.'

I included the number for one of my cheap burner phones, wrote his full name with all his post-nominals on an envelope marked confidential, and hand delivered the letter to his surgery.

Two days later the phone pinged and I read his text message:

'Bring all copies of evidence to 14 Cavendish Avenue at 6 pm tonight. Come alone. Cash waiting.'

He was inviting me to his home address, which must mean he was either single or, if he had a wife and kids, they'd be out.

"Have you got everything with you?" he asked me on the doorstep. "Does anyone else know about this?"

I told him yes and no and, as he stepped aside to let me enter, I felt a sharp prick on the side of my neck.

I would have assumed it was an insect bite if I hadn't glimpsed the movement of his arm. The effect was instantaneous and amazing. Within seconds I felt woozy and my knees buckled. Grimshaw had to hold me up and half drag me into his kitchen. I was euphoric, enjoying the best trip ever as he sat me down and began gaffer taping me to a chair. I was too happy to object.

"Midazolam injected straight into the jugular," he offered by way of explanation as he strapped my wrists to the wooden chair arms.

"Wears off after about half-an-hour. I use it as a pre-med when I do major reconstructive work. Nice isn't it?"

"Wha ... wha ..." I managed, unable to form any coherent words.

"Sorry about this, but I can't risk you disturbing the neighbours," my captor said as he used more of the tape to gag me.

Grimshaw emptied my pockets and placed everything, including the burner phone, on the grey soapstone countertop. He rifled through my wallet and found my Rockford business card.

"So, a snoop eh? Or should I say private investigator? I suppose my wife hired you to keep an eye on me. Well, whatever you've found out isn't going to do either of you much good now is it?"

The effect of the midazolam was wearing off but what he was saying still didn't make any sense to me. He picked up the SD memory card I'd removed from my dash cam to fulfil my part of the bargain.

"I assume this is your video evidence, yes?"

I nodded enthusiastically and mumbled agreement through the tape, hoping he'd be satisfied and let me go.

"Well, we better get rid of that straight away."

He lit one of the gas rings on the six burner range and, holding the tiny plastic card with a pair of stainless steel tongs, incinerated it.

After he'd flushed the ash down the sink he blew out the pilot lights for the gas burners then dragged me closer to the range before spreading plastic sheeting around and between the legs of my chair, all the time keeping up a nervous chatter.

"I don't want a repeat of last week. My wife made a terrible mess. She 'let go' if you get my drift. I hope you don't do the same. I can't have your DNA spread all over the floor... took me hours to clean up after her."

"What the hell is going on?" I demanded. "All you did was run over a dog. What's it got to do with your wife? I'm only asking for a couple of grand to save you any embarrassment!"

Unfortunately, it came out as *'Whuummmph, mmrrph. Mmmmppphhh!'*

"I could finish you off with an overdose of midazolam," Grimshaw explained, ignoring my pathetic grunts, "which would be much more pleasant, even enjoyable, but if your body is ever discovered and traces found it would throw suspicion on me, being a dentist. The tiny amount I gave you will be undetectable after a few hours."

I felt sweat break out on my forehead as I realized he really did intend to murder me ... and that's when he went off to get more gaffer tape.

Grimshaw has just returned and is prattling incessantly as he's taping a huge polythene bag around the range, carefully sealing all the gaps.

It's obvious to me now that he's going to seal me inside and then turn on the gas. Not quite as messy as I feared but just as terminal.

He tells me that he used the same modus operandi to dispatch his wife on September 4th and then buried her body that same evening in Brampton Woods. He can't understand how I know about it. He thought he'd been exceptionally careful.

Not being the sharpest arrow in the quiver, it finally dawns on me that Grimshaw thinks that's why I'm blackmailing him. It's all a terrible misunderstanding.

"*Mmmrrrphh ... whhaammph!*" I plead, meaning: 'I only know about the dog ... I had no idea you'd murdered your wife!'

Grimshaw takes no notice whatsoever.

So that's the reason he's going to kill me and I have no way of putting his mind at rest. Even if I could, it wouldn't make any difference because, of course, now I do know.

"We only bought the new mattresses last month," Grimshaw says cheerily as he drapes the bag over me and begins to tape it down.

"Lucky I kept all the packaging, it's come in really handy and is rather appropriate don't you think?"

My eyes fill with tears when I notice the irony of the brand name '*Heavenly Sleep*' emblazoned multiple times across the polythene.

He reaches in and twists the knobs for the gas rings before quickly sealing the last few inches. I hold my breath as long as I can and shake my head violently, feebly trying to overturn the heavy wooden chair.

I'm forced to take a breath and the stench of rotten eggs fills my nose making me retch and I see Grimshaw through the hazy plastic, smugly watching me die. Then my consciousness ebbs away and I'm left with the bitter certainty that he'll go on hiding behind a mask of respectability long after I'm lying in an unmarked grave, somewhere in Brampton Woods

The Other Face

Joel makes the sandwiches with tomato ketchup, because there's nothing else in the cupboard. The bread feels rough, too; it's been left on the side overnight, next to the pots and the crusted cutlery. He should toast it, really, to hide the staleness—but there's no time, not now. The clock tuts at him from the kitchen wall, sliding closer to eight.

He runs upstairs, feet thumping. When he knocks on his mother's door, there's only silence, so he nudges it open with his fingers.

"Mum," he says. She faces away from him, curled in a hump under the duvet. "Mum, I'm going."

She doesn't stir, so he rounds the bed to look at her. That's when he notices it. Something different about her face—an unfamiliar jut to her cheekbones, a strange thinness to her lips. Unease grips his stomach.

"Mum," he repeats, giving her shoulder a little shake. "I'm going to school now. I'll be back about six, because of rehearsals."

She mumbles something, but doesn't open her eyes. Joel fights the urge to shake her harder, to peel her eyelids back, to squint and check the colour of them. The alarm clock blinks on her bedside table—he can still make the bus, if he leaves now.

He brushes her hair with his fingers, briefly, gingerly, and finds the texture not quite as he remembers it. When he leaves the house, guitar case slung over his back, he sets off at a run. The case bumps in time with his heart.

Joel makes it home on the dot of six, and the door is locked. He has to cut around to the back of the house and wrench the kitchen window open, straining on the tips of his toes. It sticks halfway, but the gap is wide enough for him to push his guitar case through first—it knocks against the taps several times, with a tuneless hum that makes him grit his teeth.

After, he struggles through himself, sweating, legs kicking. The house is heavy with silence, but he checks all the rooms anyway. He calls his mother's name once, then presses his hands over his lips. His voice sounds too thin, too high.

An hour passes. He rings her mobile twice, before he finds it on the floor by her bed, buzzing silently against the carpet. When he checks the coat rack, a few things are missing—her green jacket, her pumps, her handbag. She took money, then. He tries to feel reassured.

Evening closes in, dragging long shadows over the carpet. He makes a second ketchup sandwich, with toasted bread this time, but it doesn't taste much better. The bread rolls over his tongue and clogs his throat, and when he forces himself to swallow it, his eyes water and water and water, even when he pinches his arm to distract himself.

He switches the television on, rests his head on the arm of the sofa. Cycles through channels until he finds a film. With the volume down low and his eyes lulled shut, he can almost imagine there's someone in the room with him, talking so softly he can barely hear.

When he opens his eyes again, the film has changed. Shadows grasp towards him from the corners of the room, and the acidic taste of the ketchup still clings to his throat. He wonders if that's what woke him, if he's going to be sick.

But then he listens: a key, scrabbling in a lock.

He wants to run to the corridor, but his legs have seized up. He knows what's coming. His eyes find the television, blurring on the characters' faces, their hands, the way their mouths close around soundless words. If he looks hard enough, perhaps the screen will swallow him.

A shadow falls across the floor from the doorway. Joel makes himself look up.

It's worse than this morning. His mother's face has changed entirely now—the cheekbones high and sharp, her lips colourless. She has a small mole on her jaw that wasn't there yesterday, and the bridge of her nose is thicker, flatter, like clay pushed out of shape.

"Mum," he says.

She looks at him, after a beat. Her brown eyes have lightened to a watery grey.

"Why're you up?" she says. There's a new timbre to her voice, and the words run together like watercolours. "You shouldn't... you should be asleep."

Her hair is still blonde, the same sandy shade as Joel's, but he can see it deepening to brown at the roots. It's like watching water seeping into fabric, like the dip-dyeing they did in textiles at school. Every time he blinks, the colour grows a little stronger.

"I was waiting for you," he says, swallowing hard. "Do you want a cup of tea?"

"No," she mumbles, pressing her face to her hands. "Just... you go. Go up to bed. You shouldn't be up."

Joel gets to his feet, his legs wobbling. When he steps into her space, a fog of alcohol rolls off her, so strong he can almost taste it. He takes a shallow breath before taking her by the wrists.

"Come on," he says quietly. "We can both go up."

She resists for a moment, snatching her hands back, but then goes limp. He puts an arm around her side, which feels more fragile than it should, the bones pressing closer to the surface. They struggle up the stairs, along the landing, into the darkness of her bedroom. When she slumps back on the mattress, Joel's hands move to her coat buttons. He can solve this, he thinks. If he looks after her, if he helps her sleep, if he brings her the tea just how she always has it, then she'll wake up tomorrow and everything will be normal—

"Stop it," she grits out, batting at his hands. "Can bloody do it myself. Leave off."

"I'm just trying to—"

"Get *off!*" She slaps his hands again, hard enough to sting, and Joel jumps back a step. "Should be in fucking bed. Get out."

In the streaked half-light, his mother's face is an alien thing, creased with fury. Her pale eyes sear into him. He holds his stinging hands to his chest and leaves the room, bumping his shoulder on the door frame as he goes.

Joel wakes long before dawn, a headache clenched behind his eyes. A single pigeon calls outside his window, rhythmic, lulling, maddening. He tumbles out of his bed to bang on the glass, and the noise stops.

He holds his head in his hands, coming more awake. The events of yesterday return to him—snatches of memories, catching the light like splintered glass. Mum. His mother, with her unknown face, those grey eyes, that new mole on her jaw. She wouldn't let him make her tea.

He steps into the corridor and opens his mother's bedroom door by inches. A slice of the room emerges through the gap; she's asleep, wheezing softly, sprawled on top of the duvet. She still wears her green coat.

Joel creeps through the gap, taking slow, heel-to-toe steps. A slat of sunlight falls through the gap in the curtains. His mother doesn't look as unfamiliar as yesterday, as though the sleep has softened her. Her hair has returned to its usual blonde, like the shore drying after the tide goes out. But the contours of her cheeks are still strange, and that little mole sits stubbornly on her jaw.

She never looks the same, whenever it happens. The first time was soon after Auntie Rachel died. She turned slow and quiet, too exhausted to dress, and one morning she came down to breakfast with a different face. Older, green-eyed, with the same reddish hair that her sister once had.

There were ways to manage it, Joel had learnt. He had to talk to her, to play the old albums on her CD player, to read out chapters from her favourite books when she couldn't get out of bed. He had to make the tea just how she liked it, with two sugars and a lot of milk. It was a breadcrumb trail back to herself, and she would always follow it eventually, if he were quiet and patient enough. The other face usually shrank out of sight for weeks at a time. Sometimes even months.

His mother shifts under the covers, mumbling something. Joel backs away, but he can't reach the door in time—her eyelids flutter open.

"Joel," she mumbles.

Her pupils are grey, but her voice, beneath the roughness of the drink, sounds closer to his memory.

"I'm sorry," Joel says. "I just wanted to check on you."

"Don't... come here, love." Her voice shakes slightly, and she holds out one hand. "Come on."

Joel slopes towards her, sinking onto the bed. This close, the dissimilarities are starker—her flesh smells of sweat and wine, not the warm, cheap-perfume scent he knows best. Her fingers are thin and hard when they comb through his hair, but he forces himself to stay still, to let her touch him. He interlinks his left hand with hers and squeezes the unfamiliar bones.

"I don't remember," she whispers, biting her lip. "When did I come back, yesterday? Did I leave you alone?"

"Not really," he lies. "You came back in the evening."

"I'm sorry." Her hand tightens in his hair, almost painfully. "I'm so sorry. I don't know what I was thinking."

"It doesn't matter."

He shuffles around to lie next to her, and they drowse, sliding in and out of sleep. Whenever he opens his eyes, she looks a little more familiar than before. Blink—her nose is narrower. Blink—her cheeks rounder. Blink. Blink.

As the light strengthens through the curtains, Joel disentangles himself and sits up. His mother looks up at him.

"Need to get ready for school," he says. "Marcy wants to do extra rehearsals before lessons."

A notch appears between his mother's brows. "Ah. Yes. Your concert, right?"

Joel nods. "It's tomorrow. You'll come, won't you?"

"Yes. Yeah, of course," she says, with a brief kiss to his hand. Her lips touch the exact spot she slapped yesterday, and his skin tingles at the contact. He tries to ignore it.

Half an hour later, Joel is dressed, another ketchup sandwich packed in his schoolbag. When he comes upstairs to say goodbye, his mother is sitting up in bed, staring out of the window. Her eyes are still grey.

Joel tunes his guitar for the third time, even though it's too loud in the wings to hear the notes. It's just for the motion of it; the press of the nylon strings on his fingertips, the way the tuning pegs give and stiffen as he adjusts them. A few metres away, Marcy squints at herself in her phone camera, dabbing concealer onto her nose.

"Stop fiddling with that guitar," she says, glancing at him. "You're making me jumpy."

Joel stops, clenching his hands into fists instead. He hasn't looked out at the audience yet, arranged in rows around the amphitheatre—only heard their chatter, the volley of their footsteps as they took their seats. He imagines his mother amongst them. She'll be sitting apart from the rest, hands in her lap.

A smattering of applause marks the end of the first act. It's a long, long wait before Joel and Marcy's turn—they're on right at the end, because Marcy is so good, almost like a proper singer already. After the ukulele troupe straggles off, Marcy walks out a little ahead of him, with a sway to her steps.

A chorus of whistles follows—cheers from Marcy's mum and dad, sitting right at the front. Joel follows her, gripping hard at the neck of his guitar. It's just the school stage, where they sit every week for assemblies, yawning and fidgeting, but it seems to have swollen to twice its usual size. The spotlights are hot, so bright he can barely see past them to the audience.

Still, he looks. For sandy hair, a green coat, and brown eyes watching him.

He looks and looks.

"Joel," Marcy hisses, her hand cupped over the microphone. "Come on."

He nods distantly, moving closer. Marcy counts in, and Joel's fingers move through the first chord. The guitar is slightly out of tune.

It's raining by the time Joel makes it home. A warm rain, carding gently through his hair, touching fingers to the back of his neck.

He sets his guitar case down in the hall, against the coat rack. His mother's green jacket hangs from the nearest peg. From the living room comes the quiet buzz of the telly.

His mother is asleep on the sofa, in the same spot he occupied two nights ago. A lamp shines on the coffee table next to her, pooling in her long hair, which has darkened almost to the colour of ink. On the floor by her bare foot is an empty bottle of something; he's not sure if they already had it in the house, or if she went out to buy it.

Joel moves to stand over her. She doesn't stir, her breath rasping in the quiet. He kicks the bottle so that it knocks onto the floor.

She twitches awake, jerking her head.

"Oh," she breathes. Slurred, again. Her eyes open a crack, then fall shut once more. "You're back. Where were you?"

"How much have you had?"

She says nothing, pushing her face into her arm. Something sparks in Joel's stomach. He takes hold of her jaw, one hand on either side, jerking it up to the light.

She's worse than before. Her flesh feels like wax beneath his fingers, spongey and unreal. He imagines how it would feel to dig his nails in deeper, to tighten his grip and pull. Maybe that's all it would take. One hard tug, and the face would come away like wallpaper, and he'd find the right eyes and nose and mouth underneath.

"Get off," she mumbles. "You're hurting."

"How much did you have?"

She doesn't answer, but her eyes finally open to fix on him, glassy and wet. In the muted glare of the lamp, they almost look brown.

"I'm sorry," she whispers.

Joel stops. The strength drains out of him at once, and his hands drip away from her face, to hang heavily at his sides.

He sinks down beside her on the sofa, not close enough to touch. For a few seconds, there is only the hum of the television, the patter of the rain outside.

"Do you want a tea?" Joel says.

Next to him, his mother nods silently. He gets to his feet to go to the kitchen.

LEE STODDART

Ham, Egg and Chips

"God, I miss their ham, egg and chips. Don't you, Janey?"
That's it, the reverential silence has been shattered.

Kobe had been staring vacantly at the burnt-out shell of the West Bay Cafe for a couple of minutes before making this momentous proclamation that only I will hear. The cafe's fire-blackened timbers stick out from the promenade like the ribs of a fossilised stegosaurus I'd seen on a school trip a lifetime ago.

Behind us, the tide has almost completed its retreat across the sands and rock pools, exposing the dark-green and black seaweed to stink poisonously in the growing heat. The last of the salt water steams off it as, with no hint of a cloud in the sky, the early morning sun scorches everything it touches, until all vestiges of moisture have been burnt off.

Other than Kobe's fidgeting and heavy breathing, the shoreline is perfectly still and silent once more, until he can't stay quiet any longer, and again he holds forth with unwanted nostalgia. "The ham was more like a gammon steak. The eggs were like two big yellow..."

He stops dead before his sentence has finished, unable to complete the lame cliché. The sound of that whiney voice of his has already dragged me back to focus on him, when I should be thinking of stuff that really matters.

"Kobe, were you about to say 'suns'? *Really?*"

His head drops and he stares at the cracked concrete of the promenade, prodding at a loose pebble with the toe of his what once passed for shoes, like a naughty schoolboy.

"Maybe, I—"

"Jesus H Christ. You're an idiot," I mutter, not quietly enough that he couldn't hear.

Angrily, I turn away from him and the cafe and brace myself against the promenade's rusty iron railings, staring at the rapidly drying rock pools below. Where the water has evaporated completely, miniature, white saltpans shimmer.

I kick myself for taking an unnecessary, self-indulgent trip down memory lane, lost in contemplation of happier times. Stupid of me, I should be more alert. I sure as hell can't count on Kobe anymore. I *have* to rely on *me*.

Glancing upwards, the sun has climbed higher than I expected. Must be about ten.

"Best get back." I sigh, and turn my stony gaze back on him, but he meets me with soft, bovine eyes and my anger leaves me.

Not that I can *really* see his eyes; or he, mine.

We are completely wrapped head to foot in loose, hooded robes made from any bit of rag we had found and stitched together. Beneath the hoods our faces are encased in cloth masks, except for a thin slot across the eyes.

I sport a cracked pair of *Reactolights*. I'd found them four years ago, digging through the carcass of a *Specsavers*. I couldn't believe my luck. They weren't the perfect prescription but were close enough.

Back then we could travel further. The temperatures didn't peak as high and Ramsgate, just six miles away, was still achievable in a day. But, as temperatures rose, and we edged closer to starvation, our energy and strength abandoned us. These days, we only just manage the three miles or so to Westgate. Not that Westgate offers much more than anywhere else, in these trying times.

"It's getting late. Heat's building and it's at least an hour home. Better move."

Kobe lifts his hessian scavenging sack, the legend 'Anston's Cattle Feed' still just legible on the weave, and shakes it at me. It's empty. No surprise there.

In mine, I have a couple of lizards and a grass snake, still wriggling. I'd managed to catch them as they basked on a rock, laid out like sacrifices to the gods. I'm sick of eating reptile, but they seem to be the only thing around here now.

I'd kill for just a taste of real beef or pork. Chicken even. Anything that doesn't crawl, slither or scuttle.

Most of the mammals and birds have disappeared. Even the rats. It's now a weekly chore to check the traps I set and used to check daily. Even then, they're usually empty.

To make matters worse, this year there's almost no edible plants to gather.

The vegetation had begun to vanish about fifteen years ago, when the daytime temperatures started to regularly peak above thirty-five. For the last few years, summer mid-afternoon highs have been over fifty, turning Kent from *Garden* into *Desert of England*.

In desperation, I've tried supplementing our diet by harvesting seaweed. Apart from being utterly disgusting, it made me sick, although Kobe went unscathed.

Going out only at night, to escape the heat, isn't a winning option, either. Surviving on such a terrible diet means our night-vision is utterly shot and bones are brittle from lack of calcium. A broken leg from a fall in the dark would be as good as a death sentence. Besides, it's not significantly cooler. The earth absorbs so much energy during the day, it's like a huge storage radiator. Once the sun sets, the baked ground gives up its heat without a struggle, maintaining the sweltering heat long into the night.

So, we stay hidden away for most of the year, only daring to come out between late autumn and early spring when the temperatures are a little lower. Even then, we only emerge in the hours between dawn and eleven, when the temperature is just about bearable with proper precautions, and we gather what food we can to last us through the summer.

"Can't we risk just a bit longer, Janey? We've got almost nothing and I'm *so* hungry. We could fish?" He fumbles in his pocket to pull out a reeled-up hook and line, but drops it in the process, the line unspooling as it rolls away from him.

Christ, he's like a child... No. He's like a newborn calf, stumbling through life on rubber legs, utterly dependent on me to be there for him.

Down at my feet, Kobe is scrambling around on the ground,

gathering up his dropped line. He guiltily looks up at me as he stuffs its unruly threads back into his pocket. Hopeless.

"Sorry, Janey..."

Even if he could get his act together, it would be pointless because the fish have finally forsaken us. The few I have managed to catch are ugly and sick. Mutated beyond recognition, they were devoured anyway. There was nothing spare for the summer stockpile.

Maybe the fish have escaped, with the birds, and headed to cooler climes?

If there are more temperate areas left.

I pray that there are, but I don't know, and there's no one here to tell me.

"No. No fishing. Come on, we'll cut across the old town. Maybe we can pick something up on the way." We wouldn't, of course, but I had to get him moving or we'd cook in the midday burn.

Recently, he'd seemed sluggish and slow-witted, prone to melancholy and longing for yesterdays which will never return. None of which is any help to me and really quite irritating.

The world has changed. There is no going back. There's just survival.

We trudge back, towards Cliftonville. Through deserted streets littered with the carcasses of long-abandoned cars. Most of the buildings are burned out from wildfires, like the cafe, but a few still stand—ransacked and empty.

As we cross the ghost of Margate town centre, Kobe suddenly drops behind a pale blue VW Beetle. It has been stopped, waiting for the traffic lights to go green, for over twenty years. Then it was a classic car. Now, it's just rusting-metal cover. Arthritically, he hunkers down and makes to grab at the hem of my hand-made robe, to pull me down with him; but I am already there, having spotted the threat at the same time as him.

His leather-gloved finger goes up to his mouth, "Shhhh..."

In the wreckage of the old Morrisons supermarket, two figures rake over the leavings. I'd done the selfsame thing so many times myself, forlornly hoping upon hope that, this time, I'd find something useful or maybe some edible treat.

But the tins have all been harvested—everything else rotted long ago. Anything electric is completely useless, of course. Grim experience has taught me there is nothing left worth liberating.

I pull out a pair of battered binoculars from their leather case hanging round my neck. Lifting my shades, I wince at the brightness, then squint through the lenses.

The pair of newcomers sort through the rubble, turning it over with spears. On their backs they each carry carbon-fibre sports bows and a quiver full of arrows. Despite their full-body coverings, they move quickly and with assurance. Judging from their size and shape they are nourished and healthy, agile and powerful; not emaciated and weak, like us.

Reflexively, my free hand falls on the hilt of the bowie knife in its sheath on my belt.

There is only one conclusion to be drawn.

"Oh, crap. Cannibals."

We wait in the withering heat for them to grow bored and move on.

When they eventually do, we cautiously break cover from behind the VW and creep back home. I hope to God they won't hang around and will bugger off out of the area in the next day or two.

As we walk, I ensure our tracks are concealed as well as possible. But I don't have anything handy to sweep away our footprints and it's hard to walk without trace in the ever-present dust. It's been so long since I've seen another human being, I've become lazy. Right now, I'm painfully aware I've lapsed into bad habits in my efforts to avoid discovery.

"Do you think they saw us, Janey?" Kobe calls out from the sofa at the cooler, rear of the cave. We'd got back home as the sun reached its zenith, and the heat was at its most unbearable. Outside it's easily fifty degrees. I glance at the thermometer hung on a rusty nail on the damp chalk wall—it's a much more comfortable thirty inside, and the humidity helps.

There's just enough light to see by, thanks to the mirrors I'd set up to direct daylight into the caves and tunnels we inhabit. But it isn't quite enough to see Kobe at the back, where he likes to lurk. Having stripped out of his surface coverings he would be, as usual, lounging about on our foraged furniture in what passes for underwear - a few dirty loose cloths sewn together—leaving me to get on with the chores.

I take a deep breath, and testily answer, "Well, we wouldn't be here now, if they had, would we?"

In the crepuscular light of the redirected sun, that bastes everything it touches in sepia tones, I try not to dwell on what my partner looks like. Kobe's a good fifteen years older than me. He's all bone and his filthy, desiccated skin makes him look like an unwrapped Egyptian mummy. He's in his mid-sixties and not doing so well. He's lost all his strength and agility in the last year, not to mention weight. He rarely speaks and leaves it to me to make all the decisions. I do the real work—sometimes he doesn't move for days, and even then, only if I coerce him.

Yet, once, he was a handsome company director, a man of strength, wealth and power—a bullish leader, not one of the herd.

I was his young and beautiful personal assistant.

Once I'd got him to rid himself of his drudge of a spouse, we had it all and lived like royalty, off the fat of the land.

Of course, that was until the complete and utter breakdown of society.

Now, I live like a troglodyte and grub around in the earth for a few roots to eat. Were it not for me, *he* wouldn't make it through another day. Actually, it's a minor miracle that I keep him about at all. But I'm stuck with him. We only have each other and I'd go mad if I had no one to talk to.

Time passes without further comment from either of us. It's not unusual. Sometimes we don't speak for days.

Maybe I'm being a bit harsh with him. He's worried, I can tell, sounding a bit panicky, earlier. After all, it's been so long since we've seen another human being.

"Look, Kobe, they'll just be passing through," I tell him in placating tones. If I say it with enough confidence, he'll believe me.

"Do you think?" He sounds hopeful. "Yes, I expect you are right. You usually are."

By my reckoning it's the autumn of '42.

Up until about '35, there was a regular flow of people moving, trying to find some fabled safe haven or other. Most often they'd head to the South of France so crossed the Channel any way they could, on rafts, inflatables and other small craft—crammed to the gunwales with desperate emigrants, in an ironic inversion of the early twenty-first century migrations of refugees.

Idiots!

Like it's going to be cooler in Monaco or Marseille than it is here. Scandinavia might make more sense. Scotland even.

At that time, those of us who chose to make the best of it in one place called them, rather disparagingly, *Nomads*. They, equally dismissively, called us *Stayers*. To choose one over the other was an act of faith—no one ever returned to testify whether they had chosen wisely or not. We remained, to hunt and gather as best we could where we knew the locale; praying it wouldn't get any worse, hoping we could make it better.

Besides, this was our home.

The last contact we'd had with anyone was a couple of male Nomads in the late spring of '39. Despite the risk, we cautiously welcomed them into our home, glad of the company and eager for any outside news. I particularly remember that they rather rashly produced a Swiss Army Knife to eat with. The height of retro-tech and *very* desirable.

The next morning, they left without a word, before we'd woken.

It seemed ungrateful after we'd shown them our hospitality, but I was pleased they were gone and Kobe never mentioned them again. At least they didn't steal any of our scarce supplies. That was the last summer we truly had enough to eat, after that it's all been downhill. Next year, I doubt there will be enough for even one.

Since then, we'd seen no one.

Until this morning, of course.

"Try not to worry about it, Kobe. They'll have gone away already. But just to be on the safe side, we'll have to lie low for a while and keep a watch out. It'll be just grazing on moss for a few days, though. Can you be a dear and go and draw some water from the well and scrape some dinner off the walls? I'll go out now and take down the mirrors."

He groaned, "But..."

"Yes, dear, I know. It'll be dark, but at least you *like* moss. *I* can't stand it.

"If they're still hanging about, we can't risk them seeing any reflections.

"First light tomorrow, I'll make sure we've left no other traces on the surface they can track back to us."

Heading for the surface, I imagine I hear Kobe tear himself from the couch and shuffle off down the tunnel, lurching like a Romero zombie. He's struggling more and more in the twilight world we live in. He would be bracing himself against the walls as he hobbles off, carefully feeling for the familiar handholds and secure footfalls, making slow progress on the slippery chalk floor. He'll give up halfway and slope off, back to his corner of the cave, defeated.

I'll end up doing it myself, like always.

Was it really fifteen years ago, when he was limber and had few issues navigating the tunnels, that we first came down here after our tribe was driven apart? Next year, I'll be fifty - the same age as he was then. I hold no delusions I'll see sixty-five.

Night comes and I sleep fitfully in the cave darkness, knowing what I have to do and worrying that the cannibals may have tracked us.

An hour before first light, I rise and leave Kobe resting in his usual spot, on the dilapidated couch; to meet the pre-dawn dressed in my usual UV-protective ensemble.

I don't like lying to Kobe, but on this occasion, it feels necessary. I only have a few hours to try to find the interlopers. Given how long we've resided in the caves, I'm sure it would be almost impossible to hide all signs of our presence and I'm certain they could easily find us—if they haven't already moved on. So, I have to find them first and neutralise the risk. My plan is to start at Morrisons and work my way outwards. I've gotten pretty good playing the tracker and hunter—although my prey is usually much smaller and never armed with powerful hunting bows.

I reach the supermarket, as the sun edges the horizon. On the top floor of the multi-storey car park, I slither onto the roof of a four-wheel drive, and keep low. Scanning the burnt-out ruins of the town, I spot the glow of a campfire, standing out like a beacon in the penumbra of the new day. It's not too far off; near the old Six Bells pub.

My God, the arrogance of these two, advertising their location so blatantly!

Perhaps, they are survivors of a paramilitary band, from before society finally and irreparably collapsed? That might explain their overconfidence.

Dangerous men.

Well, I have something they'll want, if I can't get them to listen.

I strike out towards their smoke signal. Prowling through the abandoned streets. Keeping to the shadows, I warily approach the pub from the street behind.

As I circumnavigate the building, I can see the smoke is emanating from a campfire, just across the road, set in the porch of St John's Church.

A gently bubbling pot of stew is suspended above it. The smell of simmering pork floats on the air and assaults my senses.

Jesus Christ, I haven't had meat in months.

No, it's been a full year since the last of the stock was consumed.

I can feel the drool building, dribbling out the corners of my mouth. I imagine biting, slowly chewing the meat. But where the hell had they got pork from?

Oh, yeah. Cannibals.

Long pork.

I creep through the lychgate and up the path; the taste of the stew in my nostrils.

Would it be *so* bad if it was also on my palate?

Hang on a minute—what the hell am I doing, charging in? This is madness. I can't let my desire to feed drive my actions.

I need to think it through.

What would *I* do, if I was them? Hold up in the coolest place...

Inside the church?

In the crypt.

Sounds about right. OK.

Having reassured myself, I continue my slow progress into the portal, my right-hand resting comfortingly on the bowie knife tucked in my belt, spurred on by the prospect of illicit protein.

The view into the church is obscured by punk-wood oak doors, which are still in place, but only just. Kicked in long ago, they hang from one hinge each, looking like a pair of rotten teeth in the otherwise empty sneer of a skull.

Drawing closer still, I peek inside. No one visible. They must be asleep. Perhaps, I can grab a mouthful of stew. I'm *so* hungry.

"That's far enough. Chuck the knife through the door and turn around." The command comes from behind me.

"Ah, shit." What else was there to say.

They're *not* in the church.

I turn, but resist losing the blade.

One man rises from behind a gravestone. The other steps out from behind a graffitied war memorial.

Bastards.

They must have spotted us yesterday and just calmly walked off to set their trap; baited with the leftovers of some poor sod they'd saved for just such an occasion.

How many times have they pulled this stunt?

Well-practised, I guess.

I can't really blame them.

You do what you have to do, to survive.

Both of them brandish their bows—arrows nocked and ready to be loosed. They must have been there all bloody night, waiting. Neither has a UV-protecting hood on, perhaps it's the arrogance of youth, or maybe just ignorance. And they are young—eighteen maybe. Well-fed and plump—by today's standards at any rate.

Fit, healthy and beautiful.

Two of the last of the bastard litter mankind ever produced—a progeny that was, for some unexplained reason, almost entirely male by 2025. It wasn't long after that all live births stopped entirely. After that, the heart went out of mankind, as realisation hit—fifty years left, then that was it. The race was over.

I'm the rarest of commodities: a survivor *and* a woman.

I know I have value.

Fearlessly, I pull off my hood and mask, then drop my robes from my shoulders—revealing my emaciated and scarred, but still recognisably female form.

"Fuck, is that...?"

"Yeah. Well, I'll be bolloxed."

Momentarily distracted, the two dip their bows. They look like they've never seen a woman before. One has his mouth flapping up and down in disbelief. For a second, I have the advantage and casually throw the robes behind me, along with the forgotten knife which, thank the Lord, I manage to cover.

"Look, lads... we all know *what* you are, and I'm cool with that. I could even manage a little bit of *whoever* is in the pot, myself. But, I bet neither of you has ever been with a real woman. We should come to some kind of *arrangement*. You know?

"Otherwise, you're just going to have to kill me; and what good would that do anyone? Sure, I'd put a bit more meat in the larder, but you'd be missing out on the only real woman within a hundred miles of here. Then, you'll be back to buggering each other, again. What do you say?"

Emphasising my point, I catch my thumb in the front waistband of my last pair of faded, ancient M&S knickers—not hand-made from found scraps of cloth, but real shop-bought pants. I'd worn them especially for the occasion, a glamourous distraction if needed. I edge them down, just a little.

I don't want them to misinterpret my intentions.

It doesn't seem possible that they can; but, they clearly aren't the brightest pins in the box.

Gravestone-man responds first. He shrugs and raises his bow again, drawing back the string until its taut. "Can't miss what you've ain't had."

"Wait, I can sweeten the deal." I interject swiftly, making him hesitate once more.

"I can provide a safe haven. Somewhere away from this heat. Somewhere easy to defend. It's got its own fresh water and a food supply. Close to the sea. We can share it. There's enough—"

Flappy-mouth monument-man nervously finds his voice, "Karl, perhaps it's worth a look. Maybe it's time to settle down. Besides, he's. *She's* a woman. Please."

Interesting. He sounds like a younger version of Kobe. Whiney.

Weak. Stupid. Led by his dick. Easily manipulated.

My kind of guy.

"Shut the fuck up, Geoff. You can get it over with and fuck her, if you want; get it out of your system. I'm not bothered. Then we can eat her anyway. Look at her, she's a withered old crone—"

"The recent hot weather has not been altogether kind to my skin, I have to admit."

"—but we are not, and I want to make this perfectly fucking clear, going to be shacking-up in a cosy, little, seaside retreat threesome with her or anyone else. It's just the two of us. Got it? Shit."

I don't know whether to be angry at the rejection or panicked by his aggression, but, somehow, I have to seal the deal.

Appeal to their bellies?

"OK, OK! Look—Karl. Geoff. I can throw in my partner. He's *really* old. Past his prime. Useless really. But there's some flesh left on him. He's yours. Sauté him, boil him up, grill him. I don't give a fuck. Just don't kill *me*."

I'll have to sort this out later, with Kobe. When this has all blown over there'll be hell to pay.

"Oh, nice. Throwing in your man. Way to go!" Karl sneers. "OK. Let's take a look. What have we got to lose?"

The sun is rising as I slip back into my robes and pull the face coverings back over my head, whilst struggling to keep the recovered knife out of sight. As I hastily shove it up my right sleeve to secrete it in the voluminous folds, the blade draws a deep welt on my forearm. I flinch, but manage to stay silent within my cowl.

This isn't really going to plan at all. I'd hoped to get the drop on *them*—despatch them before they got a chance to defend themselves.

From behind, Karl shoves me roughly on the shoulder, and we set off to find Kobe, *my* sacrificial gift to them.

Still, Geoff seems nice.

I walk between them: Geoff on my left, Karl on my right. Occasionally, I feel Geoff's hand brush mine.

Christ, is he trying to hold my hand?

Does he think this is some kind of date?

I allow my hand to peek out of the robe sleeve, and return

the compliment with my gloveless fingertips. He curls two digits around my little finger—a small child holding their mother's hand. Like I once did...

I brush the hood back from my face a little and smile lovingly at him from beneath my rag veil. *Yes, Geoff. Yes, I can be your mum. Or your lover. Or both, if you want me to be.*

I will my thoughts into his head before turning a steelier gaze on Karl, who remains blissfully unaware of the flirtation going on next to him.

It doesn't take long to get back to the cave.

I call out as I cross the threshold, "Kobe. Kobeeee? We've got visitors. Where are you?" Karl leans on his spear beside me. Geoff is skulking around the back of me, bow in hand, nervously pacing up and down.

My words echo back at us, but there is no answer. "Perhaps he's gone to the well. It's deep inside, through some tunnels. Or else he's still asleep on the sofa."

Karl doesn't look like he believes me. "Better go inside then," he says, stepping forward, spear thrust out in front, prodding me onward. As the sun ascends behind us, I reset the mirrors to light our way in the dark.

I drop my hood and cast my mask to the floor.

It's time to stop the deception, to reveal the truth. Even to myself.

Reaching the inner cave, I point at the sofa in the corner. Kobe is there, supine in the deep shadows, where he's been all along.

Karl strides forward, ready to turn poor Kobe into a human kebab, but stops short as the reflected rays of the rising sun catch up with us, illuminating Kobe's rictus grin.

"What the hell?"

Seizing the moment, I yell wildly and leap at Karl, bowie knife raised high to slash downwards across his back. But, in my haste, I slip on the treacherously slick chalk, lose my footing and crash noisily to the ground. Dropping the blade, it skitters into the dark, out of reach.

I try to regain my feet, but get only halfway before Karl turns his attention on me. He looms over me, a murderous look on his face as he wields the spear. "Double-crossing bitch!"

In desperation, I throw my hand up to protect myself from his thrust.

Then, the air between us is sliced apart as I feel the shaft of an arrow glance off my shoulder. Geoff must have taken a wild shot at me.

Dropping back down and retreating into a foetal ball on the floor, I wrap my arms around my head and brace myself to face death.

But, the seconds slip by and death does not come.

Peeking out from behind my fleshy barricade, I see a hand reaching down to grasp my forearm. Awkwardly, I push myself off the floor as Geoff pulls me up.

Karl lays, looking back at me in vacant disbelief, an arrow through his neck, his body pinning poor Kobe down on the sofa.

Poor, long-dead Kobe.

For the first time in a long while, I can see the rotten flecks of flesh that still cling to the knife-scarred skeleton where I have carved the meat from his bones; his skull crushed from the flint I used to brain him. Kobe's only good for soup, now.

Out of the dead man's bony grasp, a faded menu photo of a plate of ham, egg and chips wafts to the floor. It settles amongst the carpet of marrow-sucked bones, next to the bright red Victorinox knife I'd used to excavate them.

Geoff picks up the laminated sheet and stares at it. His eyes dart from Kobe, to Karl, to me and back to Karl before welling up in tears. "Oh, shit, shit, shit. What have I done?" Wailing, he throws himself on top of Karl and hugs his lifeless body.

"Nothing you shouldn't have, my love. Now, come on. Let's get this mess cleared up, and dinner put on. Waste not, want not. There's a good boy."

Three weeks later and I don't know what I would do without lovely Geoff. I think I'd go mad without him to talk to, even if he is a bit whiney. Still, there's plenty of flesh on those bones, when the time comes.

SARAH TOWNEND

The Beauty Parlour

As Skip pulled the last steel whisker out and through the final cheek-pad hole of her face, Rhea yelped. Sixteen bores had been pierced either side of her philtrum, through each of which a short length of fishing wire protruded. It had stung a little, but her quest for beauty was never painless. Skip knew how it felt. He'd given himself facial fur using a similar technique when he had transitioned to kangaroo.

Rhea stood and surveyed herself in the salvaged Baroque mirror which hung on the far wall of the beauty parlour. The mirror, seized most likely from one of the museum raids which had taken place long before the Dust had got so bad, shouted back a reflection of pure beauty. Morphed from kitten to lioness in a little under three hours, Rhea's new form was nearly complete. She was a riot of fur and tail and paws, the cat who had got the cream. After thrumming out a purr and stroking her thread-whiskers, she sat back down, placed her hands on the table, palm side down, and tilted her head at Skip.

"Claws next," she said, her aquamarine cat's-eye contacts almost glowing with feline demand.

Skip nodded. He was tired, but he knew this customer was worth the effort for not only did she pay well, but she was also the hostess of the Unmasked Ball, and she'd promised to reward him with a ticket in exchange for a successful cross-species transformation. Skip was the best beautician in the district and Rhea was the most influential—and also the most demanding—of the Beauties.

"How long are we going this week, with the nails?" he asked, proffering a display wheel of mounted acrylic and natural keratin talons which ranged from guitar pick to nightmarishly Kruegeresque in their sharpness and in their length. Rhea took the samples in her hands and ran her finger along each blade-like claw—firmly enough to leave a linear indentation on the skin of her finger pad, but not firmly enough to draw blood.

"Oh, let's stick with two inches. I'm not brave enough to go longer," she replied. "I love the way they would look, but it's impossible to wash my face without injuring myself. You know, I'd slice open a cheek—or worse."

"I understand. I rarely went longer than a half inch myself when I was feline. It wasn't practical. I kept scratching solar units, which made them totally inefficient," said Linux, a second customer, an energy engineer, a friend of Rhea's.

"Yes, I can imagine," Rhea replied, despite not having a clue about the ins or outs of photovoltaic energy or biodome construction. She had gotten this far on looks alone.

Linux flashed his finger stumps at his friend. "Now that I identify as Philippine Cobra, I've done away with talons completely. I'm thinking about a semi-permanent finger binding next. Clump them all together with bone staples so I can strap my arms down against my torso and be done with upper limbs altogether—just for the ball, just for one evening." He stood and lifted his T-shirt to reveal a taut stomach, shelled in overlapping black scales. "One hundred percent snake, well, ten percent waterproof adhesive and reptile leather."

"You'll have to go over to Millia's for binding or webbing," said Skip as he filed and prepped Rhea's nail beds. "We don't do anything that requires anaesthetic here."

"Oh, I know. She did my neck hood, and a fabulous job she did too," said Linux, cupping his hands behind the yellow and black skin wings which stretched from his shoulders to his ears, fanning out either side of his neck.

"I can see the appeal of going reptilian. Julian from dome thirteen has gone iguana and the scale work the tattooist has done down his back is to die for," said Rhea.

Linux flicked out his forked tongue and reached for Skip's

portfolio of his influencer sketches and of drawings of his most recent work. Once Skip had finished Rhea's claws, Linux was going to enquire about non-surgical options to enhance his dentition. He had wanted all but his canines cracked and pulled and then all four remaining canines built up with loaded faux-venom chambers, ready to spray on compression, but he knew tooth removal was a permanent modification and might limit future transitions. He knew he'd like to be a large mammal of some sort again in the not too distant future—perhaps a polar bear or one of the other Arctic creatures who were some of the first to go—so he wasn't quite ready to give up his bite altogether yet.

Linux looked with admiration and great sadness at the display of images, at all of the hundreds of torn magazine and book pictures and drawings of creatures which decorated Skip's beauty parlour walls. All bar the hardy brown anoles, the cockroaches, the locusts, and a few resilient fish species had been lost since the Great Dust came many years ago. There were thousands of extinct species to choose from, to become, to impersonate, yet so few still alive. All that was left of life was survival and art, but he knew at twenty-three that he only had a short time left until his lungs succumbed to the force of pollution. Not a soul lived to see the other side of thirty. He already felt the crackle and tightness in his chest on exertion, which they all knew was the beginning of the end.

Most of the human survivors had been forced underground, partially due to the thick Dust which whipped up into ad hoc towering, erosive tornados, destroying everything organic in their wake, partially due to the particulate matter too small to see or feel but just the right size to cause almost instant emphysema, and partially due to the power of the new Elite.

When the Dust came, the capitalist society which had reigned eternal toppled like a stack of cards. Overnight, bankers, bitcoin trust-fund kids and sport stars became worthless, fame and money lost value instantaneously, and the new Elite formed. The new Elite consisted of Those That Could: solar panel technicians and bottled gas suppliers, weapon hoarders and hydroponic scientists, engineers, farmers, and the Beautiful. Those That Could rose upward.

As the value of all commodities and all abilities rocked and shuffled over the years that followed the beginning of the Great Dust, so did what the Elite considered to be beautiful. Reptiles, amphibians and mammals all dropped from existence in a matter of months, animal carcasses littered deserted roadsides until scavenged, and scavengers lasted only a little longer, but soon, all who existed under the natural sky became blighted by the perilous toxic dusts. The air held a dryness like no other as the humans kicked Mother Earth into premature menopause; Earth's wildlife, Earth's fruits became desiccated, powdered like trampled sandcastles. The biota of the planet was decimated ten-fold and ten-fold again.

Those That Could built glass-roofed ecosystems with clever ventilation, air purification and toxin extraction methods, and Those That Could survived. And Those That Could, formed allegiances with Those That Had Weapons, and Those That Could and Those That Had Weapons took in Those That Were Beautiful. The Beautiful traded in the Oldest Profession, and together, they formed the Elite.

And the Elite separated from Those That Just Survive.

Beauty had in the past been the slim, symmetrical face of youth and muscle, and those genes still remained, however a quest to become—or to at least imitate—what had been lost evolved. Beauty parlours cropped up in between the glass domes and the Elite and the Beautiful travelled bravely from their places of safety—where the air was breathable and the water was pure—to the parlours for their modifications, to become animal, to decorate themselves with relics of organisms lost and only now present in posters and books and paintings and myth.

"Excuse me Skip, I need a comfort break," said Rhea, standing and swishing her leonine tail behind her. The tail, a gift from a taxidermist in exchange for tickets, had been anchored into her behind, into the ligaments of her sacroiliac joint, under lidocaine injection. "It's such a palaver taking this suit off to use the bathroom."

"Sure. I could use a drink gel anyhow," replied Skip, wiping sweat from his brow. "You know, we sell beta-carotene supplements—take a high enough dose and your skin will yellow all over from within.

You could give the skin suit the old heave ho." She peeled down her lioness cloak until it sat, an emptied sack, on the floor. Made from 'donations' from Those That Just Survive, it was not only buff yellow, but also soft and downy, and unbelievably pelt-like.

Those That Just Survive were a collective of hardy families who were not Beautiful and who were not Those That Could. They'd fled straight underground when the Dust came. They were the underworld, they were redundant. They had nothing to offer bar their own tissues. They bred like rabbits and bartered with the flesh of their own weak in exchange for foodstuffs and pure water. The Survivors, with their average and below average appearances, and their simple fashions, would never be allowed to attend the Unmasked Ball. And they had no gas masks with which to travel through the Dust in to reach it anyhow. They were trapped in their caves. But their skin was young and supple and Those That Died were peeled and broken apart like scrap heap cars, and those spare parts were offered up to the Beautiful Elite for their costumes and their modifications and their surgeries. In this process of desperate up-cycling, the Elite and the Beautiful worked hard to bring about the look of the rarest animals and the look of the animals long since lost to the Dust.

The skin, hair and nails of the Survivors were all good—all good for bargaining with—as they were all young. No one lived beyond thirty in this time. The Dust, the radiation, the tropical illnesses that spread like wildfire as the planet warmed, and the wildfire and the dust that spread like the tropical illnesses: all of these things kept anyone from reaching death due to age. Time rarely killed the Survivors or the Beautiful or Those That Could. Old age was as much a distant memory as the dragonflies and the snow leopards and the orang-utans and the pangolins.

"Good idea. Add some to my list, wouldn't you be a darling?" Rhea shimmied to the bathroom and on her return, her talons were fitted and she paid Skip in tickets. Skip thanked her profusely and his tapered pseudo-ears, brown and soft, flapped as he did so.

Rhea and Linux donned their protective suits—yet a further

layer of costume, this one essential when taking on the Dust and solar glare—and pulled their gas mask helmets onto their heads. Skip poked Rhea's whiskers under and in, ensuring not to bend them in the process as the pair got ready to leave.

"The Dust is bad today," said Skip, tucking the tickets into his kangaroo pouch. "Make for home with haste."

"We shall," Rhea replied, voice muffled through inches of filter and tubing. "See you at the ball on the morrow."

The Unmasked Ball came and went. Five hundred Elite from the network of biodome cities met and celebrated and compared their transitions and their costumes.

Each month that the Ball took place, Those That Could tried to outdo each other with their extreme modifications. Ivory elephant tusks taken from a museum long ago were surgically affixed to a young man's upper lip. Brightly coloured toucan bills fashioned from acrylics and resins were welded to the exposed, sanded jaw bone of another. Plumes of feathers mounted to sockets drilled into the soft tissues of a lady's back created a bird of paradise. One young reveller, both his legs bound together and smashed to smithereens, like crushed packets of crisps beneath unbroken skin, tarnished himself with grey body paint; an eel he became.

Each month, the competition grew for most modified and most dramatic transition. Slashes to cheek and neck were made and stitched and healed as a Beauty re-identified as an axolotl. Survivors' teeth were mounted on steel hinges and fastened to foreheads: and so, a megalodon attended the Unmasked Ball.

One half-orbit of the planet about the sun later, the Dust had thickened. The Dust became more corrosive than it had ever been and Earth cried tears of acid and grit.

Rhea barged through the safety lock, pushed open the second door and marched into Skip's beauty parlour. Many of her friends were getting prepared for the final ball of the year, the Christmask Ball, the annual pinnacle of the Elite calendar. Those attending would no doubt pull out all stops to come in their most revered, most outrageous and most fanciful attire to bring in the end of the year.

"Skip, darling. You simply must see what I have in my bag. I have a look I want... I *need* you to help me attain. It will be worth five tickets—no—I will give you ten tickets. Bring all of your parlour friends along; Christ—bring Survivors! I care not who you bring if you will only help me achieve this look."

In the parlour room, which stank of epoxy resin and burnt flesh, all the customers turned to look at the Hostess and what she was presenting. "I have found the rarest of images. The most rare of all creatures. You will not believe this when you cast your young marsupial glare upon it, Skip. No one will beat this. All eyes will be on me, as they should."

She pulled out a folded sheet from her bag, unfolded it, and thrust it forward into the audience.

"There. Isn't it a thing of beauty? What will it take to make me, this. Say you can do it for me, Skip."

Skip's brows rose like banners above his brown eyes. He had never seen anything like it before.

"What is it? What are they meant to be?" He could tell it was something like a human, for it had a face, and all the parts of the face were where they should be, if somewhat compressed and clouded with sagging skin; it had elements of Shar-Pei dog, folds of horseshoe bat, facial hair of a piglet. Hair sat on the top of its head like that of a sheep—white, yet wispy, like smoke.

"It's...it's some kind of mammal, humanoid, I'd say, but most peculiar," he replied, his chin cupped in his hand, his thumb and forefinger poking at the corners of his mouth, his brow now screwed, lost in thought and consideration.

"Can you do it? To me? Do you think you can?" asked Rhea, keen as mustard.

"Where did you find this photograph?" he asked.

"My guard ransacked the Survivors who live to the east of the Apricot Desert," she replied.

Pulling up a chair, she reached for the myriad tray of hair weave samples, searching for something to match the greyness of the image.

"Held them up at gunpoint, demanded they fill his sack with keepsakes; something for us to look through of a dull, dusty evening.

I'd instructed him to go out and forage for inspiration, and this is what he came back with."

Linux hissed from the corner, "It's an old person, Rhea. A 'geriatric'. Long before the Dust came and the planet could breathe—and we could breathe outside without our masks—in the great Apricot Desert, people lived double, treble what we live now. Rumour has it, some managed until they were one hundred. Can you believe it?"

"That's what I thought," said Rhea, cheeks flushed with excitement. "I've never seen one in such detail before. Look how the eyes nearly slide under drooped lids, see how there is the same white, wiry hair as on the top of the head sprouting like clouds of dust from the ears and the nostrils. Isn't it marvellous? Do say you can do this to me, Skip."

Skip took the photo from her hand and brought it close to his face. The crowd waited, breath baited, for his answer.

"I'll have a go," he replied, fumbling through his drawers of accessories, piercing tools, glues, searching his refrigerator for sheets of fresh-primed skin ready for grafting, sterilised needles for stitching, tattoo inks for blemishing and marking and pocking and furrowing. "I'll do my best."

He stripped back her yellow make-up, pulled off her lash extensions and unthreaded her steel whiskers. He scrubbed near raw her yellowed hands and dissolved the bonding chemicals anchoring claws to her nail beds. He worked, folding, cutting, charring and stitching, to try to recreate the look of time and age that she'd presented as the other customers sat and watched Skip with wonder, surrounded by his constellation of tools and materials.

As Skip reached completion, the spectators erupted a volcanic fever of applause, the ash of which resonated in Rhea's eardrums, an opiate snare. Skip swivelled her chair around for all to see his creation.

She looked ancient.

Skin folded over on skin, some prosthetic, some her own, some borrowed, her face corrugated and creased akin to a brain coral. Her hair stood curly and white like the Dusts laced with sharp ice crystals that came in the winter. Her hands, now covered in brown liver spots looked better than anything Skip had ever achieved before when transitioning customers to leopard or Dalmatian or Friesian cow. Rhea looked marvellous: a thing of time and of many winters witnessed, an epoch of generations collected.

As she stood to examine herself in the full-length mirror, she gasped. Never before had she looked so rare.

"I wish the ball was tonight, I don't know how I'm going to contain myself for twenty-four further hours," she said, hugging him tightly, placing a ream of golden tickets into the palm of his furry hand.

Skip, swollen with pride, blushed and thanked her for allowing him to work on the canvas she had provided him with. He helped her back into her safety suit and slid carefully her gas mask, all tubes and filters and inches of Perspex and glass, back over her newly old skull.

"Journey safe, home with haste, my most precious piece," he said as he opened the air lock for her, the audience clapping majestically as she left.

Outside, the Dust was spinning, a zoetrope of grit and particulate pollution. The air was custard-thick as she set off on the treacherous journey back to her biodome.

Plodding onward, full of glee and following the route her feet knew by heart even in the blinding desert smog, she could just about make out the wall of hexagonal panels in the distance which she would need to enter.

The guard which stood up on the balcony did not seem to be present. *How odd,* she thought, *that the Dust is so thick, it obscures the guard.* Was the guard lying down up there, snoozing in his safety suit, under the protection of his gas mask helmet...whilst on duty? She would certainly be having words with security about staff taking absence without leave, napping on paid time. Rhea placed one foot in front of the other and bee-lined toward the port under the familiar hexagonal structure. She needed to parade impetuously her most magnificent transformation from lioness to 'elder' in front of her community before dealing with lollygagging guards.

Out of nowhere through the thick of the evening, a hard clunk to her head came. A Survivor with a club of sorts, manufactured from layers of swathes of wound and bound leathered skins, took a strike, knocking Rhea out cold on first attempt. The Feral tucked his baton into a crudely fashioned belt pocket, knelt over his prey and tugged and tugged and unscrewed and unhooked the connectors on Rhea's gas mask and ripped the device off and away from her head before placing it into his sack. Grabbing next her boots and the trouser cuffs of her outer suit, he lifted and tipped the young old girl upside down. The suit peeled away from her lifeless body, and out of it she slid, paste from the tube, onto the white-hot sands of the desert. Rolling up and bagging the costly protective gear, he grinned a smile that only the Dust would see; this one would be his best find yet.

His own appearance, worthless by all current standards, had taken a battering an hour before as he had stepped outside of the Survivor's cave to take on the guard that had returned for a second time. The guard had returned after an earlier theft of skins and nails and photograph albums to request that further sacks be filled with knick-knacks, entertainment for the Elite. The Survivor had snapped and had taken a swipe with his club, knocking the guard to the floor. His average face had taken a chemical peeling from the acidic reflux spit-up of the desert and his lungs had pulled sharply upwards and inwards, as scorched toes in the bath do, at the heat of the Dust they'd inhaled.

But it had been worth it, as with one swift blow of the club he had fashioned from remnants of human fabrics, he had taken down the guard. The guard had then provided him with a gas mask which he had donned and used to venture out and into the Dust and out toward the second guard who was manning the nearby biodome. Then, the Survivor was blessed with winning a third gas mask and Dust suit even less rudimentary than the other two.

The feral Survivor ripped out the purse of coins and tickets from the Beauty's bag and stormed off into the Dust, to his cave, to share news and findings, to launch the next round of attack—that night, the Survivors would snowball the Elite. Three masks would become six, twelve, twenty-four, and the Christmask Ball would become theirs.

And the young old girl's hair blew in the wind as the dust whipped up, a writhing vertical snake of sand and grit, a maelstrom of particulate smog. Her hair spread out and into the Dust and melted like licked candyfloss. The layers of skin that were hers and layers of skin that were not hers un-bandaged, melted, dribbled and blew away, and were carried off into the air with the cosmic grime.

The dust and the sand blasted against her cheeks and her nose caved in, a fallen pyramid, releasing her un-mummified ghost to the ether. The vile force of ruined nature, acidic and potent, lifted off the cartilage and sinew and tendons and fat that lay underneath her skin. Up, up, and away it all went, dissolving into the Dust. The weather took years from the girl's face, tens and tens of years, until her skull was all that remained of her head.

Fatty brain corroded, liquefied into sludge, and slid out through her ear canals. Neurone rivulets vanished on contact with the hurricane of pollution that chipped and gnashed and bit at her remnants. On her neck, solar lasers breaking through the Dust burned and teased away young and old and young again skin, layer after layer, until a passing locust swarm moved in to tidy away what the weather had yet to claim.

Her body—all accelerated and modified tissues and trims, all falsely aged arms and legs and torso—followed suit, layer after layer rubbed clean.

Bones and titanium piercings were all that remained of her on the floor of the Apricot Desert as the Dust settled, satisfied, well fed. Never before had she looked so rare.

DAN VANVIK

The Enemy Next Door

"You're not going to say anything to him, right?" Marcie asked her husband. She was sitting at her stool at the black granite kitchen island, Sunday paper spread out in front of her. Pen in hand, she was halfway through the Sudoku puzzle, her Sunday ritual.

Her husband was standing at the condo door, down the short hall from the kitchen, one eye peering into the peeper. No reply. He simply reached behind his back and vigorously waved her off.

She persisted, "Please, John, don't start trouble with the neighbors."

Again, no reply. She flipped up her middle finger to the general direction of his backside and resumed her puzzle, sipping coffee from a chipped and faded mug that read 'Teacher of the Year'. She introduced this unseen one finger salute about a month into the pandemic, nine months ago now. *The Bird* somehow served to assuage her anger and she regretted not using it in the earlier decades of their marriage. It might have helped to avoid petty bickering.

John finally turned back from the door and began his usual grumbling about their condo neighbor, "Damn! I missed him again! Since the mask mandate, he's apparently been skulking around like a cat burglar, even closes the door more quietly. I'm having a hell of a time catching him maskless—even when I sprint to the peeper."

"C'mon John," Marcie said. "The email from the association said masks are a 'recommendation'. You're getting all riled up about nothing."

"Nothing? Look, an unmasked face is like an unholstered gun, a threat to us as well as the rest of the people in the building. Keep in mind the infectiousness, who knows how many people his political beliefs are putting at risk?"

She agreed with most of John's rantings but didn't tell him outright, fearing he might take it as an endorsement and actually act on one of his threats. Instead, she pushed back a bit.

"Political beliefs? You're just guessing. Maybe he can't wear a mask because of a preexisting condition."

"I doubt it. He looks to be in pretty good condition, I'd say early fifties, and if he has a condition, it's either a bad case of machismo or runaway Trumpism. Either way, anti-maskers and virus deniers are sick fucks and if they get Covid they should either get their health insurance premiums doubled or lose their citizenship because they don't give a fuck about their fellow citizens."

John's use of F-bombs—not a common occurrence—put her on red alert and she stopped sipping her coffee and placed it back on the countertop too quickly, slopping a bit on her paper in the process. His unsettling anger was scrambling up the same steep slope as the soaring death toll.

"That's crazy talk, John," she said. "Whatever happened to the mild-mannered man I married? Please, let's not get on bad terms with the neighbors. They've been here just a few months and they're pleasant enough when I see them in the lobby."

"I'm going to talk to him," he said, as he turned to walk back to the condo door. "He can run, but he can't hide."

She looked him over as he turned away, wearing his 24/7 uniform of grey University of Minnesota sweatshirt over red plaid flannel pajama bottoms. White tennis, unlaced. Matted grey bed hair. Once a week he had what he called a 'spa day', when he showered, shaved his stubble and changed to his other quarantine uniform—the blue flannel pajama.

"Are you going like that?" she asked. "Maybe you can at least put on a pair of jeans?"

"Why?" he said. "I've got underwear on. It's not like I'm going commando here."

"Crude, John. At least don't forget your mask."

He gave her a look, but pulled an N95 mask out a of pocket. "If I contract Covid," he said, as he put it on, "I'm taking our unneighborly neighbor down with me."

She spoke, more firmly now: "So, you've tried the anonymous note on their door and glaring at him in the hallway, and now you're giving up on the civilized approach?" She folded the paper over the sudoku, her peaceful ritual violated.

He gave her a look but opened the door without answering and let it slam behind him as he stepped out into the hallway.

She flipped him off again. Soon she heard John's knock on the neighbor's door followed by unintelligible voices.

She turned back to concentrate on the puzzle, but her thoughts soon drifted into recalling the months in lockdown. The minor thrill of pandemic perks like scant traffic and abundant parking spaces in the city, had waned early on. To break the monotony, Marcie planned 'contactless' day trips to Minnesota state parks and wooded hikes around scenic towns along the St. Croix River. She also tried the smaller pleasures more frequently, like candles at dinner or flowers delivered from Trader Joe's.

As high school teachers—he math, she biology—they only considered the guidelines of science and medicine, not the buffoons, not the conspiracists, and they frequently reminded themselves that their circumstances were less dire and more comfortable than most of the world.

The guidelines were necessary, but irksome, particularly when they visited their daughter. Hugs were prohibited. Their daughter banished them to a corner of the backyard, safe-distancing in matching lawn chairs, mere grandparent yard ornaments, barely acknowledged by the grandkids playing at least six feet away at all times. Their son quickly followed suit, suggesting they use the same protocol when they visited him.

When Minnesota's weather prohibited lawn visits, they grudgingly settled in to Zooming with family and friends and hunkering down with books and Netflix.

As the epidemic dragged on, Marcie was surprised to realize she was faring much better than John. He became more taciturn and, when he did speak, he was quicker to anger, especially when he yelled at the news clips of the president peddling falsehoods about the pandemic or making dangerous comments about ingesting Clorox or comparing Covid to 'a bad flu'.

Marcie finally returned to the sudoku but, unable to focus, soon gave it up and turned back to the front page of the paper and the overwhelmingly bad news she was trying to avoid—Covid, racial unrest and the uptick in shootings and general violence in Minneapolis. After reading a couple of pages of negative headlines, she fell back to worrying about her husband. As the long months passed—death toll ticking up relentlessly—his dark eyes had grown dull, the quote mark frown between them deepening. Seemed to her that he was either angry and in a very dark place, or he was listless, a sail without a wind, a face without a smile, a chin without a shave.

She felt his anger stemmed from the huge scope of the pandemic and the fact that he couldn't directly help his family to escape the virus. He simply couldn't get his arms around the problem—too many versions of the truth, too many people disputing the facts. He was accustomed to the absolute truths of discrete, tidy problems and there were none to be found in the politics of the pandemic. Too many people were listening to fake news, like that spewed by the talking heads at a particular network who all agreed that the coronavirus was 'nothing more than a bad cold or flu, nothing to worry about'.

John needed a specific target to vent his anger, not the politicians in Washington DC, and not the intangible virus itself, spread through invisible respiratory droplets by the unwitting to the unwitting. He eventually was able to parse the problem down to the anti-maskers and, more specifically, the convenient target living right next door.

When she heard the key in the lock, Marcie snapped out of her musings and looked up as John entered. He closed the door quietly behind him, and began moving down the condo's entryway, shoulders slumped, mouth slightly agape, and pallid as she'd ever seen him.

"So, what happened?" she asked.

"Dead."

"Dead!" she said. "What did you do?"

"Hold your horses. I did nothing. Covid killed him."

"But what happened," she said. "You talk to his wife?"

"Yeah. So, his wife's crying when she opens the door, tears soaking her mask, and there's a couple of bouquets of flowers on the countertop in back of her, so I figure right away that he's sick or dead, so I ask how he's doing—in that sort of concerned way—and she says, 'He died of Covid two days ago.'"

"My God, what did you say to her?"

"I said what people always say, 'I'm sorry, my thoughts are with you...et cetera.'"

She gave him a long look.

"Seriously," he said. "I felt sorry for her."

Marcie nodded her head for a moment without changing her expression and asked: "But how do you feel about him? And please don't say anything about 'just rewards.'"

"I have to think about that for a bit," he said quietly, moving past her toward the study.

Death seemed to have mollified him, as it often does, to the enemies left behind.

She returned to her sudoku still shocked. But also relieved, and hopeful that the neighbor's death might mark John's first steps back to his pre-pandemic self.

She decided against flipping the bird.

Area 37

1

"Dr Bok?" Scudamore stared at the yellow smiley face that filled his laptop screen. "Dr Januarius Bok?"

"This is he."

The scratchy, high-pitched reply somehow matched the grinning icon. Scudamore paused, and wondered again at the wisdom of contacting this—well, whatever this individual claimed to be. But what option did he have? "I'm not a fan of avatars, Dr Bok."

"Do you suffer from visiosubrideophobia?"

"Suffer what?"

"Have you a phobia of smiling faces? Or perhaps of emojis in general?"

Scudamore thought it better to withhold the fact that smiley faces, along with those of clowns and ventriloquist dummies, all creeped him out. "Consider it practicality not phobia. I prefer to look people in the eye, see who I'm dealing with."

"But we have no deal. Indeed, I have no idea with whom I converse."

Scudamore gave his name. "My colleagues speak highly of your gifts. They tell me your advice has led to convictions."

Silence. Scudamore stared at the banana-coloured image on the screen. "Are you there, Dr Bok?"

"Yes."

Scudamore inhaled diaphragmatically, as the mindfulness

quacks had told him to do at the first sign of anger. "I should like to consult with you on a case."

"If your profession is that of police officer then let me save us both some time. I have no interest in affray, assault, arson. Retail theft, robbery, and racketeering do not—to use a barbarism—float my boat. I will never..."

"I'm not police." Tempt the weirdo, Scudamore's colleagues had told him, like using maggots to lure a carp. "I'm Head of Risk at a government research agency. And I'm up against a locked room mystery. A puzzle that puts the security of our nation at stake." Was it his imagination, or did the smiley face twitch? Scudamore pressed on. "The case will prove difficult even for you, Januarius Bok. The law restricts what I can tell you."

"Restrictions spur creativity," Bok replied airily.

"Well that's... dandy," Scudamore said. "Look, I'm authorised to offer a reward. The money could run to six figures."

"I decide upon my fee after the successful completion of an assignment," Bok said. "A warning: I place a high value on my time. But you intrigue me, George Scudamore, so I offer my service. Send me an outline of your puzzle. Focus on the main points of interest."

The smiley face collapsed into a blob of pixels.

Scudamore slammed the laptop shut. He had wasted valuable investigation time on a charlatan. A ridiculous, pompous, blathering charlatan. Tomorrow he would re-interrogate witnesses, reanalyse the system logs, reconsider the forensic evidence. He inhaled, deeply, and tried to concentrate on the exhalation. But his mind returned to the mystery, like a tongue to a hole in a tooth. He prodded and poked at it, but the problem remained. The events baffled him. He needed fresh thinking. Even a charlatan such as Bok might provide some insight. Scudamore opened his laptop and began to type.

2

Two days ago, someone punched a hole through our security protocols. I need to know who made the hole and how they did it.

Scudamore lifted his fingers from the keyboard and considered how much information he could share with Bok.

The agency contains an Institute, Area 37, which carries out its work in a three-storey building situated in the middle of the back end of nowhere. CCTV cameras outside the building cover every brick, every window, every access road. The building has a single entrance, which requires the successful completion of biometric checks before it opens. The door time stamps all activity. We know who entered and left the building, and we know when they did so. The tech gurus confirm that our systems remain unhacked. The logs don't lie.

As he typed, a familiar feeling descended. Despair. The crime, though impossible, had happened. Unless someone was playing a practical joke? No, a prank made even less sense than a crime. He pulled the notebook from his jacket, even though the details it held were fresh in his mind.

The day before yesterday, four people worked in Area 37. Rebecca Tipstaff, personal assistant to Charles Melchior, the Institute director, entered at 7.30 a.m. Nine minutes later she was joined by—let's call him N. He works as a neuropsychologist. You don't need the details. Twelve minutes after that a biologist—let's call him B—entered the building. The fourth person, a chemist—he's C—arrived at 8.01 a.m. Tipstaff left the building at 11.53 a.m. and returned at 12.17 p.m. At 12.20 p.m. she called me from the phone on Melchior's desk and said an intruder had been in the director's office. I entered Area 37 at 12.24 p.m. The CCTV cameras, the biometric door system, and the phone records all agree with that chronology—and with the accounts of the five people involved: B, C, N, Tipstaff, and me.

Scudamore replayed the scene in his imagination.

Tipstaff seemed agitated. Confused, I think, more than upset. She'd returned from the canteen to see a man standing by the director's desk. When he saw her, he left. She checked the office then ran out to confront him. The intruder had gone. We have no cameras inside the building, so we don't know where he hid. Fingerprints, fibre analysis, DNA ... forensics examined the room and found nothing unusual.

As you can see, Bok, I have a locked room mystery on my hands. More precisely, a locked building mystery. If the intruder can penetrate Area 37 then he can enter any building in the country. None of our labs is safe.

Scudamore's finger hovered over the send button. He felt the same shame as that time in Missing Persons, when he'd asked the spirit world to help find a body. Januarius Bok was a bigger fraud than that medium. But what were his options? He pressed send.

3

"Tell me about the three scientists." The smiley face appeared unbidden on Scudamore's desktop. Bok's thin voice echoed off the walls and out into the corridor.

Scudamore closed his office door. "How did you get this number? It's restricted."

"We can discuss your security, or lack thereof, at some later time. For now, I need more information."

"Lack of security? No, we'll talk about that now." He hadn't had a chance to grab his morning caffeine boost but, despite himself, Scudamore felt a growing excitement. "You found a bug? A fault that permits unauthorised entry?"

"Your systems, as far as they go, are robust. No, you presented me with an accurate chronology: Tipstaff, B, C, and N—tinker, tailor, as it were—entered the building at the times you stated. No one else entered until you arrived."

"So who did Tipstaff see? A ghost?"

"I have no need for such an hypothesis." Bok sniffed. "Concentrate on the corporeal. Four bodies had access to the office."

"Did you read my account? Tipstaff saw the intruder. He was not one of the scientists."

"If she saw him then you must have a description of the trespasser?"

Scudamore paused. "I find this conversation difficult. Please, Dr Bok, turn on your camera."

"No. Continue with Ms Tipstaff's description of the man she saw."

Scudamore swore, not caring whether his absurdly named interlocutor heard. In interrogations, *he* dictated the pace of conversation. How could he do that when talking to an avatar? He massaged his temples, another of those tips the wellbeing wheeler-dealers told him to practise. Fine for them to hand out advice. They didn't have to deal with Januarius Bok. "The description lacks precision," he said at last. "Medium-sized man, dark hair, wearing

Institute-issued coveralls. I can't hang a photofit on that."

"Fascinating," Bok said, strangling each of the syllables separately and in different ways. "Was anything stolen?"

Scudamore shrugged. "I can't rule it out."

"Hmm." Bok's voice whined out from the speakers like high-pitched interference. "Do you fear for your job?"

Good question. Scudamore considered. "In truth, no. If some punter can swan around Area 37 whenever he wants then I've identified a national security risk. I get a gong, the director gets the sack."

"Ah, the director. Where is Melchior?"

"Abroad. He doesn't deserve the kicking he'll get when I report the breach. He's a first-rate scientist, an outstanding administrator, a skilled political operator. And a good man. He takes care of his staff. I have to nail this before he returns tomorrow."

"In which case I suggest you contemplate what information you can provide regarding those three scientists. I have yet to break my fast. Expect my return call in two hours."

The smiley face shrank to a point.

4

The screen came back to life precisely two hours later. Scudamore looked up at a water stain on the ceiling, the result of a plumbing problem that the Estates department had resolved to the satisfaction of no one except those working in Estates. "Please understand, Dr Bok, that I am limited in what I can say."

"Yes, yes. Government secrets, hush hush. I grasp the nature of the constraints. Divulge what you can. Biologist, chemist, neuropsychologist. B, C, N. Tell me something about them."

"Three middle-aged white men," Scudamore said. "Our Head of Diversity has yet to make much impact."

"Start with B," Bok pressed. "Have you ever had reason to run a security check on him?"

"We check everyone." Scudamore considered whether to continue. Bok's line of questioning led nowhere. Then again, all other paths led nowhere. Might as well humour him for now. "B gambles. Plays slots to chase money to pay the debt he racked up playing slots. You're thinking motive, yes? That he plans to sell secrets to fund his addiction? Forget motive. We need to focus on whom Tipstaff saw in the director's office. It wasn't B, C, or N. Someone else got into Area 37."

"The Institute's name intrigues me. I assume Areas 1 to 36 do not exist. What, then, is its significance?"

"No idea," Scudamore said. "I believe the previous director proposed it. Before my time."

"Then let us return to B. His research is…?"

"Classified," Scudamore said at once. "A freedom of information request will tell you he researches the anthrax bacillus. True, as far as it goes. For you, it goes that far."

The speakers fell silent, but the smiley face still filled the screen so Scudamore waited.

"Let us move on," Bok said at length. "Suspect C?"

"He's not a suspect."

"Suspect C," Bok repeated. "What can you tell me of his work?"

"He investigates clean-up methods for nerve agent attacks. No money worries, little in the way of a home life, spends a lot of time in the lab. Loves his job. Devoted to it, to the point of workaholism. We have nothing on him, except he likes a drink."

"Which I take to mean he is a functioning alcoholic as well as workaholic. Does that not concern you?"

"The director ordered him to take a medical. I told you, Melchior looks after his staff."

"Perhaps C sees it differently," Bok said. "A medical examination imperils his job. He might seek information with which he could threaten the director, force Melchior to change his mind."

"Dr Bok, I repeat: our eyewitness rules out the chemist. And the biologist. And the neuropsychologist."

"Ah yes, N. Tell me about N."

"He's brighter than you," Scudamore said, savouring the taste of the words. He imagined the yellow smiley turning green. "N investigates super-identifiers. People who can recognise an individual amongst a crowd."

"I know what a super-identifier is," Bok snapped. "What else?"

"He founded the Institute."

"And then Melchior replaced N? Tell me why."

"I told you, before my time. A dispute over research direction, I believe."

"From what I know of researchers, N must hate Melchior. All three thus possess motive. B wants money. C wants to blackmail. N wants revenge."

"But none did it," Scudamore insisted.

"Do you have photographs of the three in their typical work garb?"

"I suppose." The conversation had started to bore Scudamore. He pulled up a database and shared three images. Three bland, bloodless, bespectacled men. Dark hair worn short; five-nine, five-ten in height; blue lab coats draped over white shirts.

"Three peas in a pod," Bok observed.

"Look at them," Scudamore bellowed. "Do you think Tipstaff couldn't identify one of her colleagues?"

"Tipstaff. I should like to talk to her. Your working day ends at five, correct? Arrange a meeting for then."

The face dissolved like the Cheshire Cat. Scudamore imagined the grin, persisting. He shoved the screen away and it toppled into the window. Fine. Estates could fix the crack while they fixed the damn leak in the ceiling.

5

A tangled spaghetti of wires bulged out of the flimsy partition wall that divided an unused storeroom into two poky interview rooms. Scudamore found an audio connection and jammed it into his laptop. Bok's whine began at once. "I presume you have ruled out the obvious solution?"

Scudamore separated the wires and tried, one after another, to connect to the room's video feed. He wanted Tipstaff to address her replies to him, the human in the room, and spare her the ordeal of staring at the rictus grin of Bok's yellow smiley face. On his fifth attempt the screen came to life. He set the laptop on the table. "The obvious solution?"

"Namely, that Ms Tipstaff herself bears culpability."

"Tipstaff?" Scudamore said. "Makes no sense. I'd be unaware of the break-in if she hadn't contacted me. Why bring about an investigation?"

"Spite, perhaps. Imagine, for example, Tipstaff and Melchior conducting an affaire de coeur. Imagine, furthermore, their office dalliance ending in rancour. If you are correct, and reports of an intruder could lead to Melchior's dismissal, then her entire story might be a concoction, the result of a lover's tiff. Hmm?"

Damn him! How did Bok know about the affair? "We have no reason to suppose Ms Tipstaff is dissatisfied with her relationships, professional or otherwise. Pick another tree up which to bark."

"As you wish," Bok said. "Let us not keep the good lady waiting."

If he ever got within punching distance of that man, Scudamore thought. But he opened the door and Tipstaff marched past him. "I have a train to catch," she muttered.

"This will not take long," Bok said. Scudamore turned down the volume on the speakers. "First, your relationship with Charles Melchior. How long has that persisted?"

Tipstaff exuded a sense of composure, serenity almost. Her blonde hair and long neck attracted immediate attention, but that soon gave way to an appreciation of the stillness in which she clothed herself.

"Are you asking how long I've worked for the director?" She levelled her question at Scudamore, seemingly unfazed at having to converse through an intermediary. Her voice carried the trace of a northern accent.

"No. I ask about your romantic entanglement. When did it begin?"

Scudamore squirmed as Tipstaff stared at him, her chin high. "I accompanied the director on a business trip to America the year before last."

"Do you recall details?" Bok pressed. "Do you remember the date?"

"October 10 to 15, if you insist. We stayed in a motel in Stowe." She smiled, a hint of colour in her flawless cheeks. "The trees were ablaze. The mountain air so clear you could see to eternity. We discovered we had feelings for each other."

"You were the personal assistant to the previous director, I believe."

"Yes." Tipstaff's hands, fingers intertwined, rested motionless in the folds of her tartan skirt.

"You had a personal relationship with the previous director too."

"I resent the insinuation." Tipstaff's voice remained level. "He asked me to dinner, once, and I accepted. At my request he made no such further offers. Do you understand, whoever you are?"

"In every respect," Bok replied. "Let us move on, then, to the break-in. At what time did it occur?"

"I don't know. I wasn't there. I left my desk between 11.50 and 11.55 to take a call in another room."

"I can confirm," Scudamore said. "The call came from our stationery supplier."

"I placed an order for toner cartridges," Tipstaff added. "You can check."

"Not necessary," Bok said. "Did you return directly to your office?"

"No. I went to the canteen, bought a ham sandwich, cherry yoghurt, and sparkling water. I returned to eat lunch at my desk but I didn't get there because I noticed the director's office door was ajar. I looked in and saw a stranger. The wall clock, directly behind his shoulder, showed 12.17 p.m. I asked him who he was, what he was doing there. He stared me in the eye then walked out into the corridor."

"Did he run?"

"No. He ambled, like he had no care in the world." Tipstaff frowned, as if puzzled at her own reply. "I dashed into the office to see whether he'd stolen anything. When I went to challenge him, he'd disappeared."

"I commend your remarkable memory," Bok said. "But you have a train to catch, Ms Tipstaff. Let me detain you no longer."

Tipstaff turned back to Scudamore. "Is that all?"

"Apparently so," Scudamore said. He closed the laptop. "I've had enough for one day too."

6

Scudamore ticked off time zones in his head as he pushed a bagel around his plate. Breakfast time here, so dead of night over there.

He'd hoped to avoid this, but he could no longer put it off. He ate his bagel then put through a video call. The webcam showed a small hotel room with magnolia walls and a single bed. "Boss? Sorry for disturbing you."

Melchior shook his head. "Rebecca told me. I return later today. Set up an appointment with the minister and take me straight to him. He needs to know."

"Agreed." Scudamore paused. "The safe. Did it hold anything that could cause embarrassment?"

Melchior tugged at his trimmed, grey beard and forced a smile. "Nothing that could embarrass the department. Personal embarrassment, perhaps."

Divorce papers, Scudamore thought. It wasn't only Bok who possessed powers of deduction. "Would you like me to hush this up?"

"I'll pretend you didn't say that. Just do your job. Have you made any progress? Rebecca mentioned some outside help."

"I've engaged the services of Januarius Bok. He comes highly recommended. Do you know him?"

Melchior frowned. "I've heard the name. Other departments have used him from time to time, following a hack, a ransomware demand, that sort of thing. His price can exceed what the hoods hope to extort. Don't trust him."

Scudamore stared out of his office window. Estates had examined the cracked pane and concluded that a strip of transparent tape constituted a repair. The ceiling still leaked. "I'll pick you up at the airport."

"Rebecca has the details." Melchior removed his glasses and rubbed his eyes. He looked old.

Scudamore killed the call. He paused, pressed another number. A smiley face appeared. "Dr Bok? I pick up my boss tonight. You have the rest of the day to make something of this case. Do you have any ideas? Any at all?"

"Manifold," Bok said. "Ideas grow like grain. One must winnow them, so truth alone remains. In pursuit of which, organise another meeting with the divine Ms Tipstaff. Let us agree to meet at noon, sharp."

7

Scudamore ushered Tipstaff into the interview room. Save for her outfit and his underwear, the room and its contents were unchanged since yesterday. Estates must have prioritised the taping of his window over the cleaning of this room. He switched on the audio. Bok's voice at once began to drone.

"Ms Tipstaff. I need to know, in detail, what you observed during the intrusion. The future of Melchior's career depends on what you tell me. Do you understand?"

Tipstaff offered a slight nod.

"Good. Let us start with the director's office. The intruder left and you entered. Describe your impressions."

Tipstaff's eyes, the colour of a darkening sky, lost focus as she recalled the scene. "The desk was disarranged. Not hugely so. Three paper files were not where I had placed them. A coaster had been moved from the right to the left side of the desk. Two drawers were half open. But, as far as I could tell, nothing was missing. The wall safe worried me, though. An oil painting, a rather florid landscape, hides the safe. I could tell someone had moved it. That painting always hangs askew, you see. It had been askew earlier that morning, when I left those three files on the desk. Now its edges aligned with all the posters and certificates and noticeboards that hang on the wall. That's how I knew the intruder must have tampered with the safe. That's why I called Security. I called from the director's phone."

"I can confirm that," Scudamore said.

"Good." Bok dragged out the syllable. "Now tell me about the interloper. What did he wear?"

"Blue, knee-length lab coat. Black trousers. Black shoes."

"Height?"

"Half a head taller than me."

"His face. Describe his face."

Tipstaff shuffled in her chair. "I... average, I suppose."

"He had an average number of eyes, noses, and mouths? Come come. Try harder."

Tipstaff pulled a lace handkerchief from her skirt pocket and began to tug on it. "I... I suppose I didn't see him too well."

"But you said he stared you in the eye, walked straight past you. I ask again: describe his face."

Tipstaff dabbed away tears then looked at Scudamore. "I've told you all I can. May I go?"

Scudamore nodded, but Bok's voice overruled him. "A final question. You worked for the first director. Did he give the Institute its name?"

"Area 37?" Tipstaff got to her feet. "I believe so. But I have no idea why."

Scudamore waited until Tipstaff had left. "A memory like a steel trap, and yet she claims not to remember the guy's face? Seems she's involved after all."

"Apply a modicum of rigor to your thought process, Scudamore. Her love for Melchior shines bright. Therefore, as you yourself noted, she gains nothing by bringing this episode to your attention."

Scudamore bit down on a reply and forced a smile. "Then you leave me with my locked-room mystery, Dr Bok. And I need a solution before I meet Melchior."

"In which case expect my call this evening. I must first confirm a detail or two."

8

Scudamore's phone shivered against his chest. He rested his forehead on the limousine window, watched his breath fog the cold glass. In the condensation he drew two dots and a curved line, then encircled them. He wiped away the smiley with a handkerchief. The phone shivered again. When he took the call, Bok's voice filled the car. "Are you free to speak?"

Although his driver had clearance, Scudamore raised the internal window. He wanted as few people as possible to know about Bok. "Well? Do you know how he got into the building?"

"No one got into the building," Bok said, his tone one of exasperation.

Scudamore could see air quotes around those words 'got into'. He told himself to breathe. "I meet Melchior in ten minutes, Bok. So tell me. Do you know who entered his damn office?"

"Of course. N, the neuropsychologist."

"How? Why?"

"The 'why' should be obvious," Bok said. "We have established his motive: revenge. He led the Institute, even gave it its name. Along with the post came a personal assistant, the formidable Ms Tipstaff, with whom he was in love. Melchior took all this from him."

"But Tipstaff saw the intruder and she didn't recognise him. Are you saying she lied? Or that N wore a mask capable of fooling her?"

"The latter," Bok replied. "Tell me, have you heard of Brodnam Area 37? Or of proposagnosia?"

"Heard what now?"

Bok sighed. "Brodnam Area 37 resides in the brain's temporal cortex. N has spent his career investigating the fusiform gyrus, a structure within Area 37. He named the Institute after his research interests."

The limousine glided to a halt in the short-stay area of the arrivals terminal. "Speed it up, Bok."

"You told me N researched super-identifiers." Bok's languid delivery showed no signs of accelerating. "His research led him to a contrasting phenomenon. Proposagnosia. In common parlance, face-blindness. Clinicians have long known that trauma in the fusiform gyrus impairs a person's ability to recognise faces. A stroke can bring about the damage, as can a tumour. Whatever the cause, the patient sees a head, a hairline, two eyes above a nose above a mouth. They understand the concept of a face. But they cannot distinguish one face from another. Your friend N has developed a way of exciting Area 37 and thereby inducing short-term face-blindness. His technique, I suspect, involves ultrasound of a particular frequency. A person within range will feel nothing, but the excitation of that person's fusiform gyrus induces temporary proposagnosia."

"The perfect mask," Scudamore said. "And he used it to get access to the wall safe?"

"Safecracking demands an entirely different skill set. No, he stole nothing. Except perhaps Ms Tipstaff's peace of mind. And yours."

"But then what did he..."

Bok interrupted. "He entered the office, rearranged items

on the desk, then walked away when he knew Tipstaff would see but not recognise him. He knew Tipstaff would call you, and you would investigate. He believed, with good reason, that you would fail to elucidate the mystery. But your report would be sufficiently damning to have Melchior removed from post."

"What he didn't know was that I'd call you," Scudamore said ruefully.

"Indeed. N possesses an ingenious mind. Ingenuity, however, does not equate with infallibility."

"Seems he committed no crime." Scudamore paused. "What do we do?

"A decision for you and Melchior."

Scudamore got out of the car and entered the terminal in time to see the director's familiar frame striding towards him.

"We never agreed on money." Scudamore stared at the grinning avatar on his phone. "How much?"

"I waive my fee," Bok replied.

Scudamore felt his guts clench. Melchior had told him not to trust Bok. "If not money, what is it you want?"

"I presume you will recreate a device based on N's work. Well, I should like one. A mask such as that will prove ... useful for me."

The smiley face disappeared.

Acknowledgements

The H G Wells' Short Story Competition is thirteen years old now and going from strength to strength. We are since 2020 fully virtual and therefore inclusive and feel very proud to be so. It is wonderful to receive entries from around the world and for all shortlisted writers to be able to participate in the awards ceremony if they wish to do so.

Thank you to our hard working committee members for their contributions and to our judges who have been very busy this year reading the 771 entries and selecting our winners.

Thanks as ever to Graham Turnill for his continued support and involvement in the competition over the last 13 years and to the late Margaret and Reg Turnill for sponsoring the annual short story prize to encourage our younger writers.

We are extremely grateful to Tim Prater, IT wizard of Sandgate, who has managed our website activity for the last five years with efficiency and effectiveness. This year as last year, Tim is shouldering more work by overseeing our virtual awards ceremony.

Thank you too to Tony Scofield, editor and publisher of this tenth anthology of stories, and for the editorial assistance of Stephanie Scofield and Liz Joyce. Many thanks also to Sarah Anthony and Tony Quarrington for their professional skills.

We should also like to thank Folkestone Town Council for their continued generous financial support which is very greatly appreciated.

Lastly, thank you to the record number of writers who have had the confidence to enter their stories this year and to all of you who read this anthology.